Copyright © 2022 by Melody Tyden

All rights reserved.

Cover design by: GetCovers

LEADING LADY

MELODY TYDEN

Chapter One

~Freya~

Some days, the stars aligned and it felt like you could do no wrong. Things fell into place so perfectly that you knew they were meant to be. Everything felt light and easy and effortless.

I was *not* having one of those days.

"No cell phones during the audition, Ms Rose." The casting assistant gave me a stern, unimpressed look as the loud chime of my text alert filled the waiting room. Literally the moment she walked in and called my name, asking me to follow her to the rehearsal room where the casting agents were waiting, my phone decided to go off. The timing couldn't be worse.

"I know," I assured her. "I'm sorry, I just need to make sure everything's okay..."

As quickly as humanly possible, I grabbed my phone and checked the incoming message, which turned out to be my boss at the restaurant, asking if I could pick up an extra shift that weekend. That could wait, so I shoved the phone into my bag and offered the casting assistant one more apologetic smile.

"It's not important."

She simply arched her eyebrow in disapproval before turning on her three-inch heels and clicking her way back down the hallway as I hurried along behind her.

That afternoon, I had been invited for a callback for a brand-new musical and I *really* wanted to make a good impression. *Any* role would be a welcome change from waiting tables, but they'd actually called me back for the lead. The role couldn't be more perfect for me, and it wouldn't even involve that much acting: an overworked, stressed-out single mom, trying to make ends meet, who gets mistaken for a missing princess and swept away on an adventure.

Maybe I didn't have any experience with the second part, but the overworked, stressed-out single mom bit? I could nail that in my sleep.

"Thank you for coming in, Ms Rose," one of the men at the table said as I stepped into the audition room. The scene that greeted me could have been from any of the auditions I'd done in my time as an actress, and I often thought how surprised most people would be to learn how unglamorous the whole process could be.

Four men sat at a rectangular table with various headshots and re-sumes on the table in front of them. They all looked vaguely the same, with short, dark hair, wearing the same business-casual clothing. Two wore glasses and two didn't, but otherwise, I couldn't really distinguish between them at a glance.

Surreptitiously, I tried to count the number of photos on the table, trying to guess just how many other actresses they were seeing for the role. Many of my competitors were familiar to me; a core group of us often went up for the same roles, and almost all of them were better known than me, and with more experience too.

Talent-wise, I fell into the same category as them, though; I truly believed that. If I didn't, I wouldn't be there.

I just hadn't had my lucky break yet.

Besides the four men at the table, another man sat at a piano just behind them, and he gave me a welcoming smile as I caught his eye. Although I didn't know his name, I recognized him from other auditions I'd done. There had been a *lot* of them.

"Call me Freya, please," I requested as I placed my bag and coat down at the side of the room and went to stand in the open space in front of the table. In September in New York, the afternoons were usually warm enough to go without a coat, but a chill sometimes crept into the morning air, so I had no choice but to wear one when I left my apartment and be stuck with it all day.

"You got the song we sent, Freya?" the man continued, and I nodded, doing my best to smile, to look enthusiastic but also at ease, to appear relaxed but still professional, all at the same time.

In the open call two weeks earlier, I'd performed my usual audition piece, but for the callback, my agent had sent me a short piece from the show itself. The beautiful, slightly sad song came from the beginning of the show, where the character lamented the life she might have led if she'd made better choices in the past.

Again, I could definitely relate.

With a nod from the man at the table, the one at the piano launched into a musical introduction completely different to the one I'd been sent. I had a theory that casting agents did that on purpose to try to see how the person auditioning reacted under pressure and if they could pick up on the cues within the music. It had thrown me off the first few times it happened, but that had been a long time ago.

That afternoon was hardly my first rodeo, and when I opened my mouth to sing my first line, it came out perfectly on time with the first note, without the slightest hesitation.

In an instant, the room disappeared, and in my mind, I sat alone on the fire escape outside my apartment, trying not to let my son see me cry when the loneliness and frustration got a little too much to bear.

People ask: would I take it back?
The love I gave on that rainy day
But if I did, then there'd be no you
And that'd be too steep a price to pay

So little acting was required that it almost felt like cheating. I knew just how the woman felt.

Tears dotted my eyes by the time I'd finished the two verses and the chorus they'd given me, and I blinked the moisture away as the last chords faded into the quiet, still air of the nondescript room in midtown Manhattan.

A stray car horn sounded from the street below as the men at the table jotted notes on their pads of paper, making marks against my name which might be good or bad. I couldn't guess.

And then...

My cell phone rang.

Disapproval and annoyance registered across several of the faces in front of me as I stepped sideways towards my bag.

"I'm so sorry, I just need to check..."

As soon as I caught sight of the name flashing across my phone screen, my stomach sank. Exactly as I'd feared, the call came from my babysitter.

Taking a deep breath, I looked back up at the men in apology, but also with determination. My son came first and I wouldn't apologize for that. "I need to take this. It's about my son."

Without waiting for permission, I answered the phone and turned my back to the room.

"Sara? What's going on?"

"I hope this isn't a bad time..." she started, but I quickly cut her off. The sooner we got to the point, the better.

"What is it?"

"Dylan can't find his blue car. Do you know where it might be?"

She had to be *freaking kidding* me. Normally, my mom or my friends would help out with Dylan as much as possible, meaning I didn't have a regular sitter I hired. That day, no one had been available, and in my desperation, I hired one recommended by my neighbour. I had told her to call me only in an emergency, which was why I had insisted on answering the phone. However, Dylan losing his blue car definitely did not qualify. For him, it might be an emergency, but I expected an adult, even an 18-year-old one, to be able to tell the difference.

"They often end up under the sofa, I'd look there first. I have to go."

I hung up before she could say anything else, wincing to myself before I fixed the smile back on my face and turned back to the men at the table, ready to apologize once again.

"It seems my babysitter and I have a different idea of what constitutes an emergency." No point in lying about it, so I could only hope they had a sense of humour.

"How old is your son?" one of the men asked, one who hadn't spoken before.

"Four."

"I've got one who just turned five." His sympathetic and kind tone took me genuinely by surprise. People were rarely so understanding. "He provided the inspiration for Michael in the show."

My eyes widened as I put the pieces together. "You're the composer."

He nodded while the other men at the table tried not to smile. "Guilty."

Normally I would have known all about the creative team ahead of time, but Jeffrey Neill was notoriously camera shy. I'd scoured the internet for photos of him and hadn't been able to find a single one, so it hadn't even crossed my mind that he would have been in the room until he just outed himself. Even when he wrote a hit show three years earlier, he hadn't attended any of the press events or the premiere, and the show we were there about would be his first production since then.

As if he could read my mind, he explained his presence: "Once the show is ready, my work is done, but making sure we get the right cast in place to bring the piece to life is very important to me. I want Julia to feel real, and she is *exactly* the kind of person who would take a phone call from a babysitter in the middle of a very important audition."

The words made me blush; both because I had done something so stupid in the first place, but mostly because he essentially just said he could picture me as the character. That counted as high praise, and would rarely be said to an actor so early in the audition process.

"We'll be in touch," one of the other men said, giving me the customary dismissal for the situation, but as I gathered up my things, he added one more question. "Is childcare going to be an issue if you get the role, Freya?"

I quickly shook my head. "No, sir. Not at all. It's completely under control."

Jeffrey's smile told me he might not totally buy that, but it didn't seem to matter. Maybe things didn't always have to be perfect to be right. Maybe it had been my lucky day after all.

My co-worker, Elyse, let out a low whistle as she strutted into the restaurant's kitchen. "Heads up, Freya: Mr Romeo himself just got seated in your section."

"You're kidding," I groaned even as my hand subconsciously went to my hair, making sure none of its reddish-brown strands had come loose from the twist I usually wore for work. "Who's he got with him?"

"Who do you think? He's still in the show for another week, so they won't break up until a day or two after that."

My surprised laugh came out almost as a snort. "Right, I nearly forgot."

Elyse picked up a couple of plates and grinned at me over her shoulder. "I almost feel sorry for the poor woman, but she knew what she signed up for."

With my own plates in hand, I followed her back through the door. "Every woman likes to think they'll be the one to finally 'tame' him. They must see it as a challenge."

"I have no such illusions," she assured me. "But it doesn't mean I wouldn't take a turn riding that stallion if I got the chance. I just wouldn't get attached."

With that sentiment echoing in my mind, I approached the table of diners whose food I had and gave them all my warmest smile. "Here we go, everyone."

Once they had their food, I pulled out my tablet and headed over to the table Elyse had just warned me about, the one where Broadway darling Rome Taylor sat with his latest co-star and girlfriend, Melissa Chilton.

Elyse and I weren't the only ones who referred to Rome as Romeo; the nickname caught on across the Broadway community a few years ago as his pattern became clear to anyone paying attention. At the age of 23, he had been cast in his first leading role, taking the theatre world by storm and winning a Tony on his first nomination, but what everyone really remembered was the passionate romance he had with his co-star, Jennifer Marshall. They were inseparable, a true case of life imitating art, and everyone thought they were the perfect couple.

At least, they thought so until he left the show at the end of his contract and moved on to a new role, and a new co-star. Within a few weeks, he'd been dating her instead.

By the time he appeared in front of me that evening, he had five starring roles under his belt, and five heated affairs. To look at the two of them, cuddled together in the booth at the 46th Street restaurant where I worked, you would think they were solid as a rock, deeply in love, but if his pattern held, in a matter of weeks, he'd be moving on to a new show and a new co-star.

Elyse was right that the women should know by now what they were getting into, but equally, it would be pretty hard to resist him. Drop-dead gorgeous, enormously talented, and from everything I'd heard, funny and charming too, who *wouldn't* want to be on the receiving end of the attention he appeared to be showering on Melissa?

However, while Elyse felt certain she could enjoy the ride and walk away with no regrets, I suspected it wouldn't be that easy for me. I always got too attached. That had always been my fatal flaw when it came to romance, but since becoming aware of it, I had been making a concerted effort not to fall for the guys who weren't going to stick around. Getting involved with someone like Rome would be the perfect recipe for heartbreak for someone like me.

Good thing he didn't have me anywhere on his radar, then.

"Good evening." I gave Rome and Melissa a smile, trying not to look too starstruck. I'd never seen either of them that close up before, but that didn't mean I had to be nervous. In the end, we were all actors. They'd just been a little luckier than I had. "Good show tonight?"

Being close to the theatre district, we often had actors come in after the shows ended for a meal or a drink. Just an hour earlier, they had both been on stage in front of thousands of people. Hopefully it wouldn't be much longer before I knew exactly what that felt like.

"*Great* show tonight, thanks." Rome turned his matinee idol smile on me and my knees nearly buckled right there. Good God, he was beautiful. I had seen him on stage before, with me sitting in the audience with the rest of the crowd, and of course he looked good then. But up close, without the makeup on and the glare of the spotlights, he somehow looked even better. His eyes were a stunning shade of blue, his short, brown hair still a little damp from a post-show shower, and his jawline looked like it had been chiselled out of marble. "Could I have the salmon and green beans, please? Hold the potatoes."

"Chef salad," Melissa added, shoving her menu at me in a clear signal to leave. Naturally blonde and svelte, she made a great foil to Rome's more angled looks. They made a gorgeous couple, and I couldn't blame her for wanting to be alone with him, especially if she suspected, as she must, that they didn't have a lot of time left.

After confirming their drink orders, I moved on, doing my best not to let my gaze wander back to their table as I spoke to my other customers. We had a few regulars along with some tourists, and one teenage girl pulled me over to her when I took her family's order.

"Is that really Rome Taylor?" she squealed in excitement, pulling out her Playbill for the show she must have seen him in that night.

I grinned back at her, remembering all too well the excitement of bumping into my favourite actors outside of the theatre when I'd first arrived in the city. Broadway had a huge advantage over Hollywood in that way. Aside from the big Hollywood stars who came in sometimes, most of the Broadway community was very tight-knit and down-to-earth. You might run into them out jogging or doing their laundry at the laundromat, or catching a bite after the show. They were all just regular people, no matter how talented they were.

"That's him. Do you want me to ask if he would mind signing an autograph?"

We didn't encourage other diners to approach actors at their tables, since they came there to relax during their downtime, but it wouldn't hurt for me to ask since I had to go over anyway. If he said no, I could break it to her gently, but if he said yes, he might make her whole year. To me, that made it worth taking the chance.

The girl's eyes grew so wide with excitement, I almost had to laugh. "Could you?"

"I'll see what I can do," I promised, giving her parents a smile before returning to the kitchen.

Rome's and Melissa's meals were ready, so the timing couldn't be better. As I placed their plates down, I made the request.

"There's a girl at the table over there who saw the show tonight and would love to get an autograph, if it's not too much trouble."

"She could have come to the stage door," Melissa pointed out. Technically, that was true; many actors were happy to sign autographs as they left the theatre through the stage door, but a lot of theatregoers didn't know that, or perhaps the girl's parents hadn't wanted to wait around.

Rome seemed to agree with me rather than his girlfriend. "It'll only take a minute," he told Melissa before turning back to me. "Of course, that's fine. You can bring her over, if you don't mind."

His politeness endeared him to me even more than his breathtaking good looks did. I also agreed with him completely: it would only take him a minute, but it would be a minute that girl would never forget.

Before he could change his mind, I returned to the girl and told her to come with me and bring her Playbill. Vibrating with excitement, she followed me back to the table where Rome and Melissa both signed the program for her, Melissa smiling as if the whole thing had been her idea, and I quickly snapped a picture of the three of them together.

When I told Elyse the story afterwards, she rolled her eyes. "Melissa should be grateful for that photo. It's probably going to be one of the last ones they have together."

That felt harsh, and I shook my head at her, even if I couldn't really argue with what she'd said.

Rome made a point of thanking me when they'd finished eating and left a large tip for me too, almost double what I would have expected. As I watched them leaving the restaurant, I couldn't help feeling a little confused. He seemed like a genuinely nice guy, not the kind of cold, self-absorbed player I might have expected based on all the stories I'd heard.

So, why didn't he seem to be able to commit for longer than the run of a show? Could it really be as simple as the fact that he hadn't found the right woman yet?

I quickly shook my head at myself. *No, Freya.* Those other women all thought exactly the same thing, and I knew better. People were who they were, no matter how much love you gave them. The wide-eyed girl I'd been in college had grown up, and I knew far better than to think that a guy like Rome Taylor would ever settle down. Not that he was knocking on my door anyway.

I'd had my one brush with him, the same as the girl who left the restaurant hugging her signed Playbill tight to her chest, and that would be the end of it. Chances were, I'd never speak to him again.

~Rome~

The walk from the restaurant to my apartment only took a few minutes, but it felt a lot longer with Melissa sulking beside me. Obviously, something had made her unhappy. Going out after the show had been intended to help her relax, and instead, it had the opposite effect.

We were both silent until we got through the door of my apartment, stepping into the large entrance hall that took up more space on its own than the whole of my first New York apartment. Once we were finally in private, I asked her to spell it out for me: "What's wrong?"

She gave me an incredulous look as she placed her bag down on the table. "You really don't have a clue?"

I honestly didn't. Generally, I was pretty tuned into what people were feeling, but over the previous week or so, I hadn't been able to read her at all. "If I did, I wouldn't be asking. Why don't you just tell me?"

Walking into the kitchen, I flipped on the soft under-cupboard lights, the ones meant for the middle of the night when I didn't want to be blinded on the way to a midnight snack. Since we'd just eaten, I had no appetite, but I poured myself a small glass of bourbon while I waited for Melissa to speak.

"You know that people are already talking about us breaking up. There's even a pool going on among some of the cast about which day it's going to happen on."

I hadn't known about the pool, but I also didn't think any of the gossip necessitated getting upset about it. "They're not the ones in this relationship; we are. People can talk all they want, it doesn't mean it's going to happen. Is that why you've been upset all week?"

"I haven't been *upset*," she tried to claim. "I'm just hurt that you went up for that new role without even talking to me about it."

"I did talk to you about it," I contradicted her mildly as I took a sip from my drink. "I told you about having lunch with Jeffrey Neill, and then I told you afterwards that he asked me to read for the role. I didn't know ahead of time that he would ask me, so it would have been difficult for me to tell you before it happened. Last time I checked, I couldn't predict the future."

My small attempt at humour didn't seem to be appreciated as she narrowed her eyes at me. "But you just accepted it without talking to me."

"I accepted the reading, yes. I haven't been officially offered the role, and you knew I would be looking for other roles with my contract ending. I really don't understand what the problem is, Melissa. I need to work. You've still got a job next week, and I don't."

She had signed a two-year contract on our current show, while I'd only taken one. I only ever took a year. Things started to feel stale if I stayed in a role longer than that, and I relished a new challenge. A year felt like just the right amount of time to feel like I'd done everything I could with a role, and then I could move on.

So far, I'd been incredibly lucky to be able to go from role to role over the last seven years with hardly a break in between. A great deal of it came down to sheer luck, but I also worked hard making connections and making sure the right people knew when I would be available, which was how the lunch with Jeffrey Neill came about. He thought I'd be perfect for his new show, and after speaking with him, I thought so too.

I would be going in the following week to read with the shortlisted actresses for the female lead so the casting agents could see what kind of chemistry we had together. The show felt quirky and fun, the music sounded gorgeous, and I was really excited about it.

My girlfriend should be happy for me too, so there had to be more to her sour mood than just the fact that I had almost landed a new role.

She quickly proved me right. Taking a deep breath, she finally got to the heart of the matter. "It feels like you're looking to move on not just from the show, but from me too. Even tonight, we were supposed to have a nice, quiet dinner, just the two of us, and you spent the whole night flirting with the waitress!"

She had to be kidding. I hadn't done anything inappropriate with the waitress. I'd noticed her, sure, since I had eyes. The woman had been beautiful in an understated way, the plain black of the restaurant's uniform making the red highlights in her hair even stronger. Her hazel eyes had been friendly and kind, and I liked the way she acknowledged that she knew who we were without being over-the-top about it, simply asking how the show went. In our brief interaction, she'd given me the impression of being thoughtful and quietly competent, without any unnecessary drama.

That sounded pretty good right then, because while I had noticed the waitress, I certainly hadn't made *any* move on her, and if Melissa thought I had, she was being wilfully delusional. That kind of jealousy and insecurity were a big turnoff for me, and I had told her that from the start.

Yes, I had a reputation. I knew that as well as anyone, but when I went into a relationship, I went all the way in. Melissa told me she could trust that, but apparently, she couldn't.

The fact that people thought my relationships only lasted a year had started to become a self-fulfilling prophecy. My last girlfriend had been just the same too; as the one-year mark approached, she got jumpy and suspicious, looking for signs that I had grown tired of her, to the point that it became stressful and, yes, I began to get tired of it.

Melissa had seemed different. I'd hoped so, anyway, but that night, it seemed I could see the writing on the wall. Maybe her attitude over the past week had been a sign that we should just cut our losses rather than drag things out any further.

"I think you should go home tonight, Melissa."

This apartment belonged to me. Although she'd practically moved in, spending four or five nights a week there, we'd never made it official. I'd never invited anyone to move in with me. It made things too messy when the relationship ended, which it inevitably did.

Melissa's eyes widened in both dismay and disbelief, but she didn't argue with me. Instead, she turned on her heel and headed out the door, slamming it behind her and leaving me alone in the silent kitchen with its soft lighting.

Thankfully, we only had four more performances together. We were good enough actors that we could convince people we were still madly in love, at least on stage.

Maybe it had never been more than that. Maybe I had fallen in love with her character more than I had with her. It wouldn't be the first time it had happened. Though we still needed to have an official conversation about it, in the still silence of my kitchen, the echo of the slamming door still ringing in my head, I felt pretty sure the relationship had just ended.

As I flipped off the kitchen light and headed to my bedroom alone, I couldn't help wondering if anyone had picked that evening in the breakup pool. Maybe it had been someone's lucky day, even if it hadn't been mine.

Chapter Two

~**Freya**~

Dylan stood on his tiptoes, his shoes already on as he tried his best to reach his coat by the front door of our apartment. I found him there when I finished going over the plan for the day with my mom, and the sight made my heart melt. My little man seemed to get bigger every day.

"What are you doing, Dill-pickle?" I asked as I crouched down to get eye-level with him. I'd been calling him that for so long, I'd forgotten how it started, but by that point, it just fit him. He was my silly, dilly pickle, and the love of my life.

"I come too," he told me with all the confidence of a four-year-old who firmly believed that no place existed where he wouldn't be needed.

"Not today, buddy. Today is for mommies only." I often used that line when I had to go somewhere I couldn't take him, and usually, he accepted it even if he didn't like it.

That day, he required more convincing. "Mommies *and* Dylans," he amended, tugging at the bottom of his coat. The top of it remained hooked on the coat hook on the wall, so he wouldn't be getting it down, no matter how hard he pulled. "I coming."

I placed my hand on his to encourage him to let go of the coat and slowly turned him around so he looked directly at me. "Not today," I repeated gently. "But I need the biggest, bestest good-luck hug ever. If I have extra good luck today, maybe we can spend more time together soon."

Besides being the only thing I'd wanted to do with my life for as long as I could remember, if I actually landed a role in an open-run Broadway production, my work schedule would drastically change. I'd chosen the restaurant where I worked because I could do mostly evening shifts there, but they were still long hours. Usually, I worked from three in the afternoon to midnight or one in the morning, meaning I missed out on evenings with my son. He had preschool in the afternoons, so during the week, if I dropped him off at noon, I wouldn't see him again until the next day.

Broadway hours weren't easy either, but once the show got up and running, I could do my training and rehearsals during the hours he went to school and wouldn't have to arrive for an evening show until around 6 pm. That would be three extra hours a day with Dylan and it would mean a lot to me.

It would mean a lot to him too.

He still looked unconvinced about staying home that day, so I threw in an enticement I knew he couldn't resist: "Grandma's making chocolate chip cookies today, and you know how much help she needs."

His eyes lit up, as I knew they would, and he immediately ran off towards the kitchen. "Grandma! Cookies!"

"Not before breakfast," my mom called back from her bedroom. "Now quick, give Mommy a hug, she needs to go."

His eyes were wide as he ran back and leapt into my arms, nearly knocking me over. I held his little body tight for just a few seconds before he began to squirm, and as soon as I let go, he ran off again.

"Break a leg, Freya." My mom's hug was longer and tighter than my son's as she came out of her bedroom to see me off. Other than a few strands of grey hair and a few wrinkles around her eyes, she and I could be sisters. Eyes the same shade of hazel as my own looked back at me as she placed her hands on my cheeks. "You've got this. They'd be crazy not to cast you."

"You've said that about every part I've auditioned for since I was six," I pointed out, but the words still meant a lot to me. My mom had always been there for me, in every way, and without her, I would never have been able to keep chasing my dream. If by some miracle I did actually get the part, it would be just as much her victory as mine. "Call me if you need anything."

"I think you better turn your phone *off* today," she instructed, shaking her head in disapproval. I'd told her the whole story about the previous callback. "You got away with it once, don't tempt fate! You know Dylan and I are fine. Just go and live in the moment, show them how amazing you are, and don't worry about us."

I certainly intended to try. I'd never gotten as far as a second callback for a Broadway role before, so everything about the day felt new, and it both exhilarated and terrified me.

Hundreds of other commuters jostled for position as I squeezed onto the A train heading downtown, the air filled with perfume, cologne, and other less pleasant smells, as those in suits pressed up against people like me in yoga pants or jeans. The apartment my mom and I lived in was in Harlem, close enough to Midtown that I could get to work and auditions easily, but far enough away that we could afford the rent.

After getting pregnant in college, most girls in my position would have been forced to slink back home to the small town they grew up in, another cautionary tale of life in the big city, but my mom refused to let that be the end of my story. Instead of me moving home, she moved to New York to support me. She and my dad had divorced a couple of years earlier and she worked from home, so she insisted she had nothing to keep her there.

Despite her assurances, I knew she'd given up a lot to be my live-in babysitter. Together with the friends I'd made during my college years who were now moms too, she had been my lifeline over the past five years, and the idea of her being able to finally sit in a Broadway audience and see me on stage brought tears to my eyes.

Don't get ahead of yourself, Freya. I shook my head to try to ground myself once more. The role was far from mine yet. I still had to get through that day, and possibly more callbacks too. If there were several different people they were considering, the process could go on for a while, but even so, I had to feel optimistic as I headed into the same rehearsal space where my last audition had been held.

When I entered the waiting room that time, four other women were already there, and my stomach dropped as I recognized all four of them. Each one was a talented actress who had already had starring or featured roles in big productions, and it seemed unlikely they would be going up for any role other than the one I'd been called back for. They must be my competition.

Pasting a smile on my face, I vowed not to let my nerves show. They might have the name and face recognition, but I was there because the casting agents saw something of value in my audition. I belonged there, just as much as any of those women.

"Good morning," I said to the room at large as I shrugged my coat off and took a seat on an empty chair. "I didn't realize they were having everyone in at once."

"Neither did we," the woman closest to me said, returning my smile in a way that seemed sincere. Her name was Harper Laney, and she'd been nominated for a Tony two years ago. I'd never spoken to her before. "I think they intentionally keep it a secret to try to psych us out."

That seemed entirely possible. "So, we won't let them," I suggested. "Obviously, any of you would be amazing in this role, so it's not a question of skill. It's just going to come down to personal preference, and that's something no one can predict."

One of the women, a short, blonde woman named Katie Schuler, appeared to roll her eyes, but the others all nodded in agreement. "What's your name?" one of the ones on the other side of the room asked.

I didn't need to ask hers; she was Jennifer Marshall, the woman who had starred with Rome Taylor in his first big show. She'd done a few things since then, but she hadn't recaptured the same level of success she had starring opposite him. How funny that I'd just been thinking about her the week before when Rome came into the restaurant, and now I was sitting there with her, both of us up for the same role.

On the other hand, it didn't surprise me at all that she didn't know who I was; she had no reason to. In my few off-Broadway shows, I'd never had the lead. Nothing that would be memorable.

"I'm Freya Rose."

"That's a great name," Hannah Ferguson piped up. She had a starring role in a show at the time, I had seen her in it just a few weeks earlier. "Like Gypsy Rose Lee. Is it a stage name?"

"No, nothing that clever. Just what I was born with."

We got talking about other stage names, good and bad, and I almost forgot to be nervous until the door to the rehearsal room opened and the same casting assistant from the previous week came out, inviting all of us in at the same time.

The table had grown, with six men and a woman sitting behind it. The composer, Jeffrey Neill, was there again too, and he smiled at us all as we came in.

"Today's going to be run a little differently than usual," he informed us, which I had already guessed based on them calling us all in together. "You've all been given the same scenes to prepare and we're going to workshop them together. I really want to see the character as you see her, so you'll have a chance to try a few different scenes and to watch your fellow actresses. We've got an actor here to play opposite you as the prince, and I want you to really have fun and enjoy yourselves."

Maybe it made me weird, but I thought that actually did sound like fun. In drama school, I always loved trying out scenes in front of the class. What he'd suggested would be just the same, except that the 'class' included exceptionally talented people on both sides of the table. Another surge of excitement ran through me as I quickly reviewed the scenes in my head, trying to anticipate which we would be asked to do first.

"Who's playing Victor?" Jennifer asked, which was a good question. I'd been so focused on who would get the part of Julia, I hadn't even thought about the leading man.

"That would be me," a voice said from behind us, and all the women turned at the same time to see none other than Rome Taylor himself walk through the door with a smile that made the butterflies in my stomach take flight. His gaze passed over all of us, and when he got to me, I could have sworn I saw a flash of recognition in his eyes.

He didn't really remember me from the restaurant, did he?

As he walked over to say hello to everyone at the table, I noticed that all the women's heads followed. He had a way of drawing everyone's eye and keeping their attention. And they wanted me to act opposite him?

Staying focused on my lines suddenly felt a whole lot trickier than before.

~Rome~

Walking into the rehearsal room on Wednesday morning, I felt ready for a fresh start.

The past week had been a whirlwind. Melissa and I kept our breakup quiet until my final performances in the show were finished, but it had been the talk of the town since then. All the usual stories circulated, the old headlines about how my relationships never lasted past the end of my contract, but I really didn't think I bore all the blame. I could take full responsibility for some of the other ones, but with Melissa, it felt much more mutual. Maybe we'd only stayed together as long as we had because of the show.

At least I had the meetings with the creative team for the new show to distract me. The more I spoke to Jeffrey Neill, the more excited I became about his vision for his new musical. It had just the right amounts of humour, interesting characters and impressive production numbers, sprinkled with quieter reflections and some really emotional moments.

The last two shows I starred in had been revivals, so the prospect of building a new role from scratch and making it completely mine excited me too. Prince Victor came off as pompous and self-absorbed at first, but gradually, the audience learned how he used his callousness as a self-defense mechanism, and as the show progressed, the accidental princess, Julia, managed to break through the surface and get to know the real him.

It had romance, adventure and comedy all in one, the music was fantastic, and audiences were going to love it. It had all the makings of a hit.

The producers officially offered me the role at the end of the week and I accepted. All that remained was to find my leading lady.

Five actresses were in consideration for the part, all of whom had been invited to audition opposite me. Though the creative team offered to tell me ahead of time who the actresses were, I preferred to go in blind. I would rather form an opinion based on how the auditions went rather than any of their previous work. Just because an actor had been perfect for one role didn't make them perfect for the next.

As a result of my decision to keep myself in the dark, seeing my ex-girlfriend, Jennifer, when I walked in the room came as a surprise, and she appeared equally caught off guard. That breakup had definitely been my fault, and I had learned my lesson, but performing with an ex would be something I hadn't done before. It made the prospect of starting a new relationship with my new co-star far less likely, but maybe that wouldn't be a bad thing. Maybe I needed a change anyway.

We'd had so much success with the last show we did that people would probably be excited to see us working together again, and I wondered if that influenced the producers to shortlist her.

Looking over the rest of the women, I recognized Harper Laney from the awards circuit a few years ago, but the other three I didn't know, at least professionally. The last woman I did recognize and it took me a moment to place her; she was the pretty waitress from the restaurant the week before, the one with the kind eyes and quiet competence.

I'd had no idea that night that she was an actress, but discovering it didn't come as a huge shock either. Half the restaurants in Manhattan were staffed with actors. Her audition must have been pretty good for her to have made it to the shortlist, and I was curious to see what she could do. Honestly, I was curious and excited about all of them. Discovering the character with the person I would be working with mostly closely had to be one of my favourite parts of the process.

The show's director quickly took the reins and laid out the plan for us all. "We're going to start with Julia's song in the middle of act one. She's just been mistaken for the princess and she and her son are taken to the penthouse suite at the Plaza. She doesn't fully understand what's happening yet and she doesn't know who Victor is. We'll do the song first and carry on through Victor's entrance and the scene that follows. Hannah, we'll start with you."

The other four actresses all moved to the side of the room to take a seat on the empty chairs set up for them there, while I went to sit beside the table where the creative team and producers were sitting. I wanted to see the same thing they were seeing, at least until my turn came to jump into the scene.

Hannah had a brassy voice, a little throaty when she spoke, and she played Julia with a lot of spunk, like someone who would make the most of the odd opportunity she'd been given. Katie performed next, and her Julia came across as more wary and suspicious of the whole situation, and a lot more sarcastic in her scene with me. I could see it getting some laughs, but I wasn't sure that kind of woman would break through Victor's walls.

Jennifer went third, and she was a consummate professional, playing Julia as a sweet and slightly harried woman, overwhelmed in an adorable way by the turn her life had taken. Each movement, although meticulously practiced, looked like she was doing it for the first time, and when I joined her for the scene afterwards, our interactions were completely free of awkwardness. She put everything else between us to the side, just as I did.

The waitress went fourth. Her name was Freya, and when she began to sing, I was genuinely impressed. Her voice was beautiful, with a rather unique sound to it. It wouldn't work for every role, but for that one, it really did. Her Julia felt like a combination of the others, veering from overwhelmed to excited to cautious in a way that exhilarated me, and no doubt would do the same to the rest of the audience too. In fact, I got so caught up in her performance that I almost missed my cue to join her.

"Where the hell is that music coming from?" was my opening line, a little joke about all the singing in musicals. I knew it would get a laugh from the audience, so I delivered it completely straight-faced and grumpily.

Freya spun around to face me and pulled her imaginary son close to her. "I'm sorry, I didn't realize there was anyone else here."

"Where else would I be? And who's the brat?"

We both looked down to where the child would be standing. "This is my son," she explained with just the right mix of confusion and indignation.

"Son?" I repeated incredulously. "Did you go out and adopt an orphan off the street, Juliette? That's impulsive, even for you."

"Juliette?" She looked around the room as if I might be speaking to someone else. "My name's Julia and this is my son. Who, exactly, are you?"

We finished the rest of the scene, after which Harper performed, the last one to go. After Freya's portrayal, though, it felt a little flat. I had a feeling we all would have been more impressed if she'd gone ahead of Freya instead.

Next came the workshopping part of the morning, with each of the women being called back up and asked to try slightly different things in both their songs and their scenes with me. When Freya's turn came, the director asked her to try it the way Jennifer had played it, and she did an amazing job of remembering all Jennifer's little nuances. She had obviously been paying attention.

It had been almost two hours by the time the director told the women to take a break, sending them out of the room while the rest of us had a chat.

"Harper and Katie aren't really working for me," Jeffrey admitted bluntly. "They're amazing, both of them, but not for this role."

No one at the table disagreed.

"Jennifer's at the top of my list," the head casting agent told us. "As long as there won't be any problems between her and Rome."

Everyone turned to look at me, leaving me frowning in confusion. "Why would there be a problem?"

Yes, we had dated, and yes, we broke up, rather badly, but we were both actors. I didn't have to *actually* be in love with the woman I starred with. It happened to me quite a lot, to be fair, but it had never been a requirement.

"I like Freya," Jeffrey countered when no one answered me. "She's a bit more raw, a bit less polished, and I think that's perfect for Julia. What do you think, Rome?"

Again, everyone looked to me for my opinion, and on that point, I could be more forthcoming. "I think she's got something special. I could absolutely see it working."

The director nodded. "I think it's possible, although I had another idea I wanted to test out, if you all agree."

He laid out his suggestion for us, and we all agreed it would be worth exploring.

The other three women were politely thanked for their time and told they'd hear from us soon, while Jennifer and Freya were asked to come back in.

"We're going to try something different now," the director told them both. "Here's a new piece of the script for you to read over. Take five minutes, and we'll give it a go."

~Freya~

I was having the time of my life. Working with the creative team and watching the other actresses trying out different things felt like a dream come true. Some of their takes on the character were completely different to mine but each one was interesting and could work; it would all depend on exactly what the composer and director had in mind.

I had been thinking a lot about what Jeffrey Neill said during my previous audition, that Julia was the kind of woman who would take a phone call during an important audition, and so I tried to build on that in my portrayal of her. I tried to make her someone who, although intrigued by what was happening and up for adventure, would still always put her child first. Honestly, it felt like a bit of a cheat, since that described me in a lot of ways.

And when Rome entered the scene in character, I was truly blown away. It would be hard to put into words just how good an actor he was, and how responsive to the person he worked with. I'd worked with many actors before who were only concerned about their own performance; they had a way they played the role and it wouldn't matter who stood opposite them, each line delivery and each movement would be exactly the same.

Rome couldn't be more different. His performance shifted significantly depending on the Julia he performed with. He fed off their energy, adapting his portrayal to suit the woman across from him, and I found it both amazing and humbling to watch. It didn't seem like an act at all. He played Victor five different ways, changing his tone and his body language to match each actress' different style, and each one felt believable and real.

Did he even know just how good he was?

As the five of us auditioning were sent out of the room, talk turned to Rome's personal life, and I couldn't help wondering if that ability of his to adapt and give the other person with him exactly what they needed helped to explain the turnover in his girlfriends.

Maybe he only ever played a part, being the person those women needed and the one who worked best for them? Who was the real Rome, and what did *he* need?

Did he know that either?

Katie turned to Jennifer as we all made ourselves something to drink at the coffee machine in the waiting room. "Did Rome let you know he was going to be here? Are you guys still in touch?"

Jennifer gave a shrug and a smile, obviously trying to play it off as if it were no big deal. "No. We're not in touch and I had no idea. It makes sense, though. He's perfect for the part."

No one argued with her about that.

"Would it be weird for you guys to work together again?" Hannah wondered, and though I knew it wasn't really any of my business, I couldn't help being curious about that too.

"You don't actually have to be in love with your co-star to pretend you are," Jennifer pointed out.

"Maybe someone should tell Romeo that," Harper added sarcastically. "At this point, I'm not even sure whether I'm auditioning for the part in the show or the role of his next girlfriend."

Hannah and Katie snickered, but that didn't feel entirely fair to me. Nobody forced the women in Rome's past to be in a relationship with him. They all made that choice willingly, and they all seemed to be pretty happy about it, at least while it lasted.

Jennifer didn't laugh either, she simply looked thoughtful as she took a sip of her coffee. "Maybe he's changed. At least this time, he actually broke up with his previous girlfriend before starting a new show."

When Jennifer and Rome broke up, everyone knew he'd already gotten together with his next co-star. As far as I knew, that was the only time that had happened, where he'd actually cheated on the woman he'd been with, and assuming those rumours were true, I wouldn't blame Jennifer for still being a little bitter about it.

Seeming to realize she'd brought the room down, Jennifer gave one more shrug. "But if you're asking for a recommendation, I'd say it's totally worth dating him. Just go in expecting it's going to end, and enjoy it while it lasts."

Elyse at work had said the same thing, almost word-for-word, and it fascinated me to hear those words echoed by someone who had actually lived through it.

Jennifer lightened the mood even further by giving us all a wink. "Anyway, you guys can fight over Rome all you want, as long as I get the part."

That steered us onto safer ground, talking about what we all thought the producers were looking for from Julia's role, until the door opened and the casting assistant came out again.

"Thank you all for coming today. Hannah, Katie, and Harper, you're free to go. We'll be in touch soon with information about any next steps."

Disappointment registered in their eyes even as they maintained a professional demeanour, and though I tried to keep my expression neutral too, excitement raced through my body. That seemed like good news for me. What happened next?

I didn't have to wait long to find out. Jennifer and I were called back into the room where the director gave us a new scene to prepare, a scene between Julia and Constance, the real princess' advisor who helped Julia out when she realized the mistake that had been made. Essentially, she played the fairy godmother role in the Cinderella story. She had a song of her own and appeared in many scenes, so it would be a really good featured part, nothing to sniff at.

The director told me to read Constance's part while Jennifer played Julia, and I tried not to be disappointed. Of course I wanted the part of

Julia, but I had to be realistic too. Jennifer had far more experience and name recognition than I did. I should be thrilled that they were even considering me for any role at all, and I tried to stay positive as I did my best to memorize the new lines and decide how to play the new role during the very short five minutes they'd allocated us.

Rome sat with the producers and creative team, watching as Jennifer and I ran through the scene. Jeffrey had some notes, so we tried it again with his suggestions, and it worked even better. I would be completely happy with that part, I tried to convince myself.

Then, they asked us to switch, with Jennifer playing Constance and me being Julia.

We both took a few minutes to look over the other lines, making sure we knew them all, and I suspected her mind must be racing just as much as mine was. What did that mean? Why were they having us both read both parts? What were they thinking?

We did the scene two times the other way, taking notes in between. Afterwards, we both stood nervously while the people at the table whispered to each other.

"We're almost finished," the director assured us once they'd finished conferring. "We'd like to do just one more scene with each of you, the second one sent to you ahead of time, between Julia and Victor."

I knew exactly which scene he meant, and against my will, my eyes flew over to Rome, deep in conversation with Jeffrey.

Part of the scene involved Julia and Victor's first kiss.

I had kissed men on stage before, but never someone like him.

Jennifer went first. Perhaps the team wanted to know if there would be any awkwardness between them given their history, but I couldn't see a hint of it. Watching them, all I saw was two people drawn together by attraction, and when they kissed, it looked so natural and intimate that I almost felt I was intruding by being there.

"Thank you," the director said to Jennifer, giving nothing away. "Freya, the same scene, please."

My legs trembled beneath me as I got up from my chair and went to stand across from Rome, taking Jennifer's place.

He gave me a reassuring smile as I approached. "Don't worry, I've been popping Altoids all morning."

Oh, crap. I hadn't even thought about my breath. "I just drank a really strong cup of coffee," I apologized, but to my relief, he simply laughed.

"I've had worse."

He probably had. He had a lot more experience with everything than I did.

Trying to put all that out of my mind, I did my best to get into Julia's head again, to put myself in the moment where she attended her first party as the princess, on Victor's arm, and though he knew by that point that she was not his fiancée, neither of them could fight the growing attraction between them.

Rome came to stand a short distance away from me, both of us looking out over an imaginary garden.

"Coming here was a mistake," I began, letting my voice fill with emotion as I imagined how overwhelmed Julia would be feeling in that moment. "I'm not who they all think I am. I don't belong here."

"No, you don't," he agreed, and I turned to look at him in dismay. His blue eyes were warm and comforting, but also betraying a little nervousness. "You're worth ten of any of them in there, Julia."

He moved closer and closer as we both recited the next lines, tension building between us with each passing second. My eyes dropped to his lips, anticipating what came next, and I almost couldn't believe how real it all felt.

He was a very, very good actor.

And a moment later, when his lips connected with mine, I had to add a very, very good kisser to his growing list of attributes inside my head.

Chapter Three

When the audition scene ended, Jennifer and Freya were thanked and sent on their way, and lunch was brought in for the rest of us while we talked over the morning's auditions.

The decision wouldn't be mine to make, but they did ask me for my opinion, and I gave it to them honestly. "Either one would be great. With Jennifer, what we saw today is exactly what we're going to get. Having worked with her before, I can tell you that she's professional, dedicated and reliable. Her performance is always consistent. With Freya, things felt a little more unexpected. I could never quite be sure of the choice she was going to make next, which some actors will find harder to work with. Personally, I like that, but I know it's not just up to me. I think she has a lot of potential, and what we saw today might not even be her best. I think she's still capable of learning and growing into the role, and I think she's willing to work to do that."

Maybe I assumed too much based on the short time we'd had together, but I really felt there were things I could teach her, ways to bring her performance to an even higher level, and she definitely had the raw talent. It would be a risk on the producers' part, though, especially for someone who had never carried a show before. That was a lot of pressure.

On the other hand, you could never tell how someone would handle it until you gave them the chance to try, and based on the way Freya had responded to the challenges she was given during the audition, I believed she deserved that chance.

If they chose Jennifer, I could work with it, but personally, I hoped they'd go with Freya, and not because I wanted to kiss her again.

At least, not *just* because I wanted to kiss her again.

I'd kissed a lot of women before, on-stage and off, and each was different. Kissing Jennifer that day felt like slipping on a pair of sweatpants, comfortable and familiar. It brought back a lot of memories for me, but in her eyes afterwards, I could see that for her, it had simply been business. We had no deeper connection, not when she had a wall firmly up between Jennifer the actress and Julia the character.

With Freya, I didn't feel any such wall. If it existed, she hid it very well. Instead, I saw the way her pupils dilated as I got closer and the way her eyes moved to my mouth in anticipation. It could be an act, but I didn't think so. Her curiosity about what the kiss would be like, the same curiosity her character shared, felt entirely natural, and, to be honest, it matched my own. When I kissed her, I was looking forward to it too.

And the kiss had been good. Really, really good. Competing scents of coconut and berries mingled as I drew closer, likely from her shampoo and lip gloss. She'd warned me about the coffee she drank, which I appreciated, but in the end, the sweetness of her lips drowned it out, along with the softness and warmth of them. For a moment, I could almost forget a room full of people were sitting there watching us.

When she pulled back, I saw surprise in her eyes and perhaps even a little flash of something more, something closer to desire.

That look made me think that, in some ways, it might be better for me if Jennifer got the part. After the way things had ended, there would be little chance of rekindling our relationship, and it might be good for me to get out of the routine I seemed to have unintentionally fallen into. I didn't set out to fall in love with every woman I starred with. Somehow, it just turned out that way, and with Freya, I could very easily see it happening again.

She had no ring on her finger, I happened to have noticed, so Jeffrey's next words took me completely by surprise. "As fantastic as Jennifer is, I think that, as a mother, Freya can truly understand Julia's struggles."

"A mother?" The words were out of my mouth before I realized I meant to speak them out loud and everyone turned to look at me curiously, wondering why I cared. Since I couldn't take back what I'd said, I asked the follow-up question as nonchalantly as I could. "Freya has children?"

"At least one," the director replied, giving me a slightly suspicious look. "Is that a problem?"

"Of course not," I quickly assured him. "I'm just surprised. I didn't know."

It created more questions for me, more things I wanted to know, but I understood that asking about her marital status wouldn't be appropriate. It didn't have any bearing on how well she could do the role, but it did make one thing perfectly clear to me: if she was married and a mother, then she would be completely off limits. Granted, one of earlier co-stars had been engaged when we met, an engagement she had broken off once we fell for each other, but with a child involved, the boundaries completely shifted. That line was one I would never cross.

The strength of my disappointment about the situation took me by surprise. I'd only met Freya twice, and never even had a real conversation with her. I hadn't let myself realize just how much she interested me until I understood that getting to know Freya in a romantic way wouldn't be an option.

We could still work well together, though. Besides, as I'd just thought about Jennifer, having a co-star that I couldn't be in a relationship with could actually be a good thing for me in the long run.

"I really liked Jennifer as Constance," Jeffrey continued, putting my interruption behind us. "I think the two of them could work well together.

That would be my choice."

He didn't have the final say either; it all came down to the producers, but they would be foolish not to take the composer's views into account. The director gave his preference for Jennifer, but conceded that he would be happy to work with either of them.

When they came back to me for my vote, I sided with Jeffrey. "I think Freya should play Julia, with Jennifer as Constance. The dynamic feels right."

The producers thanked us all but they didn't tell us which way they were going to go. I wouldn't find out until the role had been offered and accepted, with rehearsals scheduled to start in 10 days' time.

With the rest of my day free, I decided to go for an afternoon jog in Central Park before catching up over coffee with some friends. My route home took me past 46th Street and the restaurant where I had first met Freya. I had no idea if she would be working that day, but for some reason, my feet took me towards the front door anyway. I had no plans for dinner, and I enjoyed the food there. If I saw Freya, I could say hi, and if I didn't, no harm done.

As it turned out, I saw her as soon as I stepped into the dining room, and her eyes widened in surprise as she watched the hostess lead me to my table. From the corner of my eye, I could see her smooth down her skirt before she came over.

"I didn't expect to see you again today." Her smile was warm but I could see the questions in her eyes, wondering what had brought me there and if it had anything to do with her.

"I don't have any news for you," I told her, not wanting her to get her hopes up about that. "But I did want to say that you did a great job today. I was impressed."

"That means a lot coming from you." She took the compliment well, and I could tell by the brightness in her eyes that she really did appreciate it. "So, what can I get you?"

"The chicken Kiev looked great the other night. And, if you have time later, I'd love to have a quick chat."

Once again, my mouth leapt ahead of my brain. I didn't know exactly what I wanted to chat about, but Freya didn't seem to mind. "That would be nice. I have a break coming up, so I could join you for dinner, if it's not too forward?"

"Not at all, I'd love that."

Giving me another smile, she went to the kitchen to place my order and I pulled out my phone while I waited. Time for me to see what Google could tell me about my dinner companion before she returned.

~Freya~

Elyse ambushed me as soon as I stepped inside the kitchen to check my orders. The tempting aroma of butter and garlic made my stomach growl while the sizzle of steaks and the clatter of dishes filled the air, but Elyse's flurry of questions drowned out everything else around us.

"Did Romeo really come here to see you? Did you get the part? Oh my God, Freya, are you going to go out with him?!"

"Slow down," I told her, trying to laugh it off even as my stomach flipped over, and not just in hunger. "He doesn't know about the part and nobody's dating anyone."

"You skipped the first question," she pointed out shrewdly, and she was right. I did, because I had no idea how to answer it. *Did* Rome come there just to see me? If so, why? He said he'd like to talk, which could mean a million different things, and reading anything into it before I had more information wouldn't be helpful.

"He said he'd like to chat, but I don't know if he came here for that reason, or if he just, you know, needs to eat like the rest of us." My stomach growled again as I thought about food. I had only had a granola bar and a banana on the go earlier in the day since I rushed home after my audition to spend some time with Dylan before I had to come to work. Having a proper meal hadn't made it onto my list of priorities, but I put in an order for my supper along with Rome's, since I told Rome I would eat with him.

"There are 25,000 restaurants in New York," Elyse pointed out, not buying my deflection. "Not to mention bodegas and hot dog stands on every corner. He could have eaten anywhere."

She had a point, I had to admit, but he had no way of knowing I'd be working that day, so it still felt like a stretch to me to think he'd come there specifically for me.

"Why don't we just wait and see what he has to say when I talk to him?" I suggested. "I'm going to have dinner with him over my break."

Elyse's jaw dropped, her eyes bugging out in disbelief. "He asked you to have dinner with him?"

I gave her a sheepish shrug. "Not really. I kind of invited myself."

"Well, look at you grabbing the bull by the horns." She looked impressed, and a little jealous too, which she admitted in the next breath. "Fuck, I want your life right now."

Elyse acted too, like half the staff at the restaurant, but she didn't sing so we were never up for the same parts. Her last paid work had been in a commercial for some kind of heart medication that had a list of side effects longer than her contract to do the ad.

"I am *not* getting involved with Romeo... I mean, Rome," I assured her as I grabbed my next plates to take out. "Even if I get the part, which is still a big if, he is not an option for me."

"We'll see," was all she said as her own orders came up and we headed back out to the dining room together.

Though I tried not to look, my eyes kept wandering over to Rome while I worked, but he kept his head down, scrolling through something on his phone. Unlike the other night, no one else in the restaurant seemed to notice they were in the presence of Broadway greatness.

When our meals were ready, I took my apron off and filled in Elyse on the current situation with my tables so she could cover me. "Do I get to come over and see how things are going with you two?" she teased.

"You know I'm going to tell you everything anyway," I replied, and she had to laugh.

"Fair point. In that case: have fun, Freya!"

With those words ringing in my head, I picked up our two plates and headed over to Rome's table. He looked up just as I approached and gave me a smile as he set his phone down on the table next to him.

"That smells great," he said appreciatively, and my stomach immediately growled again, making him laugh. "Long day?"

"The usual," I demurred. "I only get twenty minutes for a break, so you'll have to forgive me if I talk with my mouth full."

"I can deal with that."

His stunning blue eyes were kind and warm, and as he took a bite of his own food, I couldn't stop myself from looking at his mouth, at that same mouth that had been pressed against mine earlier that day. I could still hardly believe that really happened.

"Tell me a little about yourself, Freya," he invited. "I've just been looking you up online, but I didn't find very much."

I nearly choked on my own forkful of food, inhaling a few grains of rice as I coughed and quickly took a drink of water to try to regain control over my breathing. *Smooth, Freya. Very smooth.*

"You... uh, you were looking me up? Why?" My throat still felt tight as I tried to say something, anything, to distract from my gracelessness.

He shrugged, not looking put off by my awkwardness. "I like to know about the people I'm working with. And yes, I know you don't have the part yet, but I already know the other women, at least by reputation."

He knew Jennifer a lot more than by reputation, I couldn't help thinking, but that thought flew out of my head as he leaned closer across the table, his voice going deeper as he lowered it to not be overheard.

"You're the wildcard, Freya Rose, so tell me: where have you been hiding yourself?"

My whole body vibrated in response to his tone in a way that hadn't happened to me for far too long. He must know how ridiculously sexy he was, and yet, it didn't come off as arrogant or cocky. If anything, he looked at me as though *I* was the most fascinating person at the table.

"What did you find in your search?" I asked him, trying to put the spotlight back on him as I took another bite of my dinner.

Grinning, he leaned back. "I learned that you've done a few off-Broadway shows. You must have gone to NYU since your bio lists some productions there. And I found an article from the Iowa 4-H society and a picture of you with your prize-winning steer in fourth grade."

Thankfully, my mouth was empty that time or I probably would have choked again. "How the hell did you find that?"

His eyes twinkled mischievously. "I've got some hidden skills."

The wink that accompanied that statement made my insides turn to liquid instantly. How could it even be possible for one man to be so hot and easy to talk to at the same time?

"Well, it sounds like you've got the basics, then," I told him as I tried to bring my body back under control. "Born and raised in Iowa, moved to New York to go to drama school, and I've been here ever since, with a few parts off-Broadway but mostly working in places like this."

I gestured around us to the restaurant we were in.

"I think you might have left out one or two things," he suggested, obviously not satisfied with my rundown. "I want to know what made you fall in love with theatre in the first place, why you moved to New York, and all about your family."

"My family?" I repeated in confusion. Had his Google search turned up something about my parents? That seemed strange.

For the first time, his smile faltered, just a touch. "Jeffrey mentioned that you're a mother. I hope it wasn't meant to be a secret."

Oh, *that* family. That made more sense, and actually, he'd given me the perfect reminder of exactly why I had to keep myself under control where Rome was concerned. "It's not a secret at all, I just wasn't aware you knew. I have a 4-year-old son named Dylan. He's absolutely amazing, and though every mother thinks so, I have my suspicions that he's actually the best kid in the world."

Rome smiled again, but it didn't feel quite as carefree as before. Something lurked in his eyes, a distance that hadn't been there a second earlier. He didn't acknowledge it though, just asking me the follow-up question I should have expected.

"And what about your husband? Partner? Boyfriend? Whatever word you want to use."

His gaze dropped to my hands for a second, as if looking for a non-existent ring, and I told him the truth bluntly. "Dylan's father isn't in the picture. It's just me and Dill, and my mom. I wouldn't be able to do any of this without her."

A different emotion flashed in his eyes, something I couldn't identify. Pity? Concern? Relief? I really couldn't tell.

I did my best to distract him from his line of questioning with a change of subject. "And as for how I ended up in the theatre, that can be a really short story, or a very long one. Which version do you prefer?"

That made him smile again, his expression clearing as he leaned back and took a drink from his glass. "The long one, Freya. Always the long one."

~Rome~

Once again, my reaction took me by surprise. Earlier that day, when I found out about Freya being a mom, I'd been disappointed even though I hadn't even fully known I had been considering her in a romantic way.

Then, as soon as she said she wasn't in a relationship, a shot of adrenaline went through me, my interest piquing again as I realized she wasn't quite as off-the-market as I thought.

Except she still was, in a way. She still had her son to worry about, and the few things she'd said about him made it clear that she took that responsibility very seriously, as she should. A mom *should* want to put her kid first.

I'd never been involved with anyone who had kids before, and the reason the idea made me hesitate wasn't the reason most people might think. I liked kids; kids were great, but when that kid might be impacted by our relationship, that changed things. I didn't want to be the guy who became a part of his life and then disappeared if things didn't work out between me and his mom, and I definitely didn't want to be the guy who took up his mom's time, leaving less for him. That was another hard line for me.

All in all, it looked like Freya and I weren't meant to be romantically, which was a damn shame when I found everything else about her so utterly appealing.

Over the following ten minutes, she told me all about how she fell into acting in high school, including a hilarious story about a performance of Little Shop of Horrors where everything that could go wrong did, including the plant falling apart in the middle of the climactic scene. Excitement shone in her pretty hazel eyes as she recalled the moment she first realized the rush that the applause of the crowd could bring, and her laugh had a musical quality to it as she recounted the disasters of that ill-fated night in Mushnik's florist's shop.

"Strangely, even though that could have put me off performing, that night actually made me realize that I wanted to do this forever." Wistfulness and determination played across her face as she thought back to it. "No matter what went wrong, we were all in it together, the cast and the crew and the audience, living and sharing a moment that could never be recreated, and one that no one involved would ever forget. Isn't that what the magic of theatre is really about?"

I couldn't have said it better myself.

A tinny, beeping sound cut us both off before I could ask another question, and disappointment crossed Freya's face as she pulled her phone out to silence it. "That's the end of my break, I'm afraid, and I spent the whole time babbling about myself and didn't even get to hear how you caught the acting bug."

I didn't mind. I'd have happily listened to her talk for a lot longer, so I just gave her a shrug. "The same thing, really. High school drama club, disintegrating stage props, the usual."

Her smile lit her face, and lit something inside me too. "I'd love to hear it sometime. Maybe when I get the part, we can have a longer chat."

That might have sounded presumptuous if not for the uncertainty behind it. Though she said the words, she didn't really believe them, or wouldn't let herself believe them. Every actor knew nothing could be counted on until the contract had been signed.

Wanting to provide some reassurance, I reached out and put my hand on hers. "You really impressed them today. I can't say for sure if you got the part, but if it's not this part, there'll be another one, Freya. You're too good to stay undiscovered forever."

"Thank you." She held my gaze for a moment, my hand still on hers as something tentative and indefinable passed between us, until she cleared her throat and got to her feet. "Can I get you dessert or anything?"

Leaning back in my seat, I gave her one last smile. "No, thanks. I think I'm finished."

Taking our empty plates away with her, Freya returned a couple of minutes later with my bill, her apron back on and her waitress persona firmly back in place. I wished her goodnight and headed home to my apartment in the dwindling evening sunshine.

Thinking about Freya's son made me reach out the next day to a guy I hadn't spoken to in a while.

"Well, well, Mr Romeo Taylor himself." Jordan's deep bass voice sounded warm and friendly through the phone. "What an honour."

"Please, drop the Romeo," I begged, though I knew I'd have a better chance of convincing the Pope to give up religion. Jordan never missed an opportunity to roast me when he could. "I'm actually single at the moment, I'll have you know."

"Until the next show starts," he teased, hitting a little too close to home. "What can I do for you?"

"Well, as you just so helpfully pointed out, I'm between shows at the moment and I've got a bit of spare time. I know it's short notice, but I was wondering if I could offer another recording session this weekend for your guys. I'm sorry it's been so long."

"Don't worry about it," Jordan assured me. "You're busy, we get that, and any time you can offer means the world to these kids. The ones who went two years ago still rave about it."

Two *years*? I hadn't realized it had been quite that long.

Jordan ran the Harlem branch of the Chosen Family organization, which helped pair up boys who needed a positive male role model in their lives with a mentor who could provide that to them. Unfortunately, my schedule made volunteering on a regular basis impossible, but I did a few event days where I could, borrowing time in my friend's recording studio to let the kids come in and lay down a few tracks that they could download and share with their friends. I'd done it a few times and always had a lot of fun when I did.

We set up a time on Saturday, and I made all the other arrangements necessary. Bright and early Saturday morning, I showed up outside the youth centre with a school bus, and we took a group of about twenty kids and their mentors to the small studio for the day.

If an activity had ever been designed to keep a man humble, working with kids had to be it. The younger ones had no idea who I was and the older ones didn't find being on Broadway very cool. They wanted to record hip-hop instead, so we did, with them giving me a hard time for my lack of street cred, as they saw it.

I didn't tell them that I grew up on the same streets they did, or that I used to go to the very same Chosen Family group they were part of. That was how I got to know Jordan in the first place.

By the time the bus dropped them all off again and I took a taxi home, I was exhausted in the best way. My apartment seemed quieter and emptier than usual after the noise and excitement of the day, and I found myself thinking, irrationally, that I'd like to tell Freya about it. Her laugh lingered so strongly in my memory, I could almost hear it as I imagined telling her about how I'd been relegated to backing vocals.

Even if I'd wanted to get in touch, though, I didn't have her number. She might be working again that night, but it would definitely start looking suspicious if I kept showing up at the restaurant for dinner, night after night.

As much as the idea of spending time with her appealed to me, I had to stay realistic too. Seeing the boys that day made it clear to me exactly why I couldn't get involved with her beyond friendship and, hopefully, being colleagues. Those kids had all been let down by a man in their lives, and the last thing I wanted was to add another kid to that list.

My relationships just didn't seem to last, and since I didn't really know why not, I didn't know how to prevent it happening again. Getting into a potentially doomed relationship when there were only two consenting adults involved would be one thing, but adding a child to the mix made it too much of a risk.

My reasoning left me with no choice: I had to keep my distance from Freya, no matter how much I'd rather not.

Chapter Four

~**Freya**~

Every time my phone rang, my heart rate spiked, anticipating the call from my agent to let me know that the producers had been in touch. And each time, when it turned out to be someone else, disappointment weighed down on me until I almost felt it would be better to simply find out I *hadn't* got the part rather than live in limbo any longer.

Almost, but not quite. Because those little moments where I imagined it happening, where I imagined the call coming and saying that they *did* want me were so good that even if it was false hope, I wanted to live in that hope just a little bit longer before reality intruded once again.

Even though I truly tried not to get my hopes up, I couldn't help picturing the rehearsals, the costume fittings, the opening night, and the applause of the crowd. Then there were the *other* daydreams: about me and Rome doing press appearances together and getting to kiss him night after night... on stage, of course. Only on stage.

After he left the restaurant on Wednesday, I realized that we hadn't exchanged numbers. I'd gotten so caught up in simply talking to him that I'd forgotten the number one rule of networking: exchange contact information. His comment about me being too good to remain undiscovered suggested that he might be willing to help me get noticed if the part didn't work out... but that would only work if we had a way of keeping in touch. Without his number, I'd either have to hope he came back to the restaurant again, or try to catch him at the theatre when he started working on the show, and neither of those options seemed as appealing to me as simply being able to text or call him.

Why hadn't I simply asked for his number when I had the chance? I could only put it down to getting distracted by those stunning blue eyes of his, which could hardly be considered professional behaviour.

After Friday came and went with no word, I suspected I wouldn't hear anything until Monday. Theatres didn't shut down for the weekend but producers kept different hours, and once I accepted nothing would happen for a few days, good or bad, I was able to relax and enjoy the weekend a little more.

On Sunday, I took Dylan to the zoo in Central Park. In the past few weeks, he had become obsessed with the snow leopards there and asked to go see them almost every other day. They had recently had cubs, and his 4-year-old brain simply could not comprehend why we couldn't get one to take home to our tiny Harlem apartment.

While we stood in front of the enclosure, his tiny face rapt with excitement as he watched the cubs playing together, my phone rang. Thinking it must be my mom calling to check in or a friend calling for a catch-up, I was surprised to see a cell phone number I didn't recognize on the screen.

"Hello?" I covered my other ear to try to drown out the chatter of the other families around us, taking a couple of steps back but keeping an eye on Dylan the whole time as he pressed his face up against the glass.

"Freya? It's Angela McIntyre."

My heart gave a painful thump as it began hammering in my chest. Angela was my agent, and she had *never* called me on the weekend before. I didn't even have her cell number in my contacts since I'd only ever contacted her through her office.

"Hi, Angela, how are you?" I made my best attempt at sounding casual, and she saw straight through it, laughing throatily through the phone.

"It's okay to ask me to get to the point. I know you're dying to know."

If she knew that, then why was she torturing me? "You're right, I am. So? You've heard from the show?"

"Just got off the phone with the producer," she confirmed. "They want you to play Julia."

The world around me seemed to shift, the colours changing and the sound distorting, like in a movie where things suddenly go into slow motion. My ears seemed to ring and I almost forgot how to breathe.

"I... I'm sorry, can you repeat that?" I needed to hear it one more time, to make sure my brain hadn't simply filled in the words I wanted to hear.

"You heard me," Angela said, laughing again. "You got it, Freya. You're going to be starring in a brand-new Broadway musical."

I got it? For real? I pinched myself, just to be sure, though the crying baby next to me should have been a pretty good sign too.

As I winced, I had to admit, it sure felt like real life. I didn't seem to be daydreaming.

"I... uh... wow, I don't know what to..." I tried to force words out of my mouth, to say *something* rather than leaving dead air between us as I internally freaked out, but all that came out was useless babble.

Luckily, Angela seemed to understand. "Take a minute, honey, it's okay. I'm going to email you over the contract, take a look through it and let me know if you've got any questions. You can reach me on this number any time, okay?"

I had obviously just been bumped up my agent's priority list, along with everything else. "Okay. Thank you, Angela."

"You're welcome, and congratulations! You deserve this."

She hung up just in time for me to see Dylan try to take a lick of another boy's ice cream cone. Muttering a mild curse under my breath, I quickly hurried back over to him.

"That's not yours, Dylan." I shot the other boy's mom an apologetic look, but she simply shook her head and looked away. It seemed my newfound success wouldn't protect me from the usual mom trials, but at least I could brush them off more easily. "Come on, buddy, we'll get one of our own, and then it's time to go home."

He wasn't thrilled about leaving so soon, but the promise of ice cream seemed to help. Meanwhile, I might as well have been walking on air as we headed back to the subway station. Everything around me seemed a little bit brighter, a little more full of promise. My whole world had changed with just one phone call.

When we got back above ground in Harlem, my phone buzzed with a waiting message from another number I didn't recognize. Holding Dylan's hand, I pressed my phone to my ear with the other hand to listen to the voicemail, and nearly dropped my phone in surprise as an unexpected voice began speaking.

"Hi Freya, it's Rome. I just heard the good news. Congratulations! I'm really excited to work with you. Let me know if you want any help reviewing the contract, I know it can all be a bit overwhelming the first time around. This is my number, give me a call back when you can. I hope you're out celebrating."

How did he get my number? I knew I hadn't given it to him; I would definitely remember that.

No sooner had he hung up than a little voice spoke up from next to me. "Mommy, I tired. You carry Dylan."

Putting the phone back in my pocket, I picked up my son and carried him the rest of the way home, my heart racing for a whole new reason as Rome's message played on repeat in my head.

After all those years, my dreams were finally coming true. I just had to make sure I didn't let myself get carried away.

~Rome~

Jeffrey Neill broke the news to me. He called me Sunday morning to see if I would be interested in going to a show with him that afternoon because he'd seen something in one of the characters he thought might be interesting for Victor's part. Getting to attend other shows was one of my favourite parts of being between roles; normally, when I was performing, it became impossible to see all the other shows that were going on because of my own performance schedule. As much as I loved being on stage, I also loved to watch other people performing. As a true fan of the art form, I could always learn something new.

Therefore, when the offer came in, I jumped at it, and soon Jeffrey and I were seated next to each other in the house seats for one of the biggest shows of the season. The show was excellent, the cast were wonderful, and as Jeffrey and I sat together over coffee afterwards, we discussed the ways that the main character compared to Victor and what elements might be appropriate for his portrayal.

"By the way, the producers have decided to offer Freya the role of Julia," he added casually on our way out of the coffee shop. "They should be calling her agent this afternoon."

"That's great." I did my best to appear pleased but not overly invested. "Does that mean Jennifer accepted for Constance?"

He nodded. "The producers wanted to get that squared away first since they don't really have any doubt that Freya will accept."

I didn't either, knowing the excitement coursing through my veins would only be a fraction of what she'd feel when she got that call. Although that moment happened seven years earlier for me, I could still remember exactly where I'd been and what I'd been doing when I got the call offering me my first starring role. I suspected it would be just the same for Freya.

I could also recall just how overwhelming the whole thing felt, and the urge I'd had to just say yes to everything without understanding all that went into the contract. So, as I walked home to my apartment, I thought it might be helpful for her to have someone to talk business with, someone who had been through it and could be a neutral party, rather than her agent who obviously had a vested interest in her signing.

Unfortunately, I didn't have Freya's number. It crossed my mind after I left the restaurant earlier that week that I hadn't asked for it nor had she offered, and I took it as one more sign that perhaps I was meant to keep my distance. That afternoon, however, I really wished I had it.

I could call Jeffrey to ask for it, but I'd rather not involve anyone else from the show, so instead, I decided to head to the restaurant again. Perhaps she would even be working that night and I could congratulate her in person. That would be nice.

However, when I inquired at the hostess' station, the women there told me that Freya had the day off. Next, I asked if I could get her number, but as soon as the words came out of my mouth, I heard just how creepy and wrong they sounded. I actually felt quite relieved when she told me she couldn't give it to me.

My hand was on the door to leave when one of the other waitresses came running up. "Wait! You're looking for Freya's number?"

The pretty brunette gave me a smile, which didn't quite compare to Freya's, I couldn't help thinking, but I gave her a smile of my own in return. "That's right, but I understand why you can't give it to me. I wasn't thinking."

"I don't think she'd mind if you had it, Rome." The woman gave me a wink, making it clear, even if she hadn't already said my name, that she knew exactly who I was. Had Freya been talking about me? The idea made me happier than it probably should have. "I'm Elyse, I'm a good friend of hers, and if she gets pissed off that I gave it out, you can blame it on me."

That sounded like a good deal to me. "Thanks, Elyse, I appreciate that."

I handed over my phone so she could enter Freya's number in, and she added hers as well for good measure.

"In case you ever need me again," she said, giving me one more wink before she sauntered back to the dining room.

I knew an invitation when I heard one, but at that moment, my thoughts were still on Freya. As I walked back to my apartment, I called her number, but to my disappointment, it went straight to voicemail. Perhaps she was busy taking other congratulatory calls from people who were smart enough to get her number in the first place.

I left a message anyway and once I got home, I did my best to distract myself while waiting for her to return my call. My nervous energy made it difficult to sit still. The more I thought about getting to work with her, the more excited I became, and I could almost convince myself it only had to do with how talented she was. It would be a privilege to get to introduce the rest of the world to her, and to help her transition into the spotlight she was so clearly born for.

At last, my phone rang, and my fingers fumbled over the screen as Freya's name popped up.

"Hey, Freya. Congratulations again."

"Thank you." She sounded breathless, which I hoped was a result of her own excitement. "I don't know if I quite believed it until I got your message. It's really happening, right?"

"It is," I assured her, grinning into the phone like an idiot. Just hearing her wasn't enough; I wanted to see the look on her face too. "Can I call you back on video?"

"Oh, uh, sure. Just give me a minute to get set up."

After hanging up, I pulled out my own laptop so I could see her on the full screen and counted down the rest of the minute until I could call again.

When she answered, she sat on a plush red sofa in a cozy-looking room. Throw pillows in shades of red and brown surrounded her, and behind her on the wall was the bottom of a photo that looked like it might be her and her son, but I couldn't see their faces. It didn't matter though, since the face I was most interested in waved at me adorably, trying to hide her smile.

"Don't hold back," I told her. "Let me see how you really feel."

Her smile immediately flashed wider, the joy in her expression setting off an answering wave of happiness inside me. I couldn't remember the last time I'd been so excited about a casting, and it wasn't even my own. "I don't even know what to do, Rome. I hardly feel like I'm touching the ground. I just want to go and shout it from the rooftop."

"So do it," I encouraged, grinning back at her. "It's New York, nobody cares."

She looked tempted for a moment, but ultimately shook her head. "There's no roof access at my building, but maybe I'll go out on the fire escape later."

I wanted to say she could come and use my roof. I wanted to shout it out with her. The words were on the tip of my tongue when suddenly, another face appeared, a curious little face close to the camera, peering in at me.

"Who's that?" The boy's voice was inquisitive as he came even closer, until all I could see were eyes and forehead.

"Back up, Dill, he can't see you," Freya said in the background, and the boy did as she said, taking a step back so I could see him fully as Freya's arms resting protectively on his shoulders. "This is Mommy's friend. Can you say hi?"

"Hi," the boy said obediently, his big brown eyes still watching me with interest.

"Tell him your name," Freya prompted.

"Dylan," he told me before turning back to his mom. "What's his name?"

"You can ask him." The smile she gave him was full of love and patience and pride, and it brought me right back down to earth, tempering my excitement as the reality of the situation hit me once again. No matter how swept up she might get in the show, this other part of her life had a claim on her, and I had to respect that.

"What's your name?" Dylan asked me, stepping close to the screen again.

"I'm Rome. It's nice to meet you, Dylan."

"Do you have laugh ears?" Those big, earnest brown eyes were back up close to the camera again, eyes that bore no real resemblance to Freya's hazel ones. He must have got them from his father, making me wonder who his father might be and why he wasn't around. Freya had said he 'wasn't in the picture', making it sound like he had chosen not to be part of their lives. I honestly couldn't imagine why not.

"I'm sorry?" I said in response to Dylan's question. I had no idea what a laugh ear was, or if I'd even heard him correctly.

"Leopards," Freya translated from behind him, though I couldn't see her behind Dylan's giant face. "He wants to know if you have leopards. We saw them at the zoo earlier."

"You have big house," Dylan added, exploring my background, and he wasn't wrong. From where I sat in my kitchen with the whole open-plan living room behind me, my apartment did look pretty spacious. "Mommy says our house is too small."

"She's probably right," I had to agree. "Leopards need a lot of room to run. I don't think my house is big enough either, so I don't have any leopards."

"Okay, Dill-pickle, that's enough questions for now, can you go and play with your cars for a little while?"

He ran out of the shot without a backward glance and Freya gave me an apologetic smile. "Sorry about that. My mom's out at the moment, it's just the two of us here."

"That's absolutely fine. He's sweet." The words came easily since they seemed to be true.

She looked more appreciative of that response than she'd been of any other compliment I'd given her so far. "He is. Anyway, you said you'd help me review the contract? That would be amazing, if you're sure you don't mind?"

"Of course not, it'd be my pleasure."

She shared her screen with me so we could review it together and I made a few suggestions of things I would go back to them with. "Are you sure it's not going to make me seem difficult?" she wondered. "I don't want to mess this up."

"You're not asking for anything unreasonable," I assured her. "It just shows that you know your own worth, and they'll respect that. Trust me, by the time you get to this point, they've got their hearts set on you. They'll agree to those requests."

The document disappeared from my screen as Freya's face returned. "Thanks, Rome. I really appreciate this."

"It's no problem. There are going to be a lot of firsts for you over the next little while, but I'll be here for you. From now on, your success is the show's success, which means it's my success too. We're in this together."

"That sounds really good." Her sweet smile warmed me again. "I guess I'll see you when rehearsals start."

"Or before," I heard myself offering before I even realized I was going to say it. "You've got my number now, so if you need anything before then, feel free to get in touch."

"I will." It almost sounded like a promise, though I could hear a touch of uncertainty in her voice too. "Goodbye, Rome."

"Bye."

She disappeared as the call ended, and silence settled over my apartment once more. In the stillness, the first thing that came into my head was to wonder how big an apartment would have to be before you could comfortably house a leopard in it.

Keeping an emotional distance might be more of a challenge than I thought.

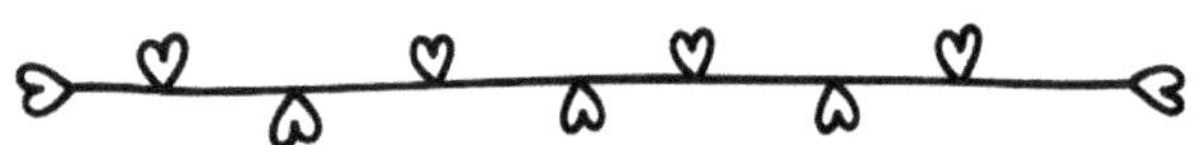

~Freya~

The following week flew by, each minute packed with activity.

After negotiating and agreeing on the contract with my agent, including asking for and receiving the additional concessions Rome had encouraged me to ask for, I had to give my notice at the restaurant. Having a lot of actors on staff, they were used to people getting roles at short notice, so they didn't make a fuss about rehearsals starting in just one week. When I told my manager about the part I'd be playing, she was thrilled for me, as was Elyse, who admitted to me she'd been the one to give Rome my phone number. I had assumed he must have got it from the producers, so I was surprised and a little flattered when Elyse told me he'd come to the restaurant to get it.

"I gave him my number at the same time," she told me with a wink. "Since you're not interested, he won't be dating his co-star, which means he's on the market, right? You want to put in a good word for me?"

I laughed along with her, trying to ignore the odd, unsettled feeling that bubbled up in my stomach at the thought of Rome and Elyse dating. I had no reason to feel that way, since she was right: I *wasn't* interested in a relationship with the one and only Romeo Taylor. If he wanted to date someone else, he was free to do so.

Though, to be fair, the Rome I had started to get to know wasn't at all what I thought he'd be like.

That's what they all think, I tried to remind myself. Every woman he dated must have gone into it thinking that with her, it would be different. It hadn't worked out before, but that time, it would. I couldn't let myself fall into that trap.

Not when I had Dylan to think about too.

With a slightly bigger paycheck on the horizon, I splurged and took Dylan on a few adventures during the weekdays. Rehearsals would last six weeks before the show opened, and during that time, I would be gone most of the day so I wasn't going to get to see him very much other than on weekends. I wanted to make those last few days count.

We spent a day at Coney Island, and another taking the ferry over to Staten Island for a picnic. Dylan loved being on the water, his big brown eyes wide with wonder as we sailed past the Statue of Liberty.

Another day, we went to the Bronx Zoo, which was bigger than the one in Central Park but still had snow leopards we could visit. Watching Dylan as he almost vibrated with excitement watching the big cats play, I couldn't help remembering the conversation he'd had with Rome about the leopards, and how sweet and natural Rome had been with him.

Stop that, Freya. Rome had been polite and nothing more. I really needed to stop reading too much into every little thing Rome did.

Like the texts he sent me throughout the week. They weren't long or too frequent, just a note here and there with something that had occurred to him that he thought would be useful for me to know. When I'd reply, he'd respond too, both of us bantering back and forth a few times, until I let it die off.

He was being friendly and supportive to his new colleague. It meant nothing more, and it *couldn't* mean anything more. I knew that.

My mom and I also discussed Dylan's care, especially over the next month and a half while I'd be in rehearsal. Normally, I would be around during the day and could watch him if she needed to be on business calls, but with the change in schedule, we agreed to get someone to come in and help out in the apartment, with my mom still there. I wanted both my mom and Dylan to be happy and productive, so although the cost would eat into my new salary, it would be worth it.

Besides getting my personal life in order, I also had to learn the rest of my part for the show. As soon as the contract had been signed, the producers sent me the full script along with recordings of the music for all my songs. I read through it at night when I got home from the restaurant, while Dylan slept peacefully in his bed, my heart soaring and racing as I imagined performing the lines in front of thousands of people every night. I listened to the music on my headphones during my commute to the restaurant, humming along until I knew every word.

Most of all, I couldn't wait to act it all out with Rome beside me. Every time I got to a kiss in the script, it took me back to that moment in the audition room when we'd kissed, smelling the masculine scent of him and feeling the soft press of his lips against mine.

There were five kisses in the show, five times I would get to have that feeling every day. Ten times on days when we had both an afternoon and evening performance.

That would be more than enough. I certainly didn't need to think about kissing him outside of those times too.

By the time Monday morning dawned, I was a bundle of nerves and excitement, and after hugging my mom and Dylan goodbye in the morning, I made my way to Midtown and the rehearsal space that would be my home base for the next month until we moved into the theatre.

Besides me as Julia and Rome as Victor, the show also starred Jennifer as Constance and Blain Carroll as Edward, Victor's long-suffering servant. A fun side plot involved Edward having to distract Constance so Julia and Victor could have some time alone together, and they ended up developing a romance of their own.

Eight other actors had speaking roles, and there were another ten in the chorus, who played multiple characters across different scenes. In addition to the adult actors, there were also the three young actors who would be alternating playing the role of Michael, Julia's son. They were only six or seven years old, just older than Dylan, and my heart melted as I got introduced to them as soon as I arrived.

"We're going to do their scenes in the morning so they can get back to school," the assistant director told me. "They'll be in three days a week for rehearsal."

Besides Rome and Jennifer, I hadn't met any of the other actors in person yet, though I knew many of them by name. Everyone was kind and welcoming, and as we were all called in to start the day, my nerves began to dissipate, leaving only the excitement behind.

"Good morning." Rome's voice sounded cheerful as he took a seat next to me in the rehearsal room, looking cool and casual in a button up shirt and blue jeans. His captivating blue eyes twinkled in anticipation. "I love the first day of rehearsal."

"Me too." I smiled over at him, glad to see that he looked almost as excited as I did. Though he'd been doing this a lot longer than I had, he hadn't lost any of his enthusiasm for it, and that both inspired and comforted me.

"I've got something for you," he added as the creative team walked into the room. "Remind me to give it to you before the end of the day."

The director started speaking before I had a chance to ask for any further details, leaving my mind racing with the possibilities.

"Congratulations to all of you, and thank you for being here," the director greeted us. "This show is going to be something special, I think you'll all agree, but we've got a lot of work to do to get us from those pages in your hands to opening night six weeks from now. I could give you a big pep talk about the privilege of being here and the talent that you all bring to the table, but I'm sure you know it all already. So, let's do what we all came here for: let's get to work."

Chapter Five

~**Rome**~

As I told Freya, I really did love the first day of rehearsals. At that moment, anything felt possible, before any decisions had been made or anything was set in stone. Though I had an idea in my head of who the character was from reading the script and talking to the show's creator, in that room, Victor would grow and develop and take on a life of his own. Some of that came from seeing how my 'audience' reacted to him, and a lot of it would come from Freya and the other actors and how they chose to play their parts too.

I had hoped to have a chance to speak with Freya before the rehearsal started, but she arrived only a few minutes before we got underway. I could understand that; she must have to look after her son in the morning, and I had no idea how far away she lived. Meanwhile, with my apartment only a short walk away and no other responsibilities, I had arrived more than half an hour early, as usual.

At least one person had expected that. "Figured I'd find you here already," Jennifer said as she came up to the coffee machine next to me. "Do you have time to talk?"

We hadn't had a proper conversation since our breakup almost six years earlier. If she had been cast as Julia, I would have reached out to her before that day, but as she hadn't, I figured I would let her take the lead. That seemed to be what she wanted to do then, so I agreed to her request and we both took our coffees into one of the small offices that bordered the rehearsal room.

Once upon a time, the woman in front of me meant a great deal to me, but looking at her that morning felt like looking at a stranger. Her glossy blonde hair was shorter and her makeup a little heavier than it used to be, but physically, she looked mostly the same. The changes that had occurred had been on an emotional level instead.

When we got cast in the show that we did together, seven years earlier, we were both not long out of drama school and it had been a whirlwind of excitement as we navigated all the firsts together. The thrill of red carpets and awards shows and the nightly applause seeped into our relationship, the line between personal and professional not only blurred but entirely erased.

I'd had other girlfriends before, but Jennifer was the first one I thought might be 'the one'. All the magazines and Broadway blogs certainly seemed to think so. Our relationship played out in the public eye and we both bought into the hype. We were labelled as 'Broadway's greatest love story' and it made the breakup all that more difficult for everyone to take, but especially for her, since it had been entirely my fault.

As for me, it actually amazed me how quickly I was able to move on, and that realization almost made me sadder than the actual end of the relationship did. Maybe our connection had never been quite as deep as it had seemed? Or maybe there was simply something wrong with me?

Our breakup seemed to be on Jennifer's mind that morning too. "I don't want there to be any awkwardness in there," she explained bluntly, her light brown eyes watching me closely. "You may have worked non-stop since we had our debut together, but I haven't. This role is important to me. I know you didn't want me to play Julia but I hope we can have a good working relationship. I'm willing to put everything behind us if you are."

Taking a sip of my coffee, I tried to figure out how to respond to that.

I had a few questions, but I started with the biggest one: "What makes you think I didn't want you to play Julia?"

"At the audition, you said you preferred Freya for the role."

I did say that, but it had nothing to do with our history, which she seemed to be implying. And how did she know I'd said it anyway? Someone in the room must have told her.

I kept my response to the point. "I gave my opinion based on the audition, but the final call wasn't mine. If they'd cast you, we would have made it work. You're a great actress and I respect that."

Her wary expression didn't change. "You want me to believe that your 'opinion' didn't play a role?"

I hadn't said that. "I don't know how much of a role it played since I had no involvement in the final deliberation. I also said that I thought you'd do a good job in the part. Maybe your spy didn't tell you that. Either way, in the end, the producers made the call and went with who they wanted."

She shook her head, and I didn't know if that meant she disagreed or that she simply wanted to move on. When she spoke again, it seemed to be the latter. "In any case, we're here now and I just wanted to put it out there that I want us to be able to work well together. I've moved on, I'm in a relationship, and there are no hard feelings, at least on my side. I want to be sure you feel the same."

Her relationship came as news to me, but I was happy to hear it. How could I explain to her that there had *never* been any hard feelings on my side because I had never felt it as deeply as she had? Since I had no kind way to say that, I simply nodded. "Absolutely no hard feelings. I'm glad that you're here, Jenn. You're going to be a huge asset to the show."

With that settled, we both went back out to mingle with the others. There were several actors I knew already and some I didn't, so I took a moment to speak to everyone, and I only saw Freya for the first time when we got into the rehearsal room itself. The chair next to her was empty, so I quickly grabbed it for myself.

The children in the show were with us for the first-day introductions so we did a few scenes with them first, and once they'd gone, the whole cast sat down for a full read-through of the show. It marked our first time to hear the other actors reading their parts and singing their songs, and the director and the composer both took furious notes throughout.

Though Freya must have been nervous, she did a great job. She already had a lot of the script memorized, as did I, so when we had our scenes together, we spoke them looking at each other rather than at our notes. Not only that, but her singing voice sounded wonderful. It had a warm, earthy quality to it, and, at least to my ears, we sounded great together on our duets. When we got to the scenes where we were meant to kiss, her eyes flicked down to my lips, just as they had at the audition, and I couldn't help wondering if she had enjoyed that kiss as much as I had.

We were going to have an opportunity to practice a lot more, very soon.

When the run-through finished, we took a break for lunch. I hoped to snag some one-on-one time with Freya then, but the director came over to speak to me before I had a chance to ask Freya if she had plans for the break, and as I spoke with him, I heard Jennifer come and ask Freya to join her for lunch instead.

Groaning internally, I watched them go. Not only was I on my own for lunch, but I had to spend the whole time wondering exactly what my ex-girlfriend might say about me to my intriguing new co-star.

~Freya~

Reading through the show with the whole cast gave me such a buzz. I'd done read-throughs before, but not since drama school had I been the lead in one of those shows. More recently, in the few off-Broadway shows I'd done, I'd been a member of the chorus, with a handful of solo lines if I was lucky. That morning, however, I featured in nearly every scene, and as I listened to the script coming to life around me, I got more excited than ever before.

This show was incredible. It would be amazing, and we were all going to be amazing in it.

Even better, no one had looked at me like I didn't belong there. In fact, several times I caught the composer, Jeffrey, nodding his head at something I'd done or the way I said a line, and though I knew there would be plenty of constructive notes coming, it also generally felt like I was on the right track, which excited me too.

Then, there was Rome. He couldn't have been more supportive, and he had a way of building up whoever he did a scene with, all without fading into the background himself. He never stole a scene but you never forgot his presence either. It was a rare talent.

The little smiles and nods he gave me after I finished a scene were incredibly encouraging, and I had hoped we might be able to have lunch together to talk over some of the lines that had been tripping me up while rehearsing on my own.

However, as soon as we broke for lunch, the director cornered Rome, and as I packed my script away, Jennifer Marshall came over to me.

"Have you got plans for lunch, Freya? I'd love to get to know you a little better."

That was very nice of her, especially when she could have chosen to be standoffish after I got the part instead of her. Since the truth was that I had no plans beyond some vague, undefined hopes of talking to Rome, I agreed. After leaving the building, we stopped at a small grocery store close by so she could grab something to eat from the deli counter. With money tight for me, I had brought a bagged lunch. Once she had her food, we made small talk as we walked the few blocks to Bryant Park and found a place we could sit among the other working people taking a break from their jobs. The late September day still felt like summer as the birds tweeted in the trees around us and the warm sun shone down, but it wouldn't be long before the weather turned and fall arrived with all its blustery greyness.

"Has it all sunk in yet?" Jennifer asked with a friendly smile once we were settled and had both taken a bite of our salads. "Do you believe that you're starring in a Broadway show?"

"Honestly, no." I returned her smile as I answered honestly. "Just when I think I've accepted it, something else occurs to me, and it hits me all over again."

She nodded knowingly. "It'll be like that for a while. There'll be interviews and TV appearances and award shows, and more. Just enjoy every second of it."

She was being very gracious about the whole thing, and I tentatively acknowledged that fact. "You would have made an amazing Julia."

"I would have," she agreed bluntly, but with a twinkle in her eyes that made us both laugh. "But the producers wanted you, and you should never apologize or feel bad for that, Freya. You've got enough pressure on you as it is. You need to trust that you deserve this, and I promise you'll never hear otherwise from me."

"Thank you." I truly appreciated that, especially since a lot of people in her position would be bitter about the way things had turned out. "I definitely feel supported. Jeffrey's been so kind, and Rome has already given me some great advice too."

Rome's name made her wince, and immediately, I felt insensitive for bringing him up. Although I wasn't naive enough to believe everything I'd heard or read about their relationship, I had to assume at least the basics of the rumours were true since she'd never said otherwise. The relationship ending hadn't been her idea, by all accounts.

"Rome is great," she told me, though her tone suggested something slightly different. "Just be aware that he's someone who will tell you exactly what you want to hear in the moment even if it's not always the truth. He's adaptable, just like he is on stage, and though it's a great quality in a co-star, it's less useful in a friend or a boyfriend."

Well, she certainly didn't beat around the bush, so I kept my reply just as straightforward. "I'm not getting into a relationship with him."

Her smile felt almost wistful and not entirely without condescension. "You aren't the first one to say that."

I didn't doubt that, but I also suspected none of them had the same reasons I did, and I told her about that honestly as well. "It's not just me I have to be concerned about. I've got a four-year-old son and he's my priority, always. I'm well aware of Rome's reputation, and that kind of instability isn't what I need in my life or my son's. I hope we can be friends, just like I hope you and I can be friends, but that's all it is."

She nodded with what looked like approval as she took another bite of her lunch. "It sounds like you're seeing things clearly right now, but just take my warning: he's got a way of changing the picture. Before you even realize it, you're seeing things through Rome-tinted glasses."

The pun made me smile, but I heard her warning clearly. She'd been there, after all. It hit differently than Elyse and I gossiping in the restaurant kitchen.

"Do you regret the time you spent together?" I asked, not quite sure if the question overstepped our new acquaintance. She'd been the one to bring him up.

She looked away from me, as if looking into the past, with a rueful smile. "It was the best year of my life. Not just because of Rome, although he played a big part in it, so how can I regret that? No, I wouldn't change it, but I do wish I wouldn't have let myself fall quite so hard. People think I was the first and I couldn't have known any differently, but that's not exactly true. He had the same pattern in college too."

Those words hit me harder than I expected, and I forced myself to swallow down the lump in my throat. "He did the whole showmance thing in college?"

Jennifer nodded again. "He was up front with me about it when we got together and talked about past relationships. He said he'd dated other co-stars before but it had never worked out long term because their interests would diverge after the show ended. I didn't put it together at the time that his only interest *is* the show. He lives and breathes the show he's doing, which again, is a brilliant quality in an actor, but not a good one in a boyfriend. Once the show's over, he'll move on, no matter who he leaves behind."

Snippets of long-repressed memories tried to push their way to the surface as I heard a different voice talking to me on a similar theme: *We got caught up in the fantasy, the make-believe. It was never real, Freya.*

It had been real to Jennifer though, and though she didn't appear to carry a grudge, the experience had obviously hardened her.

"Are you seeing anyone at the moment?" I asked, trying to move on from Rome and learn more about her at the same time.

It worked, as she smiled a softer smile that time. "I am. It's kind of a secret, at least for now, but I'm hopeful about it."

The word 'secret' twisted like a sharp knife in the already tender spot of my memory that had just been opened up, and I struggled to keep from grimacing. "I hope it works out for you. If you ever want to talk about it, I'm here. I might as well live vicariously through someone else's love life."

That made her smile, and soon the lunch break had flown by and we needed to head back. Rome had already reclaimed his seat inside the rehearsal room, sitting there chatting to another of the cast members, but he gave me a warm smile as I walked in.

"How was your lunch?" he asked, flashing a curious look over in Jennifer's direction.

Obviously, I couldn't tell him what we talked about, so I simply said I'd enjoyed it and asked him about a line from the reading that morning that had caused me trouble. Immediately, he put his actor hat on and we chatted about the script until the director returned and the real work of the afternoon began.

~Rome~

Though Freya still seemed friendly and engaged all afternoon, a new wariness lurked in her eyes. Maybe I was being paranoid, but I couldn't help thinking that Jennifer might have said something to her about me over lunch that caused the distance I could feel between us.

What could she have said, though? The facts of our breakup were common knowledge. I had no dark secret to hide, so why was I worried about being exposed?

And why did I care, anyway? Nothing was going to happen between me and Freya romantically, I'd already decided on that, and she'd given me no indication she wanted it to anyway.

When rehearsal ended for the day, Freya quickly grabbed her bag to pack up her script and notes. Although we'd spent the whole day together, we hadn't had a chance to talk about anything outside of the show, and it disappointed me whether I wanted it to or not.

"I don't suppose you have time to get a coffee?" I suggested as I grabbed my own things. "There's a cafe on the corner next to the subway station."

Freya shook her head apologetically. "I can't, I've got to get home. I've already missed the whole day with Dylan, I'll only have an hour or so before he goes to bed."

Of course. She was a mother who actually wanted to spend time with her child.

That did, however, remind me of something else. "In that case, let me get you your gift."

"Gift?" Freya repeated curiously as she followed me out of the rehearsal room. They were people trying to catch my eye, wanting to talk to me about various things to do with the show, but they could wait. First, I had to dig out the small gift bag I'd hidden in the production manager's office earlier.

I'd kept it small. There had been other things I'd considered buying, but I remembered that she would have to carry it home on the subway, so I tried to be practical. "Here. There's something for you and something for Dylan too. I hope that's okay."

I held out the bag to her and she took it from me tentatively, a look of confusion on her face. "What's the occasion?"

"The first day of rehearsal," I reminded her with a laugh, gesturing around us. "I always get my co-stars something. It's an exciting day, and hopefully, it will be a fond memory someday."

Freya still looked almost bewildered as she examined the bag. "Thank you, Rome. I didn't expect this at all. Was I supposed to get you something?"

I knew what she meant; she wondered if this was some kind of Broadway tradition that she wasn't aware of. "Not at all. This is just me, it's something I started doing with my early shows and have never stopped."

I didn't tell her the reason I'd started doing it, which had to do with trying to impress the girl I starred with in my first high school show. My methods of seduction had improved since then, and the gift no longer factored into it. I just genuinely wanted to do something nice for her, as a friend and a colleague.

"I'll see you tomorrow," I added, so she felt free to go. "Great work today."

"Thanks. You too. I mean, you're always great, but today was fun."

She seemed slightly flustered, the gift having really thrown her off, and it was kind of adorable. I simply smiled as she collected herself and headed out the door. As soon as she'd gone, a steady stream of people appeared, wanting to claim my attention, but the whole while, part of my thoughts remained with Freya and Dylan and hoping they would like their presents.

~Freya~

Curiosity ate away at me the whole way home, holding Rome's gift bag in my hand. What did he buy for me? And for Dylan too? For my son's sake, I hadn't opened the gift immediately, since I knew he would get a huge thrill out of opening it himself. My own curiosity came secondary to his excitement, as usual. Though it drove me crazy, I would wait.

The babysitter had already left by the time I got home and my mom and Dylan were in the kitchen, making supper together. He loved to help and my mom made the most of it, putting him to work on any tasks appropriate for a four-year-old and inventing things for him to do if she had nothing he could actually help with. She was amazing with him and I learned so much from her.

"Mommy!" Dylan's squeal of excitement as he caught sight of me melted my heart, and a second later, he launched himself at me, jumping into my waiting arms.

"Hey, Dill. Did you have a fun day today?"

He proceeded to tell me all about his day while he and I set the table. It seemed the new babysitter got his stamp of approval because she liked to colour, but frustrated him because she said they couldn't go to the zoo every day.

As we sat down to eat, Dylan kept up his steady stream of chatter while my mom tried to throw in the odd question about my own day. I simply told her it went well, planning to fill her in more once Dylan had gone to bed.

Only when we finished supper did I tell Dylan about his present. "Do you remember the man Mommy spoke to on the computer the other day? The one with the big house?"

Dylan nodded, though I couldn't be sure if he actually did or if he just agreed because it seemed easiest.

"He sent you a present, I left it at the door. Do you want to go find it and bring it here to open it?"

His little mouth formed a perfect O shape as he hopped off his chair and ran down the hall.

"A present for Dylan?" my mom asked, a touch of wariness in her voice. "From Rome?"

I nodded, trying to look as though it were perfectly normal and not at all unexpected. "He's a nice guy, as I told you."

Her lips pressed together as Dylan returned, and I suspected she would have more to say about that later.

"What is it?" Dylan asked breathlessly, placing the bag on the table and climbing back up onto his chair.

"I don't know, you'll have to open it up and see. There's something for you and something for me."

My mom's eyebrows shot up even higher, but she said nothing as we both watched Dylan pull the bag open. His chubby little hands immediately pulled out a book, and his eyes widened once more as he looked at the cover.

"Mommy, look! A leopard!"

He still had the book facing him, so I couldn't see a thing. "Show me, sweetheart."

Adorably, he turned his whole body around so that I could see it but he could still see it too. He had it exactly right; the book was all about a snow leopard. Had I told Rome that Dylan liked snow leopards? I remembered talking about leopards, but I didn't say snow leopards in particular, at least not that I could remember.

"Read," Dylan instructed, pushing the book at me and trying to push his way onto my lap as he jumped off his chair again.

"Wait, hold on," I teased him. "Maybe this one's for me. What else is in the bag?"

As sweet as the book might be, I was more curious about what Rome had bought for me.

When Dylan reached in again and pulled out a small Tiffany's jewellery box, my mom gasped in surprise and my eyes widened in disbelief. *Seriously?*

My son, meanwhile, turned the box over in frustration. It didn't look nearly as interesting to him as the book in my hands, and he told me so.

"No, leopards are mine!"

"You're probably right," I agreed with a smile. "Can I see that one though?"

He handed it over to me as I returned his book, and my mom leaned forward curiously as I popped the lid of the box open. Inside was a silver necklace holding a shooting star. My fingers fumbled over the delicate pendant as I lifted it and turned it over. On the back, my name and that day's date were engraved.

"It's beautiful," my mom correctly pointed out. "And expensive."

That seemed likely, but Rome was a single man with a very successful career. What seemed like a lot of money to me probably didn't have the same significance to him. It didn't mean anything more than what he'd said it signified: a gift to a colleague to celebrate the start of rehearsals.

Once Dylan had been tucked up in bed, having read through his new book at least twenty times, I sat down on the couch with my mom. She knew all about Rome, I'd told her the whole story about his background before I even got cast, so that night, she looked at me thoughtfully over her glass of wine.

"I thought you said you weren't encouraging him." The words weren't accusatory, just curious, but I winced anyway.

"I'm not. I'm not trying to, anyway. I think this is just how he is. He's a passionate man, he likes the gestures and the big drama. He's an actor, after all."

"And the book for Dylan?" my mom prompted, and once again, she had a point. The necklace for me was one thing, but buying something for my son went a step further. Still, I didn't want to read too much into it.

"Honestly, I think he's just being kind. He knows Dylan's important to me. I've already made that clear."

My mom cut straight to the point. "You know I want you to be happy and fall in love again, Freya. I'm just not sure about this guy. The last thing you need is..."

"... someone like Matthew," I filled in for her. "I know. Trust me, Mom,

I know. I won't lose sight of it. Rome is a colleague, and that's all."

Her silence on the matter suggested she didn't entirely believe me, but I meant it. I felt sure I did. One present, no matter how thoughtful and generous, wouldn't make me forget everything at stake.

My priorities were my son and the show. Romance, if it waited out there for me at all, would just have to wait.

Chapter Six

The next morning, Freya arrived wearing the necklace I'd given her, and the sight of it against her skin sent a warm glow of appreciation straight through me, settling in my chest. The V-neck of her red sweater framed it perfectly and her hair, pulled up into a messy bun, showed off the chain around her neck. Her smile as she sat down next to me made it worth every dollar I'd spent.

"Thank you for the presents, Rome," she said before I could even wish her good morning. "It's too much, but since you had it engraved, I guess I can't give it back."

"I wouldn't accept it anyway. It looks great on you, and you deserve it. This is a big deal, Freya. Enjoy it."

"I'm trying to," she promised. "Dylan loved his book too. How did you know snow leopards are his favourite?"

"An educated guess," I admitted. "You said you saw them at the zoo. I figured that probably meant the Central Park Zoo, and they only have snow leopards there."

"Clever," Freya conceded, giving me a teasing smile. "So, you're not just a pretty face, huh?"

The playful taunt had me grinning. "Don't tell anyone else. It's a well-kept secret."

She would have had a retort for that, I felt certain, but we had no more time to chat as rehearsal got underway for the day and we were swept up in the show. The hours flew by, as they did the next day, and the next. Working with Freya was wonderful; she was responsive and almost completely without ego, willing to try just about anything, and I could already tell that being on stage with her would keep me on my toes. She never played anything exactly the same way twice, always keeping my attention focused entirely on her to see what she'd do next.

I'd had people tell me similar things about my acting, and though there were some people who would prefer a more predictable partner, Freya didn't seem to be one of them. She fed off my energy, and several times, we found ourselves improvising new lines that seemed to fit better in the moment, and often, the show's creator agreed. Other times, he told us firmly to read the line as written, which we took in stride. The experimentation was half the fun, and neither of us took offense if something didn't work. Rehearsals were the perfect time to figure all of that out.

I looked forward to every scene we had together. So far, we hadn't kissed again; every time we'd get to that point in a scene, the director would skip over it, saying we could work on it later. Apparently, he felt the kiss didn't require much rehearsing, but I begged to disagree, and not strictly for professional reasons.

Not kissing Freya wasn't my only frustration over the week either, despite how well things were going in general. I never seemed to be able to get her alone. She made friends with the other cast members quickly, and on breaks and over lunch, she'd often be with them. I could join them, but we never had a chance to have a private conversation, just the two of us. It started to make me a little paranoid. Was she avoiding me on purpose, or was it just a coincidence? I really couldn't tell, and knowing that her time after rehearsals was off-limits because of her son, it didn't leave me with many other options.

By the time Friday came around, I'd decided I would have to get a little creative, and as soon as Freya took her usual seat next to me in the morning, I jumped in with my offer.

"What are you up to this weekend?"

The soft smile she gave me always seemed to accompany any talk of her son. "I'm spending it with Dylan since I've hardly seen him this week."

That was exactly what I'd been anticipating, but not all I wanted to know. "Do you have anything in particular planned?"

She shook her head. "No, we'll probably just go to the park and play at home, nothing too exciting. What about you?"

"Actually, I've been thinking of going to the Bronx Zoo. Dylan got me thinking about the leopards and it's been ages since I went."

Freya's laugh sounded warm and genuine. "He'll be thrilled that he's influenced you. He doesn't understand why everyone doesn't want to talk about the leopards all the time."

She'd given me just the opening I needed. "Actually, if you're not too busy, you could both come along too. I'd enjoy the company, and I think there's even a special VIP experience you can get where you get to go 'behind the scenes' in the leopard enclosure."

Saying I 'thought' so was a little disingenuous, since I'd already booked it in the hopes that she would agree.

Freya's eyes widened in both surprise and a hint of wariness. "There is, but it's very expensive. I can't afford it."

"I can." I hoped it didn't come across as a boast, but I didn't want her to worry about the cost.

Freya reached for another excuse. "I'm sure you have better things to be doing."

"I really don't." Perhaps sadly, that was true. On Saturday evening, I had tickets to a show with some friends, but during the day, I had no plans at all. "And it would be my pleasure. We've spent the whole week together and aside from being impressed with your talent, I don't know anything more about you than I did on Monday. I'd like to get to know you better, Freya, but I understand that you need to spend the time with your son. There's no reason we can't all have some fun together."

She obviously still had some reservations, making me wonder exactly why. Had Jennifer said something to sway her opinion of me? Jenn had been fine with me all week, friendly without getting too close, so she didn't seem to be out to sabotage me, but I honestly didn't know what else would have Freya looking so leery.

I did my best to guess, though, and to put her mind at ease. "This is only as friends, of course, and you can make that clear to Dylan. It's not a date."

Once again, I took Freya by surprise, but that surprise, she appreciated. Obviously, she hadn't expected me to consider things from Dylan's point of view. "He hasn't spent a lot of time around men," she admitted to me. "He's with me and my mom most of the time, or my friends who are female, or his nursery teachers, who are female. You'd be a novelty, but you're right, I don't want him to misunderstand."

"I don't want that either." I had no intention of causing him any confusion, but if we were up front and honest with him, I couldn't see it being a problem. "So, I'll pick you up around noon?"

That got her smiling, finally. "You're very persistent."

"How else do you think I ended up here?" I asked, gesturing to the rehearsal room around us. "Not by giving up when I could still win someone over."

She hemmed and hawed, still undecided, but a smile pulled at her lips as she looked away that gave me hope. After a further moment's deliberation, she finally gave in. "Alright, we can go to the zoo tomorrow, but you better be prepared to learn a lot more about leopards than you ever thought possible. If you regret it, that's on you."

I could almost guarantee I wouldn't have any regrets. "Great. Send me your address then, and I'll see you both tomorrow."

~Freya~

"Mommy?"

A little finger poked at my face, waking me from my sleep. Squinting, I opened my eyes to the darkened room and the eager little face looking up at me. "Dylan? What time is it?"

I wasn't sure why I asked; obviously, he didn't care. Rubbing my hand across my face, I glanced over at the clock on my bedside table which read 6:12. So much for sleeping in on my day off.

"Time for zoo," Dylan declared, clapping his hands in excitement, and I groaned, knowing I had only myself to blame. I shouldn't have told him about our outing with Rome in advance, but I couldn't help it when I knew just how excited he would be.

I hadn't even said anything about possibly getting special access since I didn't know if that would be available on such short notice, but it didn't matter to Dylan. Just getting to go to the zoo was exciting enough for my little boy, especially when I told him the man who gave him the book would be coming with us.

"He doesn't know much about leopards," I warned Dylan when I gave him the news the night before. "You'll have to tell him everything you know."

Dylan nodded seriously, running off to his room to 'research', and my mom shook her head at me in mock disapproval. "You're going to make that man regret his kindness."

Maybe I would. Maybe I wanted to. It would be easier to keep my distance if he wasn't so damn nice all the time.

The week of rehearsals had been incredible, and a lot of that came down to Rome. He was a pleasure to work with, encouraging me to try new things as he experimented himself. We laughed together over line readings that didn't work, we made suggestions and brainstormed ideas, and the whole thing felt wonderfully collaborative and exciting. Never once did he make me feel like I didn't belong there or that he thought himself better than me. For someone who'd had so much success, he was remarkably down-to-earth, which probably played a huge part in why he kept getting cast in things. Who *wouldn't* want to work with him?

"It's too early for the zoo," I mumbled to Dylan from my bed, pointing to the window where the sun had just started to come in. "All the animals are still sleeping. We have to wait until the clock says 12, and right now it's only 6."

Dylan leaned over to put his face right in front of the bright red numbers. "How many more is 12?"

I counted through the numbers with him from six to twelve. "It's a while still," I summed up.

He frowned in disagreement. "I can make it go fast: six, seven, eight, ten, 'leven, twelve." He ran through the numbers as fast as his tongue would go, missing one along the way.

"That's not how it works, Dill-pickle. Come on, climb up and we can snuggle until it's time to get up."

Seeing he wouldn't win this argument, he pulled himself up into my bed as I moved over, curling up so his little body was spooned against mine.

"Mommy?" His head lay on the pillow, looking away from me as he asked the question.

"Yes?" I honestly never had any idea what would come out of his mouth next, but he rarely disappointed me.

"Leopards aren't sleeping now. They like the night."

Since he was right, I simply kissed the top of his head. "Close your eyes, sweetheart."

In a few minutes, he had fallen asleep again, but I had no such luck. Instead, I lay there listening to his deep breathing and the occasional sounds of early morning traffic that drifted up to my bedroom window.

Dylan hadn't batted an eye when I told him that Rome would be going to the zoo with us that day as our friend, not seeming at all concerned or confused about it. The leopards were far more interesting to him, but as for me, I couldn't think of anything else. We weren't friends, really, were we? We were simply colleagues, but Rome said he wanted to get to know me better. He'd made absolutely no move to indicate he wanted more than that, and he made it clear he didn't consider it a date.

So, why did my stomach flutter when I looked at him? Why did my heart beat faster when he winked at me across the room? The naive college girl I'd once been had disappeared a long time ago, but maybe knowing that Rome was off limits for me made the thought even more enticing?

It frustrated me that I couldn't simply turn my body's reactions off the same way I tried to control my thoughts. Wanting Rome was self-destructive and self-defeating. Getting into a relationship with him only made sense if I could keep it casual, and casual didn't work for me, not with my son to think about as well as my own heart.

By the time we were ready to go meet Rome, I'd convinced myself that I could handle the day as friendly colleagues and not read too much into it. Dylan having fun remained my top priority, as usual. Rome's text came through to let us know he'd arrived, and we went downstairs to find him standing outside a sports car that looked like one of Dylan's toy cars come to life.

Leaning casually against the blue car in his dark blue sweater and blue jeans, Rome's blue eyes stood out even more than usual beneath his artfully tousled hair. He hadn't shaved that morning, leaving a small trail of stubble along his chin, and when he caught sight of us and smiled, my knees nearly buckled. How was it even possible for one human being to be so attractive?

"This is your car?" I asked in surprise as Dylan pulled on my hand, wanting to get closer. The fact that Rome could afford it didn't surprise me, it just seemed rather showy for someone who had struck me as so down-to-earth.

"Only for today," he explained, grinning at us both. "When I spoke to you on video, you told Dylan to go play with his cars, so I figured he would like this."

He'd rented a car for us? Was he serious? "I thought we were taking the subway," I stuttered. I didn't want to seem ungrateful, but I had to consider safety. "Dylan needs a car seat and I don't have one."

Having a car of my own in New York wasn't practical, not to mention the expense.

"Mommy, it's blue, like my car!" Blissfully unaware of my objections, Dylan hopped up and down as Rome opened the back door to reveal a car seat already set up inside.

"The guy at the rental said this would be the right size for him. Does it look okay to you?"

It looked perfect, and I could hardly say no after he'd gone to all the trouble, not to mention how excited Dylan was. Rome stepped back while I helped Dylan up into the seat and got him buckled up. There were some books and toys in his bag that he could keep busy with, but he'd probably spend the whole time looking out the window. Being in a car was a rare treat for him, even aside from the fact that it looked just like his toy one. He would be talking about this trip for days.

"This really wasn't necessary," I protested again as Rome held the passenger door open for me. "We're fine on the subway."

"We can talk better in the car," was his reply to that, brushing my concerns aside before closing the door and hopping in the driver's side himself. "Besides, I don't have an excuse to drive very often. It's good for me to keep in practice."

"*Now* you tell me that." My teasing complaint made Rome laugh as he pulled out into traffic.

"I actually grew up around here," he told me, looking around at the Harlem streets. "Just a few blocks away, actually. I was surprised when you sent me your address."

"What was that like?" He said he wanted to spend the day together to get to know each other better, so it gave me an excuse to satisfy my curiosity about him without being too nosey.

He shrugged as he pulled up at a red light. "It had its ups and downs. I love the city and the park, so having it all close by was definitely a bonus."

I couldn't really imagine; my own childhood had been so different. "So, you were a Broadway baby then? Going to shows as a kid?"

"No, not at all. I didn't actually see my first Broadway show until high school, and then only because I went on a school trip. Even though it's only 70 blocks away, it felt like a different world. I grew up in different foster homes, so having money for that kind of thing never really happened."

None of that had ever been mentioned in any of the articles I'd read about him. "What happened to your parents?" I asked before wincing at my tactlessness. "I'm sorry, I don't mean to pry..."

He shook his head. "It's okay, I brought it up. I never knew my dad. My mom raised me until I was... well, about Dylan's age, I guess, and then she met someone else and decided life would be easier without me around. She left me at a neighbour's house and never came back."

I gasped so loud that it got Dylan's attention in the back seat. "What, Mommy?"

"Nothing, Dill, it's okay," I called back to him. "Are you counting all the blue cars?"

Whenever we went walking, he liked to play that game, even though his counting usually got confused around ten, and he happily turned back to the window while I looked back at Rome, my heart aching for him.

How could any mother do something like that? Just the thought of walking away from Dylan brought tears to my eyes.

"Come on, now, none of that," Rome admonished me gently, catching sight of my reddening eyes. "I didn't tell you so you'd feel bad for me. Things turned out pretty good for me, right?"

"I just can't imagine..." I tried to say, but my throat closed up before I could get the words out. So much for the emotional distance I'd promised myself to keep that day.

"I know you can't. I could tell that from the first time you mentioned Dylan, and this isn't something I tell everybody, so if you could keep it to yourself, I'd appreciate that. I just wanted to make it clear that I'll never ask you to put the show, or anything else, ahead of your son. I know all too well what that feels like."

Did that 'anything else' include him?

No matter how much I told myself I wouldn't lose my head, Rome Taylor kept finding ways to surprise me, and at that moment, he certainly had my full attention.

~Rome~

I didn't actually set out to tell Freya anything about my childhood that day. I didn't usually tell anyone about it, and certainly not out of the blue, casually, with no lead up at all. There were women I'd dated for a year and never told them as much as those few sentences I gave Freya. And yet, I blurted it out anyway, starkly, almost as a method of self-defense.

Meeting Dylan in person reminded me exactly why I couldn't pursue anything more than friendship with Freya. He'd barely spared me a glance, far more interested in the car than in me, and honestly, that was just what I wanted. Even by his age, I had been wary of the men my mother brought home. A new man meant I would see less of her, right up until the day I never saw her at all.

Dylan had no such worries. Secure in his mother's love and trusting that he would always be the most important thing to her, it didn't even cross his mind to consider otherwise, and that was exactly as I wanted it to stay. So, when I told her about my past, I did it to explain to her that I would never put her in a position where Dylan would have a reason to feel threatened, and to remind myself of that fact too.

I needed the reminder, since when she walked out of the building in her pretty floral skirt and yellow blouse, drawing attention to her hazel eyes and contrasting perfectly with her soft brown hair, it would have been much too easy to forget that I'd only arranged the outing to get to know my new co-star better.

On a sunny and inviting September afternoon, the zoo bustled with visitors when we arrived. Freya tried to pay for their admission, but I had no intention of allowing her to, not when I had invited them, and especially not when she'd already told me there were things she couldn't afford. Adding to her worries was the last thing I wanted to do.

"Were you able to book the leopard experience?" she whispered to me as Dylan tugged on her arm, eager to get going.

I nodded, still pretending I hadn't had it all arranged before I even asked her to come. "It's booked for two o'clock, so we've got a bit of time before then."

Immediately, she dropped out of my line of vision, squatting down to talk to her son. "Plan time, Dylan. We're going to see the leopards a little later, okay? What do you want to do first?"

He looked rather adorably confused. "Leopards first."

"We usually do the leopards first," Freya agreed. "But this time, we're going to try something different. I promise we'll go see them later. Can you pick something else first?"

He thought about it hard, obviously struggling with being thrown off his routine, before finally looking up at me. "You choose," he command-ed.

Freya looked up at me too, curiously, waiting to see what I would say.

"I like monkeys," I told him. "I like to watch them chase each other."

Bending over and letting my arms hang loose, I did my best monkey impression as Dylan squealed and ran away with me in close pursuit.

"Be careful," Freya called after us, but her warning was swallowed up in Dylan's shouts and peals of laughter as I breathed down his neck, getting close but never too close. After letting him get away a few times, I finally caught him as he shrieked in surprise. A second later, I released him, not wanting to go too far when he hardly even knew me.

"Okay, let's go find your mom and then find some monkeys!"

Freya came up quickly behind us and I led them both over to one of the zoo's motorized carts where a young zoo employee stood with a friendly smile. "Good afternoon. Mr Taylor?"

"That's me," I confirmed before turning back to Dylan. "Do you want to ride in the front or back?"

"What is this?" Freya asked in surprise.

"There's a lot of walking and I don't want Dylan to get tired out before we get to the leopards. Hop in."

She had her mouth open, no doubt to protest about the cost again, but as Dylan bounced with excitement, she closed her mouth again and got in the back with me while Dylan rode in the front with the driver.

"This is too much," she admonished me quietly as we got underway. "I don't want him to think he gets this every time we come here."

"I don't think he will," I countered. "He seems pretty grounded, and it's nice to have a treat once in a while. Relax and enjoy it, Freya. There are no strings attached. I just want you both to have a good time. I already am."

That seemed to help, and Freya took a deep breath, trying to relax. The woman driving us around told us all about the monkeys we were going to see, and after looking at them for a while, Dylan asked me to chase him again, which I was happy to do. Freya watched with a mixture of amusement and exasperation as I had to apologize several times to people we almost ran into.

"Aren't you worried this is going to end up all over social media?" she wondered as we got back in the cart to head to the next exhibit. "Rome Taylor, Broadway legend, making a fool of himself at the zoo?"

That made me laugh. "I'm not nearly as famous as you seem to think I am. In the Broadway community, sure, but out here? None of these people know who I am. If you think this show is going to make you a household name, you're wrong about that."

She immediately shook her head. "That's not what I want."

I didn't think it was. Stage actors generally weren't in it for the fame, and Freya seemed even more down-to-earth than most.

Our next stop was the giraffes, where, as if to prove me a liar, a couple of young women actually recognized me and asked for a photo. Though I happily obliged, I asked them to hold off on posting it until later in the afternoon. Despite what I'd said to Freya, I did have some enthusiastic fans who would probably head to the zoo and try to track me down if they knew I was there. I would rather avoid that, if possible, especially with Dylan around.

Finally, the time came to head to the leopards, and Dylan rattled off facts about them as we got closer, impressing both me and our guide. When we arrived, he tried to make a beeline for the front of the viewing area, but Freya held him back. "Hold on, buddy. Rome has something different planned for you."

I squatted down to talk to him, as I'd seen Freya do earlier. "How would you like to go into the back and watch them have lunch?"

His eyes were wide as saucers. "Mommy says we can't go in there."

Of course she had. I suspected it had come up a few times. "Normally, she's right, but this is something special, just for today. Do you want to go see?"

He nodded seriously, his eyes still huge, and when I stood back up, his hand slid into mine without any prompting at all. His little fingers were soft and warm, and I glanced over at Freya to see if she minded. She had obviously seen the whole thing and though there was a slightly conflicted look on her face, she nodded to let me know it was alright.

Our guide took us through the employee-only door that led into the enclosure, where the snow leopards' keeper awaited us. She had some facts prepared, but Dylan already knew most of them, jumping in excitedly to finish her sentences and making us all laugh. Smart kid.

The keeper explained to us how they fed them at the zoo, and then she invited Dylan to help prepare their meal. He listened carefully and seriously to everything the keeper said, and when they'd finished, they moved on to the most exciting part. Dylan would get a chance to hand-feed the youngest leopard, under careful supervision. The keeper held his hand to keep it on the right side of the fence as the curious cat came over and grabbed the piece of meat right out of his hand, with Freya videoing the whole thing.

As I went to stand next to her, tears had filled her eyes again, but these ones were tears of happiness.

"Thank you for this," she whispered, her eyes still glued on her son. "He'll never forget today."

That made two of us.

Nothing would compare to that for a while, so when we'd finished with the leopards, I suggested we go get a snack before seeing the other animals. At the outdoor cafe filled with families who all had the same idea, I left Freya and Dylan at a table while I went inside to go and get some food.

Though it could hardly be called a typical Saturday for me, I was truly enjoying myself. When I got back to the table, they were still talking about the leopards, so I found myself completely unprepared for the question Dylan asked me when I handed him his hot dog.

"Wome?"

He was having trouble with the 'r' at the beginning of my name, which I found pretty cute. "Yeah?"

"Can you be my daddy?"

Chapter Seven

To give Rome credit, he didn't completely freak out when Dylan asked him, entirely out of the blue, to be his daddy.

When Dylan and I sat down at the table, I noticed him looking around at the other families around us, as he often did when we were out together. From the TV shows he watched and from his friends, along with just observing the world around us, he knew what dads were, and he knew that he didn't have one.

However, rather than commenting on anything like that, he'd started talking about the leopards again, and so I believed his thoughts were entirely focused on his favourite animals.

Apparently, I was wrong.

It broke my heart the first time Dylan asked me, about a year ago, if he had a daddy. He didn't seem upset, merely curious, and though I had tried to prepare for it, knowing the question would come eventually, when those big brown eyes looked up at me innocently, the words almost failed me.

When he got older, I would tell him everything, or at least as much as he wanted to know, but on that day, I kept it very straightforward and simple. "Lots of people have daddies, but some people don't. There are all kinds of families, and you've got a grandma instead. Isn't that lucky?"

He nodded in agreement, content with that for the moment, but of course, it didn't end there. A few days later, he asked again, and again a week after that, and each time, I tried to give him a little more information without ever making him feel abandoned or unwanted.

"Your friend Charlie has two daddies, but no mommy," I reminded him one of the times he asked. "Everyone is different, but you've got people who love you and that's what's important."

He seemed to accept that, but there were still times he dwelled on it. One of his favourite TV shows featured a blended family, and I noticed how he particularly liked the episode where the little boy gets his new daddy. He asked me straight out after watching it one day: "Can we get a daddy?"

I tried to explain to him that it wasn't just a matter of going to the store and picking one up, but that he didn't have to worry. "Sometimes, people get new members of their family and sometimes, they don't, but the one thing that never changes is you and me, okay?"

Although he never pushed me on it, always taking his time to think over what I'd said, I knew he still thought about it from time to time, so when he ambushed Rome with the question, it surprised but didn't entirely shock me.

After all, that afternoon had been the first time he'd spent any real amount of time with a man who acted the way the daddies in his books and TV shows did. Rome had done nice things for him and played with him, and from Dylan's perspective, it made total sense that he would just ask him outright. He didn't have a daddy, so why shouldn't he get to pick the one he wanted?

Rome's eyes darted over at me, unsure whether he should say something or if I wanted to answer, and again, I appreciated his consideration. He had been incredible with Dylan all day, easily winning him over but never overstepping his boundaries, and deferring to me when it was something I should handle, as his mother.

This was definitely one of those times.

"It doesn't really work that way, Dill-pickle." His eyes moved over to me, his lips turning down into a frown as he tried to understand why not. "Rome is Mommy's friend from work, and a daddy is different from a friend. He would have to know us for a long time and live with us too."

"Jamie's daddy doesn't live with him," Dylan protested, completely accurately. Sometimes, he was almost too clever.

"Well, he would have to love us both a lot too."

That answer didn't please him, and his frown grew deeper. "You don't like us?" he asked Rome, putting him on the spot again, but that time, Rome answered without waiting for me.

"Of course I like you," he answered, looking Dylan straight in the eye. "But your mom's right. We just met, so we don't know each other very well yet. I'd really like to be your friend though, if that's okay?"

"Okay." Although my little boy agreed, sadness and resignation lingered behind his words, threatening to bring tears to my eyes again, and Rome quickly stepped in once more.

"You know, I don't have a daddy either."

That got Dylan's attention as he looked up at Rome curiously. "You don't?"

Rome shook his head. "Nope. And when I was younger like you, it made me sad sometimes, but other times, it made me glad."

"Why?" My son hung on every word. It didn't hurt that Rome was an incredible storyteller, drawing his listeners in like they were in on some kind of secret.

"Because I could do naughty things and not get in trouble for them." Rome gave him a wink that had Dylan smiling again. "What kind of things do you think leopards do that would make their dads mad?"

And just like that, they were back to leopards, and Dylan forgot all about Rome being his daddy. I would talk about it with him again later at home; we often had our serious talks when he was getting ready for bed, but at least he could enjoy the rest of the day and not feel like he had said anything wrong or upset anyone.

"Thank you for the way you handled that conversation over lunch," I told Rome when we were back in the car later that afternoon. Dylan fell asleep almost as soon as he was strapped into the car seat, worn out from his exciting afternoon. "I'm sorry he put you on the spot like that."

"It's not a problem," he assured me. "I get where he's coming from, and it's natural to be confused. It's great that he feels comfortable asking about that kind of stuff, and if you ever want him to have more of a male presence in his life, I'm good friends with the head of your local Chosen Family group. They could find Dylan a great match if you're interested. Anyone would love to have him as a little brother."

The offer was very sweet, and it made me curious, based on what he'd told me earlier. "Did you take part in it growing up?"

His grip on the steering wheel tightened for a second, making me wonder if I'd crossed a line, but a second later, he relaxed and flashed me a smile. "That's right. They were a big help to me. I'd love to take part myself, but time is an issue."

I had no doubt that he meant that sincerely, not just as lip-service. I also suspected he probably donated to them pretty generously if it meant that much to him. He'd already shown me today just how generous he could be.

It also happened to be a really good idea. I'd thought about doing it sometime in the future, but maybe with Dylan's questions about dads, the time had come, not to mention it would be great to have a personal introduction to someone Rome knew and trusted. "I would like that, actually. I don't have many men in my life that he can spend time with, but I know it would be great for him to have more of a male influence."

"His dad doesn't see him at all?" His mild tone made it clear that I could refuse to answer if I wanted to, but surprisingly, I found I didn't mind telling him.

"No. He doesn't even know Dylan exists."

Rome's eyebrows raised in surprise but his eyes still held no judgement. "Are we talking about a one-night stand where you never got each other's names? Maybe he's a secret prince who'll return some day to sweep you off your feet. Freya Rose, you dark horse."

His gentle teasing made me laugh. "Nothing as interesting as that, I'm afraid. We were in a relationship and it ended. I didn't find out I was pregnant until afterwards, and when I told him, he suggested I get an abortion. He said if I chose to keep it, I could, but he wanted no part in it."

Rome's hands clenched on the steering wheel again, harder this time. "Does that mean he doesn't provide any support?"

"No, and I don't want him to. He wanted no part in Dylan's life, and he's got it."

Rome's jaw tightened as he thought that over, looking ahead at the traffic in front of us. "What if he suddenly changed his mind? What if he showed up and wanted his parental rights?"

That had been a concern of mine from the beginning, but as each year passed, I worried a little less. "He's had five years to find me. I haven't hidden myself away. I know where he is and what he's doing and I'm sure he could know the same about me if he really wanted to."

"You've kept tabs on him?" Rome asked curiously, glancing over at me before looking back at the road ahead.

"He's... sort of in the public eye. Well enough known that it doesn't require any particular sleuthing to know what he's up to, anyway."

That only made Rome more curious, I could tell, but he didn't outright ask for a name, thankfully. Matthew was hardly my favourite topic of conversation.

However, what he said instead wasn't a lot more comfortable. "You're about to reach a whole new level of fame yourself when the producers make the casting announcement next week. People are going to want to know who you are, and the fact that you've got a 4-year-old son is bound to come up. He might not have looked you up before, but if it's shoved in his face, it might be harder to ignore."

He had a point, and I had worried about that too, but ultimately, I had reached a decision not to let it control me. "If that happens, then I'll deal with it, but I'm not going to make any of my life decisions based on what he might or might not do. He lost the right to have any say in my life a long time ago. And if he suddenly wants to be a part of Dylan's life, then great. You heard him today: he wants a daddy. I'd find a way to make it work, but honestly, I don't think I have anything to worry about. If he really cared about having a son, he'd have turned up a long time ago."

I couldn't tell if I'd convinced Rome, but we'd reached our apartment building anyway. Pulling up in front of it, he helped me out of the car and offered to carry the still-sleeping Dylan up to my apartment, but I assured him I'd be fine and sent him on his way, thanking him again for his generosity that afternoon.

We'd already gotten to know a lot more about each other that day, getting far more personal than I would have expected on what was not a date. With all that in mind, I needed to take a step back and rebalance, before I let myself get too attached.

~Rome~

Usually, the minute the lights went down in a Broadway theatre, the show transported me, my mind focused entirely on what happened on stage until the last note had been sung, but that Saturday evening, it didn't quite work that way.

Although the actors on stage did their best to pull me in, my thoughts remained stubbornly on the two people I had spent the day with.

Getting to know Freya outside of work had a dual purpose: first, I simply wanted to know her better, and second, I hoped that by separating her from the character we were creating together, I would be better able to control the way I was already starting to feel about her. The woman I worked with every day intrigued and captivated me, but was that Freya or Julia? Telling the two apart wasn't always easy, as my past experience showed.

And by spending the day with Dylan too, I hoped to remind myself about why any kind of casual relationship with her wouldn't be possible. Since I only did casual relationships, since I didn't seem to be *able* to do anything else, that left no possibilities for us at all.

When I set out that morning, that had been my plan, but instead, I'd ended up even more intrigued than ever.

Freya was sweet and funny, easy to talk to and easy to confide in. I still couldn't quite believe I'd told her the things I had. And that quality to draw me in and set me at ease was on top of how beautiful and talented I already knew her to be. The calm and undramatic way she told me about Dylan's father only made me admire her more. It must have been hard on her, but she had dealt with it and hadn't given up, still going after her dream all while raising a pretty great kid. I had to be impressed.

None of that made it any easier to convince myself I didn't want to get to know her in a more intimate way, and if I thought Dylan would help with that, I was proven wrong about that too.

The kid was amazing, smart and self-assured in a way that made it clear just how valued he always felt. His unapologetic love for all things leopard-related reminded me of my own passions growing up. I never just liked something; I had to know everything about it and completely immerse myself in it, just like I did with my work as an adult.

And when he asked me to be his daddy, it touched something in me I didn't expect it to.

When it came to having kids, I sat firmly on the fence. I would need a committed relationship first, and none of mine had lasted long enough to get to the point where I'd be considering it. Fear also cropped up whenever the thought crossed my mind: fear I wouldn't be good enough, fear I'd mess it up, fear I wouldn't have a clue how to be a good dad since I'd never had one of my own.

But in just a few hours, Dylan decided that I would be. Things were comfortable and easy with him, and apparently, he felt it too. I didn't want to flatter myself, but Freya's reaction made it pretty clear he didn't just go around asking anyone to join his family.

Even as I offered to connect Freya to Jordan at Chosen Family, what I really wanted to do was offer to spend more time with him myself. Which would be crazy. Ever since I found out about him, I'd wanted to protect him from getting too attached to someone who might not stick around, not encourage it.

But that would be true of anyone from Chosen Family too. The relationships formed there might last a lifetime or they might not. There were no guarantees. Dylan could be matched with someone whose life got too busy or who had to move away in a few months' time, and then he'd be just as upset as if I were the one who disappeared.

Looking at it that way, would it really be such a bad idea if I spent a little more time with him?

Needing an impartial opinion, I called Jordan the next day. After I'd explained the situation and asked what he thought, a long pause followed before he answered me in his usual sarcastic tone. "We usually try to discourage the guys who only sign up to hit on the single moms."

I rolled my eyes though he couldn't see it. "That's not what I'm doing. In fact, that's exactly what I'm trying not to do. By doing it through you guys, it makes it a little less personal, you know? I'd be another volunteer and he'd be another participant, just like anyone else."

"And you don't think the fact that you're working with his mom is a conflict of interest?"

I honestly didn't know. "That's why I'm talking to you. What do *you* think?"

"I think if you like this woman, you should just date her and get to know her kid that way. But if it's really just about the boy, then we'd love to sign you up, Rome. You're always welcome here."

That feeling of belonging was exactly what I wanted Dylan to have. If things didn't work out, at least if he was already in the program, he'd get to know some of the others too, and he could be placed with someone else afterwards. It felt like the safer option all around, especially for him, and therefore, the better one.

After I hung up with Jordan, I sent Freya his contact info, not mentioning anything to her just yet about my conversation with Jordan. I wanted her to sign Dylan up only if she wanted to, not because she thought I expected it.

A few days into the next week, she mentioned it to me again on a coffee break during rehearsals. We'd been working on Julia and Victor's big love song all morning, and so far, it felt really good.

"I had a great talk with Jordan last night," Freya told me as she sat in the break room with her coffee and script. "He's such a nice guy."

I could only agree with that. "He's great. Does that mean you're thinking about signing Dylan up?"

She nodded before taking a sip from her cup. "I was on the fence about it until I talked to him. He told me to think it over, but I signed up right there and then."

Things must have gone even better than I expected, and it made me glad to see her looking so excited about it.

"In fact, he said he already had someone in mind for Dylan who he thought would be a great fit."

I had to assume he meant me, so I came clean with Freya. "Actually, I think he's talking about me."

She nearly choked on the liquid in her mouth. "You? But I thought... you said you didn't have time to volunteer."

"It would have to be around my work schedule, but if it's okay with you, I'd really like to. Dylan's a great kid."

Freya couldn't look more surprised, and before she had a chance to tell me what she thought of the whole idea, we were being called back in.

"We're going to work on fully blocking the scene from this morning," the director told us as we got back to our places. "We'll run through it from beginning to end."

Freya cleared her throat tentatively. "Does that include the kisses this time?"

I wanted to know that too. There were two kisses in this scene which we'd skipped over so far every time we ran it.

"The whole scene," the director repeated. "Let's see how it looks."

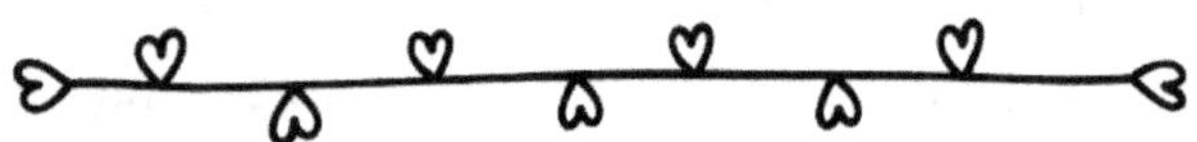

~Freya~

As the director gave us our instructions for the scene, my mind kept reeling over what Rome had said about wanting to be Dylan's mentor at Chosen Family. After the time we spent together on Saturday, I had spent the rest of the weekend trying to convince myself that involving Rome any further in my personal life would be a bad idea and that we should keep our relationship strictly professional. Just when I thought I'd succeeded, he sprung this on me, offering to insert himself even more deeply into my life, and especially my son's.

Dylan hadn't stopped talking about him ever since the zoo. He woke up as I carried him up to our apartment after Rome dropped us off, and he couldn't wait to tell my mom all about his day. While feeding the leopard had definitely been the highlight, he sounded almost as excited to tell her about all the things he and Rome had done together too. The special treats had been fun, but just playing with him had made as big an impression on Dylan as anything Rome paid for. He wanted to know when he would get to see Rome again and I had to tell him I didn't know.

When I finished putting Dylan to bed that night, my mom had a glass of wine waiting for me in the living room. "Sounds like you're not the only one who's falling for that man."

"I'm not falling for him," I tried to protest as I tucked my legs up on the sofa next to her.

"Freya, for an actress, you're a terrible liar." Her words were tinged with amusement and not accusatory in the least, but concern lurked beneath them, that same concern that I shared when it came to Rome.

"He was amazing today," I had to admit. "So good with Dylan, and so easy to talk to. I even told him about Matthew."

My mom's eyebrows raised in surprise. "You did?"

I knew why it surprised her; I didn't really tell anyone about Dylan's dad. "Well, I didn't tell him Matthew's name, but he asked me about Dylan's dad and I told him the truth. He shared some personal things with me too. Don't worry, though: as nice as it was to talk to him and to have someone that Dylan enjoyed spending the day with, I haven't lost sight of who he is."

At least, I hoped I hadn't. I was certainly trying not to.

To remind myself, I spent some time on my phone that night once I had gone to bed, scrolling through old articles and gossip columns about Rome and his past relationships. Melissa Chilton, his most recent girlfriend, had apparently said that he grew more distant as his time in the show drew to an end, as if he had been preparing himself to move on even before they were finished.

I couldn't find a direct quote, and I didn't usually trust secondhand gossip, but it matched up with some of what the other women said too: he would be devoted and fully invested at the beginning until it suddenly seemed to switch off at some point, leaving them wondering if there had ever been anything real there in the first place.

He *was* an awfully good actor. How much of what I had seen that day at the zoo had been the real Rome, and how much was the persona he'd created for himself, the person he thought I needed, adapting to me as surely as he did in the rehearsal room?

Since I had no way to be sure, I resolved to try harder at keeping my distance over the coming week, and I'd been doing a damn good job of it too, until I mentioned the conversation with Jordan to Rome and thanked him for putting us in touch. When he told me he wanted to be Dylan's partner himself, it set off a whole new conflict inside me.

Dylan would *love* that. Each day that week when I left for work, he asked me if I would see Rome that day and if he could come too. It didn't seem that time had dulled the memories they had made together, and my son would be over the moon to spend more time with Rome. But was it the right choice, for me or for Dylan?

Before I had a chance to properly process any of that, we were called back into the rehearsal room and told we'd be running through the whole scene, including the kisses that we had avoided so far.

Rome and I hadn't kissed since the audition, though I had thought about it several times since then. That day, I hadn't known much about him besides his acting skills and his generosity as a customer at the restaurant. Weeks later in the rehearsal hall, I knew much more about him and that only made the kiss feel more dangerous and volatile, like something simmered beneath the surface, waiting for a spark to ignite.

"Mint?" Rome's voice pulled me out of my reflections, and I turned to see that he did, in fact, have a pack of Altoids in his hand, holding them out to me with a smile as he popped one into his own mouth.

"Thanks." I grabbed one and quickly shoved it in my mouth, just as I would if I were kissing anyone else. I had kissed people on stage before. Nothing about this had to be different.

I was almost sure of it.

We took our places on the floor as other members of the cast sat back to watch along with the director, the composer and the pianist. Nothing about this was romantic, I reminded myself. It might be romantic for Julia and Victor, but not for Freya and Rome. For us, this was simply work.

"Did you even think about how much danger you were putting yourself in?" That was Victor's opening line, hard with frustration as he had just had to rescue the 'princess' from a precarious situation, and immediately I put myself in Julia's shoes, feeling her anxieties rather than my own.

We argued, the tension growing higher between us as the music kicked in and we switched into song, until finally we were face-to-face, only inches apart, both refusing to back down, and Rome reached down and kissed me.

Or Victor did, rather. Victor kissed Julia. It had nothing to do with

Freya at all.

The shivers of excitement that travelled through my body weren't mine; they belonged to her, and the scent and taste of him that made me weak didn't come from Rome. That was Victor.

I tried to remember it as we broke apart, staring at each other in surprise. The room seemed to be spinning as his blue eyes looked into mine, full of unspoken emotions. Was the surprise ours, or did it belong to the characters? At that moment, I found it really, really hard to tell.

I had the next line, but I let it go a beat longer, needing a moment to collect myself, needing a moment for *Julia* to collect herself, and then we launched back in, repeating the chorus of the song, but the meaning of the words changed now in the wake of that electric kiss.

When we kissed again at the end, in passion rather than frustration, marking the end of the scene, hoots and applause rang out from the others gathered in the room, bringing me back to reality.

"Wow." The composer looked genuinely delighted. "Freya, I loved the little pause you added before the second chorus. I held my breath right along with you."

I nodded and thanked him for the feedback, pretending I had done it for exactly that reason, and not just because the kiss had left me in a momentary stupor.

The director had a few notes before the rehearsal moved on to a scene between Rome and another character, so I went back to my seat where my new friends in the cast were waiting, full of compliments.

"That was amazing, Freya! You guys have some serious chemistry."

"I think I might be pregnant now," one of the guys chimed in, making us all giggle.

Another of the women around my own age looked over at Rome with thinly veiled jealousy. "Did it feel as good as it looked?"

My cheeks flushed as I tried to play it off. "It was just a stage kiss. You guys know how it is."

Their nudges and smiles to each other told me they didn't entirely buy it, and neither did Jennifer, who gave me an encouraging nod with a touch of concern in it.

Honestly, I was concerned too. Maybe my mom had been onto something when she suggested I lied about not falling for Rome. If I hadn't been doing a good job of it before, how on earth was I supposed to keep lying to myself after a kiss like that?

Chapter Eight

~Rome~

Halfway through our rehearsal on Friday morning, Freya's phone began to ping. She ignored it the first time, continuing with the scene we were working on, but as it went off a second and a third time, it became harder to overlook.

"Shit," she muttered under her breath before apologizing to everyone else in the room. "Sorry, just give me a second."

She hurried over to her purse where she'd left her phone and I pulled my own phone out of my back pocket. As I expected, messages were flooding in for me too, but I had my notifications off.

"They've made the announcement about the show's casting," I explained, not just to her but to everyone else in the room. "Those will be messages of congratulations."

That's what all mine were, at least. A few of my close friends already knew about my new role, but the producers had held off on the official announcement until they knew everything was working out with the cast. A lot of people were hearing about it for the first time that morning.

"I guess I'll have to turn it off," Freya mused with a frown. "Hopefully my mom doesn't need to reach me."

"Give it here," I instructed, holding out my hand for her phone. She passed it over tentatively, and I showed her how to silence it for all but certain numbers. "Now, it'll ring if your mom calls, but not for anyone else."

She gave me a sheepish smile. "Thanks. I didn't know that was possible."

"Can we get back to work now?" The director glared at Freya in particular and a wave of annoyance went through me. I'd noticed his attitude towards her at certain times over the last two weeks, and more often over the last few days. Once, he even asked Jennifer to come and demonstrate a part of the scene when Freya struggled to get the line readings as he wanted them, which felt inappropriate to me. He had spoken in support of Jennifer at the auditions, I remembered, so possibly, he still would have preferred her as Julia. However, the decision had clearly been made, and to keep comparing them not only wasn't helpful to anyone, it actually undermined Freya in front of the rest of the cast.

I resolved to talk to Jeffrey Neill about it later that afternoon, and the opportunity arose once everyone else had left for the day.

"Tell me if I'm being paranoid," I started out, trying to keep my tone light. "But it feels to me like our director isn't particularly happy with our Julia."

Jeffrey grimaced, making it immediately clear to me that I hadn't read too much into it. "I've felt the same thing too. He keeps pushing her closer to what Jennifer's interpretation of the role would have been, but if we wanted that, we would have cast Jennifer instead."

It relieved me to know I wasn't just being paranoid. "I don't think Freya's even noticed, or if she has, she thinks it's normal. Can the producers have a word with him?"

"I'll be speaking to them about it this weekend," he promised, and I left it in his hands.

On Saturday, I made my way back to Harlem by mid-morning. To my relief and delight, Freya had agreed to having me as a Chosen Family partner for Dylan, at least on a trial basis. The first few meetings between a new pairing were always done in a group setting with plenty of supervision to make sure the participants got along well and there were no concerns for the child's wellbeing. A few nerves played in my stomach as I made my way up the familiar streets, but mostly, I just felt excited. I felt certain that Dylan and I would click, since we already had, and it excited me to get to play a part in letting him know that even if he didn't have a dad, it didn't make him any less valued.

I'd spent a lot of years wondering exactly what was wrong with me that made my parents both leave, one after the other. A few times, I flirted with unhealthy ways of working out the emotions I couldn't seem to control, until I discovered acting and found a way to both escape and channel those feelings into something productive.

With the right role models around him, hopefully Dylan could find his thing too, whatever it might be, and in the meantime, we could simply have some fun.

Jordan stood in the entrance area when I arrived, waiting for me, and we were quickly swarmed by some of the kids who had gone to the studio with me a couple of weeks earlier. "I love you for that experience you gave them," Jordan said as he shooed everyone away so we could talk in private in his office. "But if I have to hear those tracks they recorded one more time, I'm going to go insane."

We both knew he was joking, so I laughed as I sat down and he handed over the extra paperwork I needed to sign to be matched with Dylan. I'd already gone through the background check when I first started working with the organization; even though Jordan had known me for almost twenty years, he made no exceptions.

"I'm looking forward to meeting Dylan for myself," he told me once everything had been signed off and taken care of. "From what you've said and what his mom told me, he sounds like a pretty special kid."

"You think they all are," I reminded him, and he grinned back at me.

"Am I wrong?"

I couldn't argue with that.

That day's activity was a magic show with some volunteers from a local magic society, and afterwards, they would have some activities set up to let the kids try out some tricks for themselves at age-appropriate levels. About thirty partner pairings were taking part, and almost as soon as I stepped into the main hall to see how things were looking, a little voice shouted out, "Wome!"

Freya and Dylan stood close to the door, obviously waiting for me, and the smile that lit up his face when he saw me was enough to make anyone feel pretty damn special. Freya tried to hold him back, but he slipped free of her, running over to me and throwing his arms around my legs without a hint of self-consciousness.

"Hey, Dylan." I crouched down once he let me go. "It's great to see you. Are you excited about today?"

He nodded at me, those big brown eyes gleaming in anticipation. "I do magic!"

"Be careful," Freya warned as she walked over to join us. "He thinks he's going to be able to make leopards appear whenever he wants."

Pushing myself back up to standing, we were suddenly face-to-face. Though we stood that close to each other on a regular basis at rehearsal, being there outside of work felt different. Looking into her hazel eyes, all I could think about was how good it felt to kiss her, and how I wanted to do it again right then and there, no matter how inappropriate it might be.

"We'll see how the rabbits go," I managed to say, clearing my throat since it seemed to have gone rather gravelly. "Maybe we can work our way up to leopards."

"What?" She whispered the word, her eyes dropping to my mouth before looking back down at her son and shaking her head. "Oh, right. Of course. Rabbits in hats. I got it."

It looked like I wasn't the only one having trouble concentrating.

I had so much more I wanted to say to her and ask her, about the reaction she'd received to the announcement the day before and how she felt about everything, but that day wasn't about her, or me. She gave Dylan a hug goodbye and headed off for some rare time alone. Once she'd gone, Dylan and I took a seat for the magic show.

With wide eyes, he stayed completely enthralled for the whole performance, and once we broke into smaller groups for the workshop, he quickly befriended the other kids in his age group, talking to anyone and everyone around, even though his eyes returned to me over and over, always checking that I hadn't disappeared. I made sure to never let my attention wander so he always knew I was there for him.

The tricks he learned were simple and fun. His favourite involved making the crayons disappear from a box of crayons, and as a professional actor, I had never had a more appreciative audience than Dylan when I pretended to be shocked by their disappearance even though I had sat through the instruction the same as he had.

"No way!" I gasped when he showed me the empty box. "How did you do that? Are you a wizard?"

As he squealed in delight, Jordan caught my eye from across the room and gave me a nod of approval. It looked like I wasn't the only one who thought things were going well.

When the kids started to get restless, we all headed outside for lunch out in the building's courtyard where there were picnic tables set up next to the basketball court, and some grass where the kids could just run and play. I had spent a lot of Saturdays there growing up, and it felt surreal, in a good way, to be there again on the other side of the table.

Basketball was a little too tricky for Dylan, but he joined in a game of tag with some of the younger kids, and before long, they'd roped me into it too. By the time Freya arrived in the afternoon to pick Dylan up, we were both exhausted.

Her warm laugh cheered me as she looked us both over. "I don't know who's going to sleep better tonight, you or Dylan."

The thought of my empty bed waiting for me back at my apartment felt distinctly unappealing and I wished, stupidly, irrationally, that I could invite her back there that night. What would she say if I did?

I didn't get a chance to find out as she leaned over and gave me a kiss on the cheek, taking me by surprise. "Thank you for this, Rome. You don't know how much it means to him, and to me."

With another quick smile, she gathered Dylan up and they left, walking off down the street back towards their apartment while I simply stood there, watching them go.

~Freya~

On the subway on the way home after rehearsal on Friday, jammed between all the other Friday afternoon commuters, I scrolled through the messages of congratulations that had come in during the day.

People I hadn't heard from in years were popping up to say hello. Those who didn't have my phone number were messaging me through social media, and I had more offers to get together over a coffee than I could possibly find time for in a year. Now that I was going to be a leading lady, everyone suddenly seemed a lot more interested in being my friend.

Shaking my head at myself, I had to admit that wasn't entirely fair; the fact that we'd lost touch hadn't been entirely their fault. My priorities completely changed when I had Dylan and I didn't have the time or energy to put into friendships that I used to, especially with single women my own age who were still focused on going out clubbing and dating. As our interests diverged, it became harder and harder to find the time to do things we would both enjoy. People dropped out of my life quietly, without announcing their departure, and to be honest, many of them hadn't even crossed my mind in years.

Now, they had all come roaring back, most of them offering sincere congratulations, but I could read the self-interest between the lines too. Many of the friends I'd had in college were actors just like me, and they would be hoping that with my newfound connections, I could help them get a leg up too. Some I would be interested in responding to, others I wouldn't, but on the way home that afternoon, I only had time to read them anyway.

Just before my stop, I got to the one that made my heart stop beating, just for a second.

Just heard the news. It's about time someone recognized your talent. Congratulations. Matthew

An icy, numbing chill settled over me, my eyes lingering on the name in disbelief. The message came through my Instagram DMs, since he definitely didn't have my number, and it backed up what I'd said to Rome just the other day: if Dylan's dad wanted to get in touch with me, he could. He always could have.

The announcement that day had said nothing about me being a mother, nothing about my personal life at all, but if Matthew was paying attention now, he would probably find out soon. The thought made my stomach lurch as the train pulled into my station, and I stumbled onto the platform along with the other commuters, trying to catch my breath and my balance.

I had told Rome I would deal with it if Matthew suddenly turned back up, wanting to be part of Dylan's life, and I would. Still, I hoped it didn't happen at all. That was one headache I could certainly do without.

Dylan had been so excited about his upcoming outing with Rome that I heard about nothing else all Friday evening or Saturday morning, and when I arrived on Saturday afternoon to pick him up, I half-expected him to look a little deflated. It would be hard for *anything* to live up to Dylan's expectations, but as soon as I laid eyes on him, I knew all my worries had been for nothing. He couldn't look any happier.

With my heart full as I took in both my son and Rome looking exhausted but happy, and before I had time to question it or second guess myself, I leaned over and kissed Rome on the cheek to thank him. The little peck paled in comparison to the way we'd been kissing each other in rehearsal over the previous few days, but it made my heart beat faster anyway. It marked the first kiss that involved Freya and Rome, not our characters, and the look in his eyes when I pulled back told me that distinction hadn't been lost on him either.

If I stayed there a minute longer, I might have done something stupid like inviting him back to our apartment to have dinner with us, so I pulled Dylan away before I could give into that urge. Lines were already blurring; I didn't need to make things any worse.

Dylan chatted all the way home, telling me all about his magic tricks and the games he'd played with Rome. They'd even let him bring one of the boxes of crayons home to show me and my mom his trick, and we applauded enthusiastically every time he did it, not letting our interest wane as long as he still got excited by it.

His energy flagged fast after supper, worn out from all the excitement of the day, and I put him to bed early, hoping the early night wouldn't mean an early morning. After helping my mom clean up, I intended to head to my own room where I had a romance novel waiting for me along with my vibrator that had been getting a lot more of a workout ever since I started working with Rome. At least I could fool my body into feeling satisfied even though I was alone.

However, as I was about to say goodnight, my mom took hold of my arm, pulling me in for a warm, firm hug.

"What's that for?" I asked curiously when she let me go.

"To remind you that I'm proud of you." Although she smiled at me, something else lingered in her expression. "You never gave up on your dream and now it's coming true. In just a few more weeks, you'll be standing up on that stage, and I can't wait to be there."

I couldn't wait for that either. I'd already got my mom and Dylan tickets for our first preview matinee. Dylan wouldn't understand most of what was going on, but he would like to see me and Rome anyway.

"You're a wonderful mom too, and I'm so proud of you," she repeated, still giving me the feeling that she was building up to something, and finally, she got to her point. "But between all the work and mothering, I don't want you to forget that you're a woman too, Freya, a woman who deserves to enjoy being young and unattached."

Those were about the last words I expected to hear from her, and she acknowledged that herself.

"I know I'm being contradictory after I warned you last week about staying away from Rome, but watching both you and Dylan, I'm beginning to think I was wrong. You obviously care about him, even if you're pretending you don't."

I opened my mouth to deny it, but the words refused to come out. She was right: I did care for him, a little more each day we spent together, and seeing him treating Dylan so well only made it harder to stay away.

"What should I do?" I asked my mom instead, looking to her for advice as if I were a teenager again. "I know what he's like. I've talked to one of his ex-girlfriends and she said it was great while it lasted, but it never lasts. I *know* that."

"Then use it to your advantage," she suggested, taking me by surprise once again. "Keep things light and casual. Don't get too attached. But for goodness' sake, Freya, right now you're going through all the angst of a relationship without any of the fun. If you're going to be a mess about it, at least make it worthwhile."

Elyse at the restaurant had said the same thing too: enjoy it while it lasts and don't get too attached.

Could I really do that? I'd never been any good at casual relationships before. And what about Dylan? If Rome and I spent more time together, wouldn't *he* get too attached?

On the other hand, Rome and Dylan were already going to be spending time together without me. The only one not getting anything they wanted at the moment seemed to be me.

"I don't even know if he's interested in me that way," I tried to protest, but my mom simply rolled her eyes.

"Do you *really* think he'd be spending all this time with Dylan if he didn't feel anything for you too? Besides, the only way to know for sure is to ask."

She picked up my phone that was sitting on the side table next to us and handed it to me, her message clear.

"Just remember the birth control this time, okay?" she added, leaving me with my mouth hanging open as she patted me on the back and headed into her own room.

My own mother was actually suggesting that I get involved with Rome Taylor? Or at least strike up some kind of 'friends with benefits' situation. *Just don't get attached.*

I honestly didn't know if I was capable of that, or if Rome would even want to, but she had one thing right: I wouldn't know until I'd asked, so, with trembling fingers, I pulled up his entry in my contacts and hit the call button before I could change my mind.

With each ring, I grew closer to hanging up, but just when I'd decided to, he answered. "Freya? This is a surprise. Is everything okay?"

He thought something must be wrong, which just went to show how rarely I got in touch. "Everything's fine," I quickly assured him. "Dylan's just gone to bed so I've got the evening free, and I was just wondering if you wanted to... I don't know... hang out, I guess, if you don't have any other plans."

Could I possibly have sounded any more awkward? It couldn't be clearer that I hadn't done anything like this in ages.

Rome muttered something under his breath which I couldn't quite make out, but it sounded suspiciously like 'shit'.

"I'm actually busy tonight," he answered loud enough for me to hear. "But if you're free another time..."

"Is that Freya?" a familiar voice said in the background, though I couldn't quite place it. "Let me say hi."

Some muffled noises followed until the voice spoke directly into the phone.

"Hey, Freya, it's Elyse. I miss you! How's the Broadway life?"

Elyse? My stomach sank as I remembered how she had told me she gave Rome her phone number when she gave him mine. And now she was with him, on a date, obviously, and I had rarely felt like a bigger idiot in my whole life.

Of course he wouldn't be sitting at home thinking about me like I was thinking about him. Why had I ever let myself think that he might be?

"It's great," I replied, calling on all my acting skills to sound light and happy and not-at-all upset. "We should catch up soon and I'll tell you all about it. I don't want to interrupt your night."

"That sounds perfect. I can catch you up then too." From the smile in her voice, I could guess exactly what she wanted to talk to me about, and my stomach twisted again at the thought of her and Rome together.

I said goodbye and hung up before Rome could come back on the phone. Leaving it there on the living room side table, I hurried to my bedroom, shutting the door behind me before letting the tears come to my eyes. *So much for not getting attached, Freya*, I admonished myself as I lay down on my bed and covered my face with the pillow. We hadn't even gone on a single date and already, I'd managed to get upset.

If I ever needed another reason why I should stay away from Rome, I had just found it. It looked like, as far as I was concerned, not getting attached had never been an option.

~Rome~

Once Freya and Dylan were out of sight, I went back inside to help Jordan and the others clean up after the day's event.

"That seemed to go pretty well," Jordan observed as we stacked chairs together. Even though he pretty much ran the place, he never shied away from doing the grunt work either. "You and Dylan seem to have a good connection, though he also seems pretty open in general."

I knew exactly what he meant. A lot of the kids who came through the doors, including me when I was younger, were wary and jaded. They'd been let down so many times, they didn't expect anything else. Dylan, on the other hand, wasn't like that at all. Maybe it came down to his age, but I suspected it had much more to do with Freya. The only person who had let him down had been his dad; other than that, he still saw the world as a good place and people as trustworthy. That kind of trust was an amazing thing and I had absolutely no intention of being the one who made him think otherwise.

"He's a great kid," I agreed. "And before you ask the question: yes, I definitely want to continue."

Jordan's deep chuckle filled the room. "You know I've got to ask, but I had a feeling that would be your answer."

By the time I finished there, it had gotten late in the afternoon and I was getting hungry. Weighing my options, I decided to call over to the restaurant Freya used to work at and place an order that I could pick up once I got back to my neighbourhood. I had never eaten there before the night that Melissa chose it, the night that I first met Freya, but it had great food and the location, just around the corner from my apartment, couldn't be beat. They were going to be getting a lot more business from me in the future.

While I paid for my meal, a familiar face appeared, giving me a friendly smile. "Hey, Rome, how are you?"

The face belonged to Freya's friend, the one who had given me Freya's number when I had come looking for it, though I couldn't for the life of me remember her name. I gave her a smile in return anyway. "I'm great, how are you?"

She looked down at the takeout bag in my hand with a laugh, holding up the matching bag in her hands. "About the same as you, I guess: heading home to eat my dinner alone. I just finished for the day."

"Do you live nearby?" I asked, making polite conversation while my card payment went through.

"No, I'm down in the Village. My food's usually cold by the time I get home, but at least I can reheat it in the microwave. You must be close since you keep stopping in here."

She's reached the right conclusion. "Yeah, I'm just a few minutes away."

"Well, if you'd like the company, I'm not rushing home for any particular reason. Seems silly for both of us to eat alone."

I looked over at her in surprise as I pocketed my card again. Usually, I picked up on subtle flirting pretty well, but I'd missed the signs with her until just then. I'd been so focused on Freya, no other woman even registered on my radar.

But nothing was happening with Freya, nothing *could* happen with Freya, so what harm would it do to have dinner with this woman? I wouldn't mind having someone to talk to, it didn't have to be anything more than that. The idea of spending the evening alone hadn't really appealed to me anyway.

"Would you like to come and have dinner at my place?"

She smiled again, looking pleased that I'd finally taken the hint. "I thought you'd never ask."

We made small talk for the short walk to my apartment and once we were there, I showed her to the kitchen and excused myself for a second to go to the bathroom. That's what I told her, at least, but what I really wanted to do was take a look through my phone contacts and try to remember her name so I didn't have to ask her directly. Elyse, I realized in relief as I reached the entry, trying to ignore the way my eyes were drawn to Freya's name not far below it.

"This place is gorgeous," Elyse enthused when I returned to the kitchen. She'd found some plates and had started arranging our meals just as they would have been at the restaurant. "Have you lived here for long?"

We chatted a bit about the apartment and about housing in Manhattan in general as we finished getting the food ready and took it over to my dining table. "Wine?" I offered as Elyse took a seat, and she nodded appreciatively.

"Red, please."

I'd just finished pouring the glasses when my phone rang and Freya's name flashed across the screen as I pulled it out of my pocket. In my surprise, it took me a second to answer, and I quickly asked her if everything was okay, worried that something bad had happened in order for her to be calling.

She assured me she was fine and then asked if I wanted to see her that evening, and I did my best not to groan in frustration. Of course I did, but I had just invited another woman over and I could hardly send her away because I'd rather see Freya instead. Despite my reputation, I wasn't that much of a jerk.

Elyse reappeared in the kitchen, having heard enough of the conversation to guess who I was talking to, and she took the phone from me to say a few words to her friend as I carried the wine glasses over to the table. Elyse followed behind me, saying goodbye to Freya, and I quickly took the phone back from her.

"Do you have plans for tomorrow?" I asked into the phone, but only dead air greeted me on the other end. Freya must have already hung up. *Damn it.*

"Just give me one second..." I muttered to Elyse while quickly typing a message to Freya, telling her I would be free all day Sunday if she wanted to do something, and then I put my phone away, doing my best to concentrate on Elyse even though in reality, my attention remained hyper-focused on the phone in my pocket, waiting for a response.

That response never came. We finished eating, and though Elyse suggested she could stay and watch a movie, making it more than clear that she'd be happy to stay for a lot more, I sent her on her way, thanking her for the company but trying to make it clear I wasn't interested in anything else. She was pretty and friendly, but I just didn't feel any spark there.

Freya didn't respond until the next morning, and even then, her message only let me know that she had plans with Dylan that day and wouldn't be available. If she had invited me to join them, I would have. As tempted as I might have been to offer anyway, I didn't want to come across as too pushy, and what did I even expect to happen anyway? Her phone call the night before had been the first indication she'd given me that she might be interested in anything more from me than simply being colleagues, and I managed to screw it up.

When my phone rang later that afternoon, I hoped it might be her, as I seemed to do every time it rang, but Jeffrey Neill's name flashed across the screen instead.

"I've got some big news," he started off. I could hear kids playing in the background, reminding me that he had a family of his own too. "I spoke to the producers about the director and we all met for dinner last night. We've decided that our visions for the show don't line up well enough, and he's agreed to leave the project."

Seriously? That was *huge* news for a show that was meant to be opening in a month. "So, what now?"

"Well, sometimes things just fall into place." The sound on the other end of the phone went muffled for a moment as he called out something to his son. A moment later, he came back. "I actually had a call completely out of the blue yesterday from Matthew Blackman, asking about the show. We talked it over and the way he sees it is almost exactly as I do. He's between projects at the moment, and I've spoken to him this morning about coming on. He agreed, and the paperwork is being drawn up now."

That qualified as even bigger news, assuming I had the right guy in mind. "Matthew Blackman, the Hollywood director?"

"That's the one," Jeffrey confirmed. "He's done theatre before, mostly in college, and he says he'd like to get back into it. The stars just aligned, I guess."

I'd say. The publicity the show would get from him joining the production would be incalculable. Matthew Blackman was one of the hottest names in Hollywood, a new, young director whose debut film had taken the world by storm a couple of years ago. His second one had just come out and already, I'd heard Oscar buzz about it.

It seemed almost unreal that he would be interested in our show, but I'd learned to never second guess that kind of lucky break.

"I'd like to set up a meeting between the two of you, tonight if possible," Jeffrey continued. "He'll need to speak to Freya too but I don't want to interrupt her weekend with her son. Besides, he mentioned that he knows her from college anyway. Apparently, they went to NYU together."

I hadn't known about that, but then, a lot still remained that I didn't know about Freya yet.

"I'd love to meet him. I'm available anytime."

By the time we hung up, my head had started spinning with excitement for all the possibilities for the show. I'd already thought it would be great, and chances were this new change would only make things better.

I couldn't wait to find out exactly what Matthew would bring to the table.

Chapter Nine

~**Freya**~

I could have invited Rome to come to the park with me and Dylan that afternoon. He would have come, I felt pretty certain, but I still had to deal with my embarrassment over what happened when I called him the night before and my reaction to it. He'd never promised me a single thing, never even asked me out, and I had practically cried myself to sleep with jealousy over another woman being with him anyway.

I didn't like feeling that way, and a little distance from the whole situation seemed to be exactly what I needed, so when I saw the message from Rome that morning asking if I had plans, I replied that I did and left it at that.

Even so, when my phone rang as I sat in the park watching Dylan playing happily at the playground with the other children, I couldn't help hoping it would be Rome.

It wasn't.

"Hey, Elyse," I greeted her through the phone, trying to sound upbeat even though hearing about what a great time she had with Rome the night before sounded like torture. "What's up?"

"Just checking if you still wanted to catch up," she answered me equally cheerfully. "Where are you?"

"In Central Park with Dylan."

Her warm laugh echoed through the phone. "I had a feeling. It's a sunny day and you've got the day off, where else would you be? I can be there in about twenty minutes. I'll bring coffee."

That gave me twenty minutes to try to put all my envy behind me and be happy for my friend, and by the time she walked up with two coffee cups, I managed to give her a genuine smile. "So?" I asked as she took a seat next to me. "Is dating the legendary Romeo Taylor all that you hoped it would be? You guys have both kept that quiet."

That almost didn't sound bitter at all.

Elyse simply snorted before taking a drink from her coffee, waving over at Dylan who had spotted her sitting next to me. "We're not dating. I definitely tried, and I thought when he invited me to his apartment that I had a chance, but he shut me down completely."

Jealousy reared its ugly head again when she said she'd been at his apartment, so strong that I almost missed what she said at the end. When her words sank in, my spirits began to rise.

"He shut you down?" I repeated curiously, trying not to sound too happy about it. "What do you mean?"

She shrugged. "Exactly that. We had dinner after you called and I suggested watching a movie, hoping it would lead to a little more, but he refused. Told me to go home. Not in a rude way, but I got the message. He's not seeing anyone in the cast, is he?"

I shook my head, trying not to smile. What was wrong with me? I shouldn't be happy about my friend being rejected, but I couldn't stop the relief that bubbled up inside me anyway. "As far as I know, he's not seeing anyone. So, where does he live? I bet it's pretty swanky."

An almost orgasmic groan left her mouth. "Oh my God, Freya, I would kill for his kitchen! It's bigger than my whole apartment."

We both giggled despite it being true. Sometimes, you could only laugh.

She fully answered my question a second later. "He's in that fancy new apartment building on 45th and 9th. It probably only takes him five minutes to walk to the theatre when he's working. He's so lucky."

He was lucky, but only as a result of talent and hard work. From the few glimpses he'd given me into his childhood, I knew nothing had been handed to him. Everything he had, he'd earned.

I told Freya all about the show and how rehearsals were going, and when I mentioned how I was having trouble with certain scenes, she frowned. "Sounds to me like the director's the one with the problem, not you."

Honestly, I had kind of been feeling the same way, and that probably came across in how I told her about it. I couldn't consider her opinion impartial. "I don't think it's personal. I'm just being paranoid."

She shrugged again, finishing off her coffee and tossing the empty cup into the garbage can next to the bench. "I wouldn't be so sure. I heard a rumour that he and Jennifer Marshall were seen together at 45 and 8."

Everyone knew the popular cabaret bar in the Broadway community, and even though Elyse usually had her gossip right, her words still took me by surprise. "Really? She told me she was seeing someone though, someone..."

I trailed off as I remembered exactly what she'd said: she needed to keep her relationship a secret, the way a director might to avoid the appearance of favouritism. Matthew had insisted on keeping our relationship a secret when he was directing me. That had been the excuse he gave me, at least.

If Jennifer really *was* dating the director, it definitely put some of the things he'd said to me in a new light.

"Maybe I'll ask Rome what he thinks tomorrow," I suggested to Elyse and to myself. "I trust he'll tell me the truth if there's really something wrong with what I'm doing."

The rest of the day went quickly as Dylan and I went shopping and made supper together to give my mom a break. In the evening, we played with his cars and read through his leopard book another dozen times until bedtime came.

As I closed my son's bedroom door behind me, the thoughts I'd been trying to push down all day came rushing back into my head: Rome hadn't actually been on a date with Elyse last night, not really. He had asked if I wanted to get together today, and my refusal had been the only reason it didn't happen.

Maybe he was interested after all?

Indecisively, I tried to decide what to do. I didn't want a repeat of the previous night's awkward phone call, and thanks to Elyse, I knew where he lived. Maybe the conversation I had in mind would go better in person?

"Do you mind if I go out for a while?" I asked my mom, who sat watching TV in the living room.

"If this is related to what we talked about last night, then have fun," she replied with a smirk, her eyes never leaving the screen. Shaking my head, I grabbed my purse and keys before heading out the door.

My pulse got faster the closer the subway got to the 42nd Street stop. He might not even be there, I reasoned, or he might tell me I'd completely misread the situation. There were a million possibilities, but at least one of them was that I would end up in bed with Rome Taylor that evening, and that thought had my whole body thrumming.

From the subway station, it took not much more than a minute to reach the building Elyse had told me about, a huge glass high-rise, impossible to miss. It looked exactly like the kind of place a successful actor would live.

The doorman greeted me with a friendly smile as I walked into the lobby. "Can I help you, Miss?"

I had forgotten that buildings that nice would have real security, not just a buzzer to let me in, but I tried to look like I had expected it. "Hello. I'm looking for Rome Taylor."

He pulled out a list of names. "Is he expecting you?"

"Um, no. I'm a colleague of his, though."

The words made me wince as they came out of my mouth. I probably sounded like an obsessed fan, and Rome probably had a few of those. Had any of them ever tracked him down before?

The doorman, however, responded kindly. "I can give him a call if you're sure he'll want to see you?"

He phrased that very diplomatically, giving me a chance to save face if Rome had no idea who I was, but since I felt pretty certain he wouldn't turn me away, I told him to go ahead. "Please tell him it's Freya Rose."

He picked up the phone on his desk and placed the call. "Mr Taylor, it's Richard from the front desk. I have a Freya Rose here to see you." He only paused for a fraction of a second before responding, "Yes, sir."

Hanging up, he pointed me toward the elevators.

"He said to go on up. 22nd floor."

"Thank you." I flashed him a grateful smile, my heart beating even faster as I got in the elevator and started the climb up to Rome's floor.

No one had told me which apartment to find him in, but I didn't need to worry. When I got off the elevator and peered down the hall, Rome stood there, dressed casually in jeans and a sweater, just outside the open door to his apartment with a warm smile on his face. "This is a nice surprise."

"I'm sorry, I should have called first." It only really hit me at that moment just how presumptuous I'd been in coming. "If you're busy, I can go."

"Not at all," he assured me. "Come on in."

I followed him into the apartment which was every bit as huge and gorgeous as it had looked on our video chat and as Elyse had told me.

"I'm actually really glad you're here, there's been a big development with the show and I want to talk to you about..."

I quickly cut him off before we got sidetracked. "I'm not here to talk about work, Rome."

"You're not?" His eyebrows raised in surprise and, I felt pretty sure, a bit of hope.

Here goes nothing, I thought.

"I'm not. I'm here because... well, because I'm attracted to you. So much so that it's hard sometimes to think about anything else when we're together. I'm not looking for a relationship, but I thought, if you were interested too, we could do something about it. If you're not, then I'll just go and we can pretend this whole conversation never happened. So... what do you think?"

My heart had never pounded as loudly in my whole life as it did while I waited for his reply.

~Rome~

Excitement buzzed through my body as I got home from dinner with Matthew Blackman and Jeffrey Neill. We'd talked for almost two hours, non-stop, about the show and what Matthew wanted to do with it. His ideas were fresh and exhilarating, and Jeffrey walked away just as pumped about it as I felt. The show was always going to be good, but with Matthew on board, it would be spectacular. We had a lot of work to do in the next month to make it all happen, but with the team we had gathered, we could do it.

The only fly in the ointment was that I wished Freya had been there to hear all of it and put in her ideas. I understood why Jeffrey didn't want to cut into her weekend time, but I valued her opinion. So, when I got the call, completely out of the blue, that she was down in my lobby, I figured it must have been some kind of sign. I went to the hallway to greet her, eager to tell her everything I'd learned.

However, she had something else on her mind, and when she explained to me exactly what had brought her there that evening, the energy inside me quickly morphed into a whole different kind of excitement.

Her words came as a total surprise. I'd hoped she might feel something for me, just like I did for her, but to that point, those feelings had only brought me frustration since I knew exactly why we shouldn't act on them.

Not only did she say them, though, she also offered me what could only be called the dream situation for most men: intimacy without commitment. She didn't want a relationship, she told me flat-out, and I knew exactly why not: the same reason I hadn't made any move with her, no matter how much I wanted to. Dylan came first, he needed stability in his life, and a guy who seemed to be incapable of making a relationship last longer than the length of a performance contract couldn't exactly be called stable.

I could have been offended, but why bother? The happily-ever-after that my characters usually got just didn't seem to be in the cards for me. If Freya saw that as clearly as I saw it myself, I could hardly blame her for that.

On the other hand, I never went into anything expecting it to be casual. The press may put an expiry date on my relationships, but that was never my intention. What she suggested would be something new for me, something casual and without expectations. Did I really want that?

As far as Freya was concerned, if it came down to casual or nothing, I knew which I would prefer. First, however, I needed to understand exactly what she was proposing.

She had been blunt and open with me, so I paid her the same courtesy in response. "Freya, I'm attracted to you too. I haven't said so because I know that Dylan is your priority. It's not that I wouldn't want a relationship with you, but I understand that it could be hard on him if it didn't work out between us."

Freya blinked at me in surprise, as if my words were completely unexpected. "You've been thinking about that?"

If she only knew how much. "I have. Dylan reminds me a lot of me, except that he's got a mom who loves him. The last thing I would want to do is hurt him."

Her surprise morphed into confusion. "If you feel that strongly about it, then why are you doing the Chosen Family thing with him?"

"Because that's got nothing to do with you," I told her, still speaking plainly. "The commitment I'm making to him is completely separate to anything that may or may not happen between us. It's not tied to the show in any way. I'm very aware of my reputation, and the truth is, I don't know why my relationships don't last. They just don't. I don't specifically set out to hurt anyone, but I know people have been hurt. The last few women I've dated, I've been very up front about that and they've gone in with their eyes open. But with you, with Dylan, it's different. Even if you could make that choice, Dylan couldn't. That's why I've been trying to keep my distance, even though it's not easy when everything about you is so utterly appealing."

Her expressive face showed off every single emotion she felt as I spoke: appreciation when I spoke about Dylan, understanding and sympathy when I talked about my failed relationships, and finally, a flare of desire when I told her just how tempting I found her. That look set off an answering call of need inside me, my body reacting instantly to the idea of being with her in a way I hadn't even really let myself imagine yet.

"I've been holding back too," she admitted. "I don't know how this would work, but I thought, maybe, we could just start with tonight. No promises past that."

"I've never been a casual hook-up kind of guy." I took a step closer to her because the distance between us was literally painful. It wouldn't take more than a second to have her in my arms if she wanted me to. "But if that's all you're able to offer, and if you're sure that we can do that without anyone getting hurt, then I'm willing to give it a try. It can just be tonight, if you want. I'll take it, because make no mistake, Freya: I want you, badly."

Her eyes scanned mine for a moment, a moment in which my breath seemed to stop as I waited for her response. Even though had come here of her own volition, I felt like the one on trial.

And when she gave me her decision, in the form of her lips pressing firmly against mine, a wave of electric energy passed through me, lighting me up and turning me on until there wasn't a single thought in my head but the desire that had been building up in me over the last few weeks and the pleasure we could give each other.

The way we kissed at rehearsals had been one thing. There was chemistry there, no doubt, but there was also an awareness that we were being watched. In the privacy of my apartment, that kiss was simply for us. No one's opinions or feelings mattered but our own. At that moment, we were simply Freya and Rome, and it felt incredible.

Freya's kiss was hungry and bold, without a hint of hesitancy. Now that she'd made her decision, she went for it, throwing herself into it just like she did everything in her life, at least as far as I'd seen. My hunger for her felt just as strong as we pushed and pulled at each other, tongues tangling, hands grasping, bodies pressing against each other, her hips firm against my stiffening cock. There could be no doubt how she wanted this to end, and I'd only be lying if I said I didn't want it too. I could barely think of anything else now that we'd started.

If I didn't move us somewhere else, we were going to end up having sex right there in the entrance hall, which wasn't the respect I wanted to show her. One night or not, I wanted her to feel special, since I already knew it would be for me.

"Come with me." My voice echoed in my ears, thick and deep, as I took her hand and led her further into my apartment. My bedroom was one of my favourite rooms, my most personal space, and normally, I would have loved to know what Freya thought of it. At that exact moment, however, we both had other things on our minds.

She hadn't worn a coat that night so it didn't take long to get her sweater up over her head, and mine quickly followed. Her hands pressed against my chest as I inhaled with pleasure. The feel of her skin on mine, combined with the sight and smell of her, intoxicated me. A thick veil of lust had descended on us both, making it harder to breathe as I kissed her shoulder and reached behind her to undo the snaps of her bra. Drowning in her, I didn't want to come up for air.

Her body was beautiful, as I had already guessed, and when I knelt down to pull her pants down, getting my first glimpse of her pink pussy, already wet and glistening for me, I didn't think heaven itself could be any sweeter.

"I... uh, I haven't done this in a while," she whispered from above me as I helped her out of one leg of her pants and then the other.

That only made me feel more special. "I don't think that will be a problem, Freya." With those words, my tongue slid between her legs, lapping at her until she spread them wider, and when I connected with her clit, Freya gasped, her hands gripping my head for support.

"Oh, fuck!"

I had only meant to have a taste before I finished undressing myself, but once I started, I couldn't stop. If it had been a while for her, I would remind her just how good it could be. Hooking one of her legs over my shoulder, I buried my face deeper, letting my tongue dart inside her as I tasted her sweetness more fully. Hearing her sighs and whimpers only made me harder and, while my tongue and lips continued to explore, I reached down to unzip my jeans, letting my straining cock free.

Without that discomfort to distract me, I redoubled my efforts, kissing and licking and sucking her as I murmured to her exactly how much I was enjoying it. "You are so fucking sweet, Freya. The best thing I've tasted all day."

My words caused her body to jolt in response, and I sucked her clit harder while my fingers pressed into her. It wasn't much longer before she contracted around me, her legs trembling as she came. Kissing my way back up her body, I got back to my feet and finally removed my pants entirely, my cock aching now in anticipation.

Freya looked down at it before glancing back up at me, her eyes hazy in satisfaction. "Well, that was the best time I've had in ages."

As usual, she made me laugh, and though I knew she was teasing, I wanted to make myself clear too. "Trust me, Freya, we're just getting started."

~Freya~

Part of me still couldn't believe we were actually doing this. It had only been just less than a month since the first time I spoke to Rome at the restaurant, back when he was still dating someone else, and a month later, I stood naked in his bedroom where he had just given me my first orgasm in years brought on by another living person.

When I told him it had been a long time for me, I wasn't exaggerating. I hadn't been in a relationship since Matthew, and I usually had no interest in casual hookups either, so it had been just me and my vibrator for, quite literally, years.

In fact, the reason I warned him about how long it had been was that I genuinely worried that I'd become so dependent on the electronic assistance that I might not be able to get off on manual manipulation alone.

I could cross that worry off the list, at least. Rome hadn't had any trouble at all. The sight of him kneeling at my feet with his face between my legs, that handsome face that thousands of people paid to watch on stage night after night, almost made me come all on its own, and that was even before his tongue got to work. Somehow, he knew just what I needed.

As he stood naked in front of me, his cock just as impressive as it had been in my daydreams, the idea of having him inside me made my body ache with need, even though he had literally just made me come.

"Do you want me to use a condom?" His voice sounded deeper and throatier than usual, letting me know without words just how turned on he was, if his fully erect cock hadn't already been proof enough.

Technically, we didn't need one. From what he'd just told me out in the hall, I believed that he didn't sleep around outside of his relationships, and I certainly didn't. Even though I'd been celibate for years, I still took my birth control pills. That had been a lesson learned the hard way. Even so, it didn't hurt to add a bit more protection. "Yes, please."

With no hint of disappointment, Rome moved briskly to his bedside table where he pulled the drawer open and grabbed a shiny foil square. "Lie down," he instructed as he ripped the packet open with his teeth.

His bed looked huge and luxurious, like everything else in his apartment, and I nearly moaned in pleasure as I crawled up onto the soft sheets. What would it be like to sleep there with him, even aside from the sex? For a moment, I wished I could stay long enough to find out.

But all other thoughts flew out of my head as I lay myself down, my eyes fixed on Rome as he rolled the condom onto his hard cock. He looked down at it too, watching what he was doing, but as soon as he had it on, his eyes came back up to me, and the lust and desire in those stunning blue eyes almost took my breath away.

"You look gorgeous in my bed," he told me as he climbed up after me, his body hovering over mine as he placed his hands on either side of me. "I could get used to this view."

I could too, far too easily. His chest was firm, the muscles in his arms clearly defined as they held his weight above me, but his eyes truly captivated me. Those beautiful blue eyes had made me weak the very first time I was close to him, and my appreciation for them only grew the more I got to know the man they belonged to.

For that night, he was mine, and I planned to make the most of it.

Reaching up, I pulled Rome's head down towards mine, and he took the hint eagerly, kissing me again with all the passion I could have hoped for. Our castmates said we had chemistry when we kissed in rehearsal, but this felt even better. This was *real*.

His body pressed down on me, his hard cock against my pelvis as my hips bucked up towards it, desperate for the fulfillment it promised. The aching inside me grew stronger with each passing second, and if he waited much longer, I would be ready to beg him to get inside me.

Luckily, I didn't need to worry. Rome's hips ground against me as we continued to kiss until finally, he couldn't stand it anymore either. Reaching down between us, he brushed his fingers across my clit, teasing me a little more, until finally, he lined his cock up against my entrance and slowly pushed in.

He took his time, moving in and out to coat the condom in my natural lubricant, obviously trying not to cause me any discomfort. He needn't have worried, though; I was so wet, he could have slid anything he wanted in there.

"Fuck, Rome," I gasped when he was fully in. He filled me even better than I could have imagined, and I no longer had any doubt in my mind that we were really doing this. My imagination wasn't good enough to come up with how perfect he felt.

"Freya." He groaned my name back at me as his hips began to move, his cock sliding in and out of me, slowly at first. "I'm so glad you came over tonight."

A laugh bubbled up from my chest and he grinned down at me, his delight in my laughter clear on his face. I loved how we always seemed to be on the same wavelength. Our mirth was short-lived, though, melting away into desire as he kept moving, a little faster each time he thrust into me. My legs circled his waist as he buried his face in my neck, kissing and sucking on the sensitive skin there while my hands grabbed at the taut muscles of his back.

His rhythm became even faster, his cock driving into me harder as I whimpered and moaned beneath its gratifying assault. It had been a long time for me, as I said, but I had a hard time remembering when it had ever felt so good, so natural, so right.

His breathing growing shallower, Rome pushed himself up, removing my legs from his waist and pressing them together in front of him instead. Leaning down onto them, his movements turned almost primal, thrusting into me with a need as old as time, and when his fingers found my clit again, I cried out his name one more time.

"God, Rome, yes!"

All the pleasure building inside me suddenly broke, the wave of my orgasm washing over me as my body contracted, and Rome groaned once more as he felt me pulsing around his cock. With a few more quick thrusts, he came too, muttering a few scattered words beneath his breath. I could have sworn one of them sounded like 'perfect'.

As soon as he released my legs, they fell back open around him, and with his cock still inside me, he leaned down and kissed me again, softer that time. "That is definitely one way to break the sexual tension."

He always seemed to know exactly how to make me smile. "Are there other ways?" I teased as he pushed himself back up, leaving my body feeling empty as he slid out of me.

"None that are quite this much fun," he conceded, grinning back at me as he got to his feet and discarded the condom in the trash can before rolling back onto the bed next to me. "I hope it was what you had in mind."

Did he really doubt it? It might have just been my imagination, but it almost sounded like the legendary Romeo Taylor wanted some reassurance.

At least I could give it to him easily, since the words were true. "Rome, that was incredible. Better than I hoped."

Clear relief flashed in his eyes. "I can usually last a lot longer, but you felt so fucking good, Freya, I lost control."

He seriously *had* been worried I would be disappointed, and affection rushed through me, mingled with the endorphins my body still swam in, thanks to my multiple orgasms. "Trust me, that was perfect. I don't know if I could have taken much more. Besides, I should get going anyway."

I sat up, and Rome quickly followed, looking at me in confusion. "Going? You don't want to spend the night?"

I shook my head. "I can't. I need to be home when Dylan wakes up in the morning."

"Oh, right. Of course." Although he nodded, I could have sworn there was disappointment in his eyes. "Well, let me call you a cab, then."

"That's not necessary," I insisted as I gathered up my clothes. "The subway's just as quick. Can I use your bathroom for a second?"

He gestured to the door of a huge ensuite bathroom I hadn't even noticed when we walked in. I'd been so focused on him, I'd barely registered anything else around me, but once I was cleaned up and dressed again, I returned to his bedroom and took a proper look around this time.

"Are these all the shows you've been in?"

He had framed Playbills on the wall, like a musician might have their gold records displayed, and he nodded proudly as I went over to take a closer look at them. He had put some sweatpants on while I was in the bathroom, but his chest was still bare, and I could still see the outline of his cock clearly, even though I tried not to look. "All the way back to my first high school performance."

He meant it. The black-and-white photocopied program from his high school production of West Side Story was framed just the same as his latest Broadway starring role. "You must have been a wonderful Tony," I commented as I peered at it.

"Actually, I was Riff," he admitted sheepishly. "They thought I was too rough to be Tony."

I looked back at him in surprise. "Rough? You?" I could hardly imagine anyone more clean-cut.

My disbelief made him grin. "I was a bit of a bad boy in high school. I told you, theatre changed me."

Affection ran through me again, along with sympathy, remembering why he told me he'd struggled. "But that must have been the last time you didn't have the lead," I guessed, moving along the line of Playbills, all the way to his latest show. There was space beside it for his next show, the one that we would be in together, and that gave me another little thrill. I would be on Rome's wall forever, at least in Playbill form.

And so were all his other ex-girlfriends, I realized just as quickly, glancing back over his past shows. *Don't lose sight of who he is, Freya.*

"Well, this was..." I started to say, turning back to face him, but something over his shoulder caught my eyes and I gasped so loudly that he jumped. "Oh my God! Are those your Tonys?"

Rome's startled face relaxed into a warm grin. "Do you want to hold them?"

"Yes!" My enthusiastic response had him laughing again and he pulled the awards off his bookshelf and handed them both to me, one in each hand as I read the inscription. *Best Performance by a Leading Actor in a Musical. Rome Taylor.*

There wasn't a theatre kid alive who hadn't dreamed of holding one of these in their hands one day, and he had two. He really was amazing.

"I can't believe you didn't notice them when you came in," he teased, enjoying my excitement.

"I was a little distracted," I pointed out, which only made him grin wider. Reluctantly, I handed the statuettes back to him. "Thank you for showing me, but I really do have to go."

I headed towards the door while he put the trophies back on his shelf before following me back to his front door. "I feel bad about this," he told me bluntly as I put my shoes back on. "Going home on the subway after what just happened... I don't want you to feel used."

"If anything, I'm the one who used you," I pointed out, checking I still had my keys and wallet. "I showed up at your door, slept with you and am running out on you. If anyone should feel bad, it's me."

He smiled at that, but not his usual grin. Obviously, he still didn't feel totally satisfied with the situation. "Well, maybe neither of us should feel bad, then. I am really glad you came over, Freya. You know where I am if you need anything, and I guess I'll see you tomorrow."

"See you tomorrow, Rome." I leaned over and kissed his cheek chastely, as if he hadn't just had me pinned and writhing beneath him a few minutes earlier, and I headed out the door.

Only as I took my seat on the subway heading back uptown did I remember he had mentioned having some news about the show, and I never gave him the chance to tell me. Although I was curious what it might be, I shrugged it off. I didn't want to look desperate or clingy by calling him again that night. Whatever he wanted to tell me, I would find out in the morning.

Chapter Ten

~Rome~

Waking up in the morning, I could still smell Freya in my bed. The scent was soft and floral, not a perfume but something lighter, maybe just her shampoo or the body wash she used. Wherever it came from, it lingered on my pillows where she'd laid her head while we had sex the night before, and I inhaled deeply in the hazy moments between sleep and full wakefulness, wishing that she hadn't had to leave so quickly. I would have liked to spend the morning with her, showering together, having breakfast, all the little things that made being in a relationship special.

Some guys liked the chase, some liked one-night stands, but for me, being settled in a relationship made me the happiest. Having someone to come home to, someone to talk to, someone I could focus on rather than being left alone with the thoughts in my own head. It had been more than three weeks since Melissa and I broke up, and for me, that was a really long time not to be in a relationship. I missed those simple little things that came from intertwining your life with another person's, and I would have loved to do them with Freya.

Except that we weren't in a relationship, and weren't going to be. She'd been very clear about that. That morning, I had to go to work and pretend that nothing had happened between us, that I didn't know how she looked naked or what she felt like from the inside.

I would definitely be thinking about it though, as I did while getting out of bed and getting my day started. How could I not? Sex with her had been wonderful. She was just what I liked in bed: a woman who let me take the lead but didn't shy away from showing what she wanted either. Though she hadn't given me any instructions out loud, her body relayed all the information I needed. Her legs tightened around my waist when she wanted me to go faster, her fingers dug into my back when she needed it harder. I understood her instinctively and naturally, like we spoke the same language. I'd had other partners where it took months until we felt so in sync, but with Freya, that connection was immediate and natural.

I almost couldn't believe how quickly she made me come. When I told her I usually lasted longer, I hadn't been exaggerating. One of the women I'd dated had teased me that if I hadn't been a theatre actor, I could have had a career as a porn star. She meant it as a compliment, which was how I took it, but I was often so focused on what my partner needed that my own pleasure took a back seat, which made it easier to hold off on my own orgasm until I gave it my full attention.

With Freya, I didn't need to do that. She made me lose myself fully in the moment so that, even though I was definitely still thinking about her, my body felt the full effects of it anyway. In a way, it felt similar to how I told her about my childhood without ever fully deciding to; she just made it easy to let go and be myself, perhaps because she expected nothing else from me.

Those were all things I would have liked to discuss with her, but in the context of our casual, one-night-only encounter, it didn't seem likely to come up. With that in mind, I did my best to put on my actor and colleague hat as I went into rehearsal that morning.

Freya hadn't arrived yet when I got there, as usual, but someone else wanted to speak with me.

"Rome, can I talk to you? Alone?"

Jennifer's tone made it clear that refusing wouldn't really be an option, so I agreed and followed her into one of the small offices in the rehearsal space, the same one where we'd spoken on the first day of rehearsal. For a moment, I thought that somehow, she knew about what happened between me and Freya the night before and had some opinions on it, but I quickly reminded myself that would be impossible. Nobody knew, and no one was going to know. Freya wanted it that way.

Her words quickly confirmed that I had been barking up the wrong tree anyway. "Did you have Ian fired?" she demanded as soon as we were alone.

'Ian' was the director who had just left the show, though it surprised me that Jennifer knew about it already. The creative team were going to be making the announcement that morning when they introduced our new director, Matthew Blackman, to the cast.

"I don't have that kind of influence," I told her truthfully. "Just like I didn't tell them to cast Freya instead of you. Those decisions are made by the producers, not me."

Her pursed lips told me she didn't entirely believe me. "Then why did they tell Ian that the cast weren't happy with him? Whose opinion would mean that much other than yours?"

I had to be missing something. "Who told him that? And how do you know any of this?"

"Don't avoid the question, Rome. Did you complain about Ian? Yes or no?" Her arms were crossed, her back definitely up, but I still had no idea why.

"I don't answer to you, Jenn," I pointed out as calmly as I could. "But yes, I raised some concerns about the way Ian treated Freya in particular. Apparently, others agreed with me, and they mutually came to the decision for Ian not to continue with the show. That decision had nothing to do with me. All I wanted was for him to back off Freya and trust her a bit more."

Jennifer's eyes remained narrowed as she considered my words. "And this had nothing to do with me and him being together? Because that couldn't be any more hypocritical, Rome, considering your history."

That stung a little, coming from her, even though she had a point: it *would* have been hypocritical of me to complain about anyone in the show being involved with each other, but that hadn't happened, since I hadn't had a clue they were seeing each other.

"You and Ian? I had no idea, Jenn. Honestly."

That took the wind out of her sails. There might be things she didn't like about me, but she knew me well enough to know that I rarely lied. I tried my best to always tell the truth, even when it got me in trouble. If I knew about her and Ian dating, I would admit it, and she knew that.

"I thought..." she began before trailing off, a grimace of embarrassment flashing across her face.

"What did you think?"

Swallowing down her hesitancy, she completed her sentence. "I thought maybe you were jealous."

That also really wasn't my style. If someone chose to be with someone else, they could make that call, and I'd be happy for them if they were happy. I didn't feel that anyone belonged to me, not in that way. I'd never really understood that kind of possessiveness, though I knew that many of the women I'd dated wouldn't have minded me being a bit *more* possessive.

"My comments about Ian had nothing to do with you," I told her gently but firmly. "I hope things work out between you if it's what you want."

She sighed, her anger completely dissipating as she accepted my response. "Thanks. We were trying to keep it a secret because of the show, but I guess that's not an issue now. What do you know about the new director?"

I didn't want to steal Matthew's thunder by going into too much detail about the plans he had for the show, so I simply said that I'd met with him and I thought the producers made a good choice. We talked a bit more about the show until someone knocked on the door and the production assistant stuck her head in. "They're waiting for you two. They're ready to get started."

Shit. I hadn't realized we'd been talking so long, and I'd been hoping to get a chance to chat with Freya before the day started. That ship had sailed as Jennifer and I walked into the rehearsal room to find the cast already assembled and waiting. I slid into the seat next to Freya, as usual, giving her a warm smile. She looked even more beautiful than usual, and it both relieved and slightly disappointed me to see that she smiled back at me as normal. It seemed she really didn't intend to let the previous night change anything between us, good or bad.

Jeffrey Neill stood up to address the cast first. "Good morning, everyone. You might have noticed that our director isn't here this morning."

There were nods and a few murmurs from around the room, but no one expected Jeffrey's next words, other than me and Jennifer.

"He has decided to leave the show, so starting today, we'll be working with a new director."

As I could have predicted, that set off a much louder round of murmurs, and Freya looked over at me in surprise. "Did you know about this?" she whispered.

I nodded while whispering back, "I wanted to tell you last night."

Understanding dawned in her eyes, making it clear she knew exactly when I would have told her: just before she seduced me.

"I know this is a big change at this point in the process," Jeffrey continued. "But I'm also very excited to introduce the man who will be taking his place. His reputation definitely precedes him, and we can't wait to see what he's got planned for our little show. Please give a warm welcome to your new director, Matthew Blackman."

As Matthew walked into the room, everyone burst into excited applause, whispering furiously to each other. I picked up a few of the things being said behind me.

"Is this for real?"

"I didn't know he did live theatre."

"This is amazing!"

The mood felt overwhelmingly positive as excitement flowed through the room, but when I glanced over at Freya to see her reaction, her face had gone completely pale. She applauded along with everyone else, but without any real enthusiasm. Her gaze had fallen to the floor and her shoulders were tight with tension.

It couldn't be clearer to me that this news didn't excite her nearly as much as it did everyone else, but I didn't have the first idea why not.

~Freya~

"Did you know about this?" I whispered to Rome when the composer told us the director had been replaced. That was a huge deal, and my mind immediately flashed back to what I'd spoken about with Elyse in the park yesterday, about how she heard that Jennifer had been dating the director. Did that have something to do with why he left? Did something happen between them?

My mind raced with a million questions, and when Rome replied that he had planned to tell me about it the night before, I almost groaned out loud. He *did* say he had big news to tell me; I had just been too distracted by my body's needs and too eager to say what I had gone there to say before I changed my mind. I didn't regret what had happened between us, not for a second, but at that moment, I did wish that I had remembered to ask him about it before I left.

A few seconds later, when Jeffrey said Matthew's name, everything seemed to go into slow motion.

Briefly, I hoped that I had misheard him, or that perhaps, there was another renowned director by the name of Matthew Blackman he would be talking about. Every head in the room turned to the door and when the man in question walked through it, any small hopes I could hold onto were quickly extinguished.

The clothes that somehow conveyed both elegance and casualness at the same time, the slightly messy hair that never stayed where he meant it to, the thin-framed glasses that gave him an air of knowing just a little bit more than everyone else; not a thing about him had changed since the last time we saw each other face-to-face, five years earlier, the day I told him about my pregnancy and he said it had nothing to do with him.

He might not be classically handsome, not like Rome, but there was a magnetism and confidence about him, a confidence that sprang directly from his talent and made him appealing anyway. That confidence had made me fall for him, learning too late that it also acted as a sign of arrogance and self-centredness.

As soon as my brain registered his presence, I cast my gaze downwards, not wanting to make eye contact. My hands clapped along with everyone else so I wouldn't draw attention to myself, but the movement felt stilted and uncoordinated, as if I'd never done it before.

Why would he be there? He'd been living in Los Angeles for years, making his name in Hollywood just like he always wanted to. Why would he come back to New York? Why would he be involved in *this* show? Could it be because of me?

That seemed like the only logical answer but it also made no sense. He could have found me at any point if he wanted to. As I told Rome, I hadn't been hiding. Agreeing to direct a show just so he could talk to me seemed incredibly far-fetched, but it couldn't just be a coincidence either. There had to be something more behind it, but at that point, I couldn't imagine what that something might be.

At least no one else seemed to be aware that we had any kind of connection. When I glanced around the room, no one even glanced my way. Everyone's attention was entirely on Matthew, excitement written across the faces of all my castmates as they adjusted to this strange turn of events.

The only one paying any attention to me at all was Rome, his brow lined with concern as he looked over at me. "Are you okay?"

I honestly didn't know how to answer that, so I simply nodded, trying to smile. "Big news."

He nodded back in agreement, but the concern never left his eyes.

"Good morning, everyone." Matthew's voice rang out in the rehearsal space, as clear and authoritative as ever. "Thank you for that welcome, and thank you to Jeffrey and the producers for giving me this opportunity. A lot of you may not know that theatre has always been my first love. I directed a dozen shows while at NYU, and when I heard about *this* show, it immediately captured my imagination. It's fun and fresh, and I could see it in my head immediately. I gave Jeffrey a call simply to talk about it, and when the position opened up, he got back in touch to see if I would be interested. My latest film just wrapped, so the timing was perfect. Sometimes, the stars just align for a project to come together, and this is one of those times."

His words mocked me, even if that hadn't been their intent. If karma had arranged this for me, I must have done something very cruel to deserve it.

"I know we don't have a lot of time to work with," Matthew continued. "So, I'm going to need your full focus at all times. You don't know me and I don't know you, with the odd exception."

His eyes flitted to me, for the first time since he entered, and that time, I didn't drop my gaze. I stared back at him, as defiantly and coolly as I could. This was *my* show, my big break, and I wouldn't let him ruin that for me. The corner of his lips twitched for just a second before he turned back to the rest of the room.

"The important thing to know, however, is that I respect hard work above all else, and any direction I give you is for the benefit of the show and not personal in any way. Is that clear?"

After everyone nodded and gave their assent, Matthew said he wanted to start from the beginning to see what we'd been working on so far. A group number opened the show, showing Julia and Victor's typical routines in their completely separate lives before they met. Rome and I were both in the scene, along with most of the cast, so we got to our feet to take our marks on the rehearsal floor.

"Are you sure you're alright?" Rome whispered to me as we walked over to our opening spots together. "You look upset."

Did I? *Shit.* I was trying not to. I would have to try harder. "I'm fine," I assured him. "Just a bit nervous."

"You've got no reason to be," he promised, giving me his warm smile. "You've got this, Freya, and I'm right beside you."

I did my best to keep that in mind, and thankfully, once the music started, I tuned everything out, as usual, and became Julia. She had her problems, but at that moment, they seemed more manageable than mine, and I found myself wishing we could swap places for good. At least I knew that a happy ending waited for her at the end of her story. What my story might bring, I still had no idea.

We worked on the scene non-stop for an hour before moving on to the next one, my opening solo number in the show, the balcony scene I'd done at the audition. Known as an 'I want' number in a Broadway show, the song explained the character's and ambitions to the audience. That moment would determine whether the actor could bring the audience on side with their character or fail to do so, which meant it had a lot riding on it.

After all the changes Matthew had suggested for the first scene, I expected him to have a mountain of notes for my song too, but instead, when I'd finished singing and the last chord of the piano faded into the air around us, he simply nodded his head. "Good. Next scene."

Seriously? Most actresses probably would have been delighted, but given the circumstances, it felt suspicious. Was he afraid to give me notes? Did he think I couldn't handle it? Was he going to treat me differently than anyone else because of our past?

I needed to find out exactly what was going on in his head, so when we finally stopped for a break, I joined the small crowd already swarming around him and spoke out above the buzz of voices. "I need to speak with you, Matthew."

My forceful declaration took everyone by surprise, including Matthew, but thankfully, he agreed. "Please excuse me for a minute," he told everyone else, and together, we walked out of the room into one of the small offices just outside.

"What are you doing here?" The question burst out of me as soon as the door closed behind us and we were alone.

His right eyebrow raised in that expression of amusement I used to know so well. "I'm directing. I thought we made that pretty clear."

I didn't smile. I had no intention of being charmed by him. "You know what I mean. Why are you *here*, at this show?"

"I hadn't heard of the show until I saw your casting announcement," he admitted when it became clear I wanted a real answer. "When I did, I looked into it, and just like I told the others, the idea of it genuinely intrigued and excited me. I got in touch with the composer and we chatted about it, but I didn't expect anything to come of it. Why would it when the show already had a director? But then the director quit and they offered me the job. So, it came about because of you, in a way, Freya, but it's not *because* of you. I hope that's clear."

He always had a way of condescending to me, of making me feel slightly less intelligent than him, and that response was a perfect example. I had never said I thought he was there because of me, but in his response, he managed to imply I thought it anyway.

Now that he had brought it up, though, I had more questions. "And you didn't think it might be worth mentioning to me that you were going to be here this morning?"

"You never responded to my message," he pointed out mildly, and I couldn't argue with that. I had ignored him, for obvious reasons. "I thought the producers or your co-star might have told you, but I didn't see it as my job to do it. If any other director had been hired, you wouldn't expect them to get in touch."

No matter how infuriatingly sound his logic might be, he was deliberately missing the point. He wasn't *any* director. He knew exactly what kind of history lay between us, but if I brought it up, I would be the one making things personal, not him.

"Why didn't you give me any notes on my song?" I asked next. If he wanted to stick to business, I would stick to business.

"Because the direction you'd been given before worked fine. At this point, I'm not worried about performance; when we get to that, I will certainly have some notes for you, but right now, I'm only paying attention to basic staging and blocking to see where the big changes need to be made. The solo numbers will need less work than the group ones."

The implication was clear once again: he had come there simply to do a job, and by making it personal, I was the one being unreasonable.

"If there's nothing else, I have a few other people I need to speak to before the break ends." He glanced down at his watch, and with no small amount of frustration, I told him to go. That had been singularly unhelpful.

I remained in the room after he left, trying to regain my composure and my equilibrium, and I had almost succeeded until Rome came through the door and shut it behind him.

"Please tell me what's bothering you," he requested before I could say anything at all, his blue eyes still filled with the same genuine consideration for me he'd shown all morning. "Is it about last night? I don't want you to..."

"It's not that, Rome," I quickly cut him off. Our night together seemed like a wonderful dream, a world completely different to the one I found myself in that morning. "It has to do with Matthew."

"What about him?" Rome's curious and open expression invited me to confide in him, drawing me in. "He said he knew you at NYU. Were you friends?"

That was one way of putting it, and I chewed on my lip indecisively, torn between telling Rome the whole story and not wanting to put him in the middle. He had to work with Matthew too, and I knew Rome's own past and the affection he already had for Dylan. If he knew exactly who Matthew was, would he be able to put that aside to work with him, as I had to try to do? Would it be selfish of me to put him in that position?

"Please, Freya," he added when I didn't immediately answer. His hand slipped into mine, warm and comforting. "We're friends, right? For the next year, you're going to be the person I spend the most time with in the world, and we need to trust each other. Tell me what's wrong."

~Rome~

I didn't understand how no one else seemed to see Freya's discomfort. All morning, the rehearsal carried on as though everything was great, and the other cast members treated her the same as always even though it couldn't be clearer to me that something had changed.

Her movements were stiff and controlled, the muscles in her face were tight and her hazel eyes had lost their warm openness. Although she still put in an amazing performance in her scenes, she didn't lose herself in them quite as much as usual. There might as well have been a neon sign over her, pointing at her and flashing *'something is bothering me'*, and yet I seemed to be the only one who could see it.

She'd just told me that 'something' was our new director, Matthew, but I still didn't fully understand. They had known each other in college, I knew that much, but in what capacity? He must be a couple of years older than her. Had they been in classes together? Did they work on a show together? Were they simply in the same social group?

There were a lot of ways they might have come into contact and a lot of different things that might have upset her, and I wanted to know the details. If I could somehow make this new development easier for her, I would.

"It's not that I don't want to tell you," she began, looking up at me with that beautifully expressive face of hers, cloaked in anxiety at that moment. "But I don't want to put you in an awkward position either. We all have to work together, at least for the next month."

What could he have done that would be so bad I wouldn't be able to work with him? My mind immediately raced with the possibilities, each one getting darker and darker until I knew that whatever it might be, I needed to know. My imagination was too powerful, and after those words, I wouldn't be able to look at him without picturing the worst-case scenarios.

"Freya, you aren't responsible for my actions. If you tell me and I choose to act on it, that's my choice, but I want to know. If I can help you through this in any way, then I want to do it. I hate to see you looking so tense. This is your big moment and you should be enjoying every minute of it. If I'd known ahead of time that this would be a problem, I would have warned you about it."

I might not have been able to do anything about it since, as I told Jennifer, I had no direct control over hiring the director. At the very least, though, if I'd known having Matthew there would make Freya uncomfortable, I would have said something.

"You couldn't have known," she assured me. "None of this is your fault, Rome. It's him I don't understand. Why would he choose to do this show? Of all the shows in the world, all the projects he could be doing, why would he come here when he knew I'd be here?"

She was getting more upset as she spoke, not less, and without thinking, I simply wrapped her up in my arms, letting the warmth and strength of my body comfort her even if my words couldn't since I still didn't know any of the details.

And just as it had that morning when I spoke to Jennifer, the production assistant's knock on the door pulled us back to reality.

"We're ready to resume," she told us, opening the door as Freya and I quickly stepped away from each other. "They're waiting on you."

Freya immediately headed for the door, but I grabbed hold of her hand as she walked past me. "I still want to hear about it, Freya. Will you have lunch with me today so we can talk?"

Her lips pursed for a moment in indecision but in the end, she nodded, so I let her go and followed her back to the rehearsal room. For the rest of the morning, I paid extra attention to Matthew, watching to see if he behaved any differently towards Freya from how he treated anyone else, but he seemed entirely focused on the task at hand. Based on his behaviour alone, no one would even think they knew each other, not any more than he knew anyone else in the room.

At last, lunch arrived and Freya and I headed outside together. A fall chill hung in the air, the warm September days finally starting to give way to the colder weather that would inevitably be on the way, and I led her to a small cafe that I knew just a couple of blocks away. A small place with great homemade soups and sandwiches, it had a pleasant spiciness in the air as we walked in. The owner gave me a friendly wave from behind the counter as we took a seat.

We hadn't had lunch together since we started rehearsals, and normally, I would have been happy just to have the extra time with her except that we obviously weren't there for a casual chat. As soon as we'd placed our order, after I'd convinced her to let me pay for her lunch, I asked the question I desperately wanted an answer to: "How exactly do you and Matthew Blackman know each other?"

Her lips pursed again, making it clear how conflicted she felt about telling me, but finally, she let the words out.

"He's Dylan's father."

In all my imaginings, that possibility had never crossed my mind. As soon as she said it, as the words settled between us like some kind of invisible divide, it made perfect sense, and I didn't know how it hadn't occurred to me before.

They knew each other in college, when she got pregnant. She told me that Dylan's dad was someone relatively famous, someone she could keep track of without any real effort.

And the eyes behind his glasses, those brown eyes I'd sat across from over dinner the night before, were just like Dylan's big brown ones, the ones I thought must have come from his dad since they weren't anything like Freya's.

Jealousy was an unfamiliar emotion to me, but I felt it then, running through my veins and tightening my heart. Matthew had been in a relationship with Freya. He'd got to have that experience with her that I couldn't have, and the sweetest little boy I'd ever met belonged to him. Dylan had asked me if I would be his daddy, but Matthew *was* his dad.

That envy only lasted a few moments, though, quickly replaced by anger and indignation, on Freya's behalf, but even stronger on Dylan's. Matthew had this amazing son and he'd never cared enough to even meet him. He'd made that amazing little boy feel less important and loved than he should, and even disregarding any pain he might have caused Freya, I didn't know if I could forgive him for that.

Freya's reluctance to tell me made complete sense to me now that she had. She must have known I would take it personally, and I did. In some ways, she knew me incredibly well considering how short a time we had actually spent together.

"Rome?" She said my name with trepidation, looking at me nervously across the table. "Say something. You're freaking me out."

Having studied improvisation as part of my acting training, I didn't usually find myself lost for words, but her revelation had managed to do it. I honestly had no idea what to say until I realized why I struggled: I was making it about *me* when it most definitely wasn't. I should be focused on Freya and how she felt, and when it came to that, I had quite a lot to say. Or rather, I had a lot to ask her about, if she didn't mind.

"Is it okay if I ask some questions?"

I did my best to keep my voice level, and she nodded, looking a little less nervous as I spoke. "Of course."

"He still doesn't know about Dylan?"

My calm tone seemed to relax her even further, her shoulders visibly loosening as she leaned back in her chair. "No. At least, I don't think so. If he does, he hasn't said anything to me."

"When's the last time you spoke to him before today?"

The questions were almost clinical, but she didn't seem to mind. She answered me readily enough. "The day I told him about my pregnancy. I haven't heard a word from him since then, not until Friday. He sent me a message after the casting announcement to congratulate me, but I hadn't replied yet. I didn't plan to."

"He didn't let you know that he'd be here today?" From her reaction that morning, I could guess the answer to that, so when she shook her head, it didn't surprise me. "And when you were together in college, were you doing a show together then?"

That time, she nodded. "He was my director so we kept our relationship a secret. He broke up with me the day the show ended. To this day, I don't know if he actually felt anything for me at all or if it had only been convenient for him since I was right there."

Regret and guilt flooded through me with those words. No wonder she didn't want to get into a relationship with me. My relationships always seemed to be tied to the shows I did too, intentionally or not, though at least I'd never left anyone pregnant on their own.

That wasn't a very high bar to surpass.

"Will you tell him about Dylan now?"

When it came down to it, that had to be the question weighing heaviest on her mind. It might be uncomfortable for her to work with him, but in the end, we were both professional actors. We could pretend not to be bothered by him if we really tried. But if he planned to insert himself into her personal life, and especially into Dylan's life, that would be a much bigger deal.

Freya obviously agreed, the anxiety returning to her face as she considered her response. "I haven't decided what I should do yet. What do you think, Rome? If you were me, what would you do?"

Chapter Eleven

Rome was handling my revelation a lot better than I expected, to be honest. I had been prepared for an outburst, maybe some swearing or threats of violence, and perhaps some of that *was* going on beneath the surface. Outwardly, however, he appeared calm and rational as he asked me questions that were focused on the immediate issue: namely, would I tell Matthew about Dylan?

Since I'd only had a few hours to adjust to the whole situation, most of which had been focused on the rehearsal, I hadn't made up my mind just yet. On the one hand, I didn't think Matthew deserved to know. He'd had ample opportunity to find out about Dylan if he really wanted to. I never lied to him; I never said I would get an abortion when he suggested it. If he assumed I had, that was on him.

On the other hand, now that we were working together, hiding it seemed pointless. Dylan wasn't a secret from anyone in the cast; I talked about him whenever I had a chance, showing off cute pictures like any proud mom would. Everyone else knew I had a son so it would only be a matter of time before Matthew found out too.

Maybe it would be better to just tell him up front and get it over with. It might not be pleasant to deal with, but at least I wouldn't have it hanging over me for the next month, waiting for the other shoe to drop.

Rome seemed to be on the same page as me, as usual. "It's not really realistic to think he won't find out at some point over the next month."

I had to reluctantly agree. "Is it awful of me that I hope he doesn't even care? In my mind, the best-case scenario is that I tell him, and he says 'so what?', but that's not fair to Dylan, is it? I should want his dad to want to be in his life."

"Dylan's doing just fine without him," Rome pointed out, a little more fiercely than necessary. That was the first emotion he'd shown, and as quickly as it appeared, he swallowed it back down just as fast. When he spoke again, his voice sounded controlled and even again. "If Matthew wants to be a real and positive part of his life, that's one thing. But if his involvement is going to be reluctant or half-hearted, then I agree, it would be better for him not to be around at all. Unfortunately, it's not up to me."

It wasn't entirely up to me either. That stupid, unprotected ejaculation gave Matthew rights under the law despite him having been a ghost in my life ever since. I truly didn't think he would want custody, but if he did, how could I stop him? He had more money and connections than I could ever dream about.

The waitress brought our food over, and although my carrot and cilantro soup was warm and spiced and soothing, I barely even tasted it. My mind remained focused entirely on Matthew's unwelcome return.

"Tell me to butt out if I'm being too nosy," Rome said after taking a bite of his sandwich. "But how long were you guys together?"

Talking about my time with Matthew didn't usually come naturally to me. I'd pushed it down for so long, but somehow, Rome made it feel less intimidating than usual. The words came out of my mouth before I had time to question them. "Only two months. Basically, the length of rehearsal and performances for the show we did together. I was in my second year of college, he was in his fourth and about to graduate. I'd played the lead in my high school productions back in Iowa, but that show was my first lead role at NYU, and I couldn't have been more excited. Matthew already had a reputation for brilliance, everyone expected big things from him, and I was a little starstruck. After the first day of rehearsal, he asked me to stay behind to go over a scene or two after everyone else left. He read the lines of the male lead, and when we got to the part where his character kissed mine, he did that too, and we didn't stop."

Rome's jaw tightened, but he encouraged me to continue. "I know how easy it is to lose yourself in the character and what they're feeling."

I supposed he did. He did keep ending up with his co-stars. "We spent pretty much every spare moment together after that. Matthew insisted we keep the relationship a secret because he didn't want anyone to think he gave me special treatment because we were together. It felt a little forbidden and exciting, and I never really questioned whether it was right. I got swept up in it and I assumed he did too."

Rome took another, rather aggressive bite from his sandwich. "And you broke up when the show ended, you said?"

I nodded, my throat constricting as I returned to that night in my mind. "At the wrap party, actually. The cast and crew had a private room rented at a local bar so we went there together and drank a fair bit. You know how it is."

He nodded in understanding. The party at the end of a show, especially in college, was always an epic affair, a release of all the pressure of putting the show on and the excitement of a job well done.

"We were dancing together and our hands kept wandering over each other. Other people must have noticed, but we were too drunk to care. Eventually, he took me into a back room so we could have sex."

Perhaps I should feel awkward about sharing all of that with the man I had slept with literally the night before, but for some reason, I didn't. Rome's expression remained completely free of judgement, interested but not too pushy.

"He didn't have a condom with him," I explained, getting to the crux of the story. "Being young and stupid and drunk, I told him not to worry. When we finished, he went back to the party first, to make it slightly less obvious that we'd been together, though I'm sure everyone knew by that point. When I got back to the bar, he'd gotten into conversation with other people so I did the same, and about an hour later, he pulled me aside again and broke up with me right there and then. To this day, I don't know if something happened within that hour or if it had been his plan all along."

"What did he say?" Although Rome's voice sounded tight, his eyes were still warm and supportive.

"He just said we let ourselves get carried away in the excitement of the show, it wasn't real, we were both meant for different things. Maybe he truly felt that way, I don't know."

"But you didn't?" Rome guessed, and I shook my head.

"I thought we were in love. I thought we were going to be together forever. I guess I'd been stupid and naive, but it honestly never occurred to me that it might just be a showmance."

The word made Rome wince, and I immediately felt bad for using it. People often used it to describe his own relationships: a pairing brought on by the intensity and illusion created by a show, which ends as soon as the show does.

"What happened after that?" he asked, eager to move on from that particular phrase.

"At first, I thought maybe he'd been so drunk that he didn't know what he was saying. For the next few days, I kept my phone glued to me, hoping he would call and either not even remember we had that conversation or tell me he'd made a mistake and he wanted to be with me after all. But he never did, and after a few weeks, I found out I was pregnant. With only a week before the school year ended, I tracked him down after one of his classes to tell him in person. After asking me first if I was sure, and second if I could be certain the baby was his, he told me he didn't have any intention of being a father that young and I should end the pregnancy, as I already told you."

"Son of a..." Rome muttered under his breath before taking a deep breath to bring himself back under control once again. "And you never heard from him again."

We'd already talked about that, he just wanted confirmation, so I nodded to give it to him. "I went home for the summer and told my mom the whole thing. She insisted that I couldn't let it stop me from living my life, and she moved here to New York to help me through it. I went back to college in the fall, dealing with all the whispers and the rumours about my pregnancy, and I took two weeks off when I gave birth. After that, my mom helped to care for Dylan so I could finish my course and keep auditioning for things ever since. She's been incredible, I honestly don't know what I would have done without her."

"She sounds amazing," Rome agreed, and sympathy ran through me as I remembered his own mother abandoning him. My own struggles paled in comparison to his, and yet he had only empathy and support for me. "Well, obviously, I can't tell you what to do. However, you asked what I would do if it were me, and I have to say I would tell him. You hope he won't care, and from everything you've just told me, I don't think he will. At least if you tell him, you'll know for sure."

As much as I hated to admit it, I felt the same way. Keeping quiet about it while we were living a country apart was one thing, but since we were back in the same room, day after day, it didn't make sense to try to hide it.

"I'll try to speak to him after rehearsal today," I decided out loud. No point in stressing about it any longer than I had to, now that the decision had been made. "I'll let my mom know I'll be home a little late, and I'll just do it."

Even though it had been his suggestion, I didn't miss the look of worry that crossed Rome's face. "Do you want me to wait for you, in case you need to talk afterwards?"

His ridiculously sweet offer gave me another idea. It might be asking too much, but I wouldn't know how he felt about it until I asked. "Actually, would you mind being there while I told him? He has a way of brushing me off and making me feel like I'm in the wrong. With a neutral party there, he might be a little less... like himself."

Rome gave an almost amused huff. "I'm not sure how neutral I am, but of course, Freya. If you want me there, I'll be there. For Dylan."

For Dylan. Of course.

"In that case, we should probably get back." The lunch hour had flown by, and after Rome paid for our meals, at his insistence, we made our way back to the rehearsal room where I did my best to calm the nerves in my stomach as I waited to see what the rest of the day would bring.

~Rome~

As the rehearsal carried on that afternoon, I understood better than ever why Freya had been hesitant to tell me about Matthew in the first place. Every word out of the guy's mouth grated on my nerves. Everyone else continued to buzz with excitement over the ideas he brought to the show, just like I had that morning, but after what Freya told me, I could only stew in my anger and jealousy.

Yes, I felt jealous. Even though the feeling was foreign to me, I had to admit it. I was jealous because he was about to find out that he had an incredible son, one that he had no moral right to even if the legal right existed, and because I knew that no matter what Freya's feelings on the subject were, if Matthew wanted to be part of Dylan's life, she would not only allow but encourage it because she wanted to make the best choice for her son. That sweet little voice asking me to be his daddy would be a distant memory.

More than that, and even more surprising to me, I didn't only feel jealous over Dylan. I resented Matthew for his relationship with Freya too. *I thought we were in love*, she told me, which meant that she had loved him, and that thought bothered me far more than the idea of her simply sleeping with him.

None of that fit my usual patterns. I didn't get possessive over women, especially not ones I wasn't even in a relationship with, so why did it upset me that she'd cared about him in a way she never would for me?

The whole thing confused and frustrated me, but the one good thing about it was that it led to me reading some of Victor's lines in a new way which seemed to work.

"I really liked that," Freya told me after one of our scenes together. "Victor sounded almost angry with her for not falling at his feet like everyone else does, but not in an aggressive way. He was just bewildered and frustrated about it. I felt sorry for him."

Her praise both pleased and annoyed me, since I knew those were my own emotions she sensed, and I didn't want her feeling sorry for me.

At last, rehearsals finished for the day. Matthew and Jeffrey immediately dove into conversation, a mountain of notes between them, while Freya hovered nearby, waiting for an opportunity to catch Matthew's eye.

I had no intention of waiting. She had to be nervous enough to begin with and waiting around wouldn't help matters at all, so I strode straight over to the table where they were gathered and interrupted them. "Matthew, Freya and I would like to speak to you."

He looked surprised by my tone, which he should be. I had been a lot friendlier over dinner the night before. With a glance over at Freya, he gave a shrug. "I can spare a few minutes. Jeffrey, will you excuse me?"

The composer gave his assent, and the three of us headed back to the small office next door, the same one where I spoke with Freya earlier that day. I smiled at the other cast members who were leaving for the day, but as soon as we were inside, the smile dropped from my face.

"Is there a problem?" Matthew asked warily, looking back and forth between us. He must have sensed we hadn't brought him there for a friendly chat.

"It's not about the show," Freya said, taking the lead while I went to lean against the windowsill, doing my best to fade into the background. This conversation belonged to her; I was simply here for support.

"You're doing a great job and I'm sure the show will be better for having you here."

Reluctantly, I had to agree with that. He made for an improvement over the previous director, at least on a professional level.

"So, what is it?" Matthew asked, his guard still up. "I thought we cleared the other thing up earlier."

The 'other thing'? Was that how he referred to breaking her heart?

"Rome knows about us," Freya said, giving him the benefit of the doubt that the reason he used those words had been to keep their past a secret.

Matthew glanced over at me with new interest. "Are you two together already?"

His implication couldn't be clearer: we *would* hook up at some point because of who I was. Maybe he also meant to insinuate something about Freya. My hands gripped onto the ledge I leaned against as I tried to keep my anger in check.

"Rome and I aren't dating," Freya answered for the both of us, and though the words were true, hearing them out loud didn't particularly please me either. "He's a friend and he offered to be here with me for this conversation. I want him here."

Matthew glanced down at his watch, making it clear he would rather be spending his time elsewhere. "And what is this conversation, exact-ly?"

Although his indifference could have shaken Freya from her decision, she pushed ahead anyway. "Do you remember the last time we spoke at NYU and I told you I was pregnant?"

At last, she had his full attention. Surprise and wariness played across his face as he looked at her fully. "I remember," was all he said, tersely.

"Well, I just wanted you to know, since you're bound to hear it anyway, that I have a son. His name is Dylan, he's four years old, and he's the best thing in my life."

A beat passed, and another, as Matthew absorbed what she'd said, his eyes moving quickly behind his glasses as he decided how to respond.

When the words finally came out, they were a surprise to us both.

"I know."

"You know?" I repeated, the words bursting out of me in fury. Was he fucking kidding? I thought him knowing there was even a possibility would be bad enough, but he actually knew he had a son and had never done a damn thing about it?

Matthew didn't look at me but Freya did, shooting me a look that entreated me to back off. Though it wasn't easy, I did my best, leaning back against the window again and keeping my mouth shut.

"How long have you known?" she asked, addressing herself back to Matthew, her voice admirably calm.

"A couple of years. You mentioned him in an interview when you did that revue show off-Broadway."

So, he'd been keeping tabs on her after all, but why? If he had been so desperate to cut the ties between them, why would he even care?

Freya also looked confused about it, but she carried on anyway. "Well, I suppose that answers my question. I wondered if you were going to want to be involved in his life at all, but the answer is clearly no, and that's fine."

She had actually hoped for that outcome, so in a perverse way, I was happy for her, even if I had lost pretty much all respect for our new director.

"Actually..." Matthew said, and my stomach sank as Freya's expression did too. Neither of us wanted to hear that word. "I thought being here in the city might give me a chance to meet him, if it's okay with you."

That confused me, and obviously Freya felt the same. "You just said this morning that coming back here had nothing to do with me."

I hadn't known that, but it didn't surprise me that he'd said so.

"It doesn't, but it does have a little to do with him. Look, I know I hurt you, Freya. I don't expect you to forgive me for that, and I didn't plan to bring up Dylan until you told me yourself. But now that you have, then the truth is that I would like to meet him."

Freya looked so lost that staying in my place became an even bigger struggle. I wanted to go and comfort her, to hug her as I had that morning and to provide a united front beside her. However, in the big picture, I was merely a spectator. They were the main characters.

"It can be on your terms," Matthew continued. "Wherever and whenever you like. Besides the show, I have no other commitments while I'm here."

While he was here. Those were the key words, weren't they? He didn't intend on sticking around forever, so what good did it do Dylan to meet him and get attached, only for him to leave again? I'd been trying to avoid that very thing myself, and now I had to stand back and watch it happen.

"I'll think about it," Freya managed to say, though even those words were difficult for her to get out.

Recognizing that he wouldn't get anything more from her at that time, Matthew thanked her, nodded at me, and headed back to the rehearsal room. As soon as we were alone, I couldn't wait any longer. In a second, I stood beside her, my arms wrapped around her while she leaned into my chest.

"Why?" she whispered into the stillness of the room, but I had no answer for her.

"I don't know, but you're not alone, Freya. I'm here for you and for Dylan. Come on, let's get out of here. Let me take you home."

~Freya~

The night before, when Rome offered to pay for a taxi to take me home, I refused. Boundaries were getting blurry enough on their own between us and I didn't want to make it worse. However, after what happened with Matthew and his completely unexpected revelation that he not only already knew about Dylan but wanted to meet him, the idea of standing in the crowded subway car surrounded by strangers couldn't be more unappealing. When Rome suggested he would take me home, I didn't even try to protest.

As soon as I nodded, he told me to wait in the office while he went back into the rehearsal room to gather all of our things, since Matthew would still be in there. A couple of minutes later, he returned, helping me into my coat and refusing to let me carry anything as he took my hand to lead me outside. Once we were on the street, he hailed a cab, got in beside me and gave the driver my address, all without me having to say a word.

Having someone else there to handle the little things made for a nice change, but it meant my mind had nothing to do but fixate on what had just been said, and as the taxi began the drive north up to Harlem, I leaned back against the seat with my eyes closed, repeating the words that had shaken me so much.

"He knew."

That had shocked me the most. Wanting to meet Dylan, I could understand. He was a great kid; who wouldn't want to meet him? But for Matthew to tell me that he'd known about him for *years* and never bothered to get in touch, that I couldn't wrap my head around.

Rome's jaw clenched as he looked ahead, his eyes on the road in front of us as if he could get us home faster even though he sat in the back with me. His hand rested supportively on my knee, though when it got there, I couldn't say. "I'm the last person in the world who would make any excuses for him, but I've been thinking about what he said about Dylan being part of the reason he decided to do the show."

I honestly hadn't even got around to processing that part yet, still stuck on the fact that he knew about him at all.

"I think..." Rome exhaled deeply, as if it pained him to even say the words. "I think maybe he felt guilty and he didn't know how to approach you. Coming into your life on a professional level like this gave him a way to speak to you without you being able to just send him away. I'm not saying that's definitely the case, and I'm absolutely not saying it excuses anything, because it doesn't and he's still a fucking selfish bastard. But that's what I got from it, anyway. I think, deep down, he knows what a jerk he was, and this is his way of trying to get back into your life, and Dylan's, without having to put himself on the line at all, which is an extremely dickish way to go about it."

What he said made a lot of sense, even if I agreed with his conclusion about it being pretty messed up. "And now I'm the bad guy if I refuse to let him even meet his son," I summed up, and Rome nodded, his face still tight.

"But just because it's his narrative doesn't make it the truth, Freya," he added, those stunning blue eyes of his looking directly down at me. "You're still in control."

It didn't really feel like it. The last time I felt things spinning out of control this badly had been when I found out about my pregnancy in the first place.

When we reached my apartment building, Rome got out of the taxi with me. "I said I'd take you home and that's what I'm doing," was his simple explanation when I gave him a curious look.

My building couldn't hold a candle to his; it had no sleek lobby and no friendly doorman, just a rusted old elevator that still had a gate you had to pull closed before it would start. Rome didn't seem bothered, though, his body still close to mine as we went up to the tenth floor to my apartment.

As we approached the door, I felt bad sending him away after he'd been so supportive to me all day, but I also wasn't sure what kind of message inviting him in would send, not only to him, but to Dylan and my mom too.

Rome seemed to sense my concerns almost telepathically, or maybe he could just see the hesitation on my face. "I'm here as a friend," he reminded me gently, and with that reassurance, I unlocked the door and let us both in.

"Mommy!"

The little shriek came from the living room where cartoons were playing on the TV, but not loud enough that Dylan missed the sound of the door opening. A second later, he came barrelling around the corner, then skidded to a stop as soon as he realized I had company. The action was so dramatic that Rome and I both had to laugh.

"Wome!" As soon as Dylan recognized him, he instantly forgot about me, launching himself at Rome instead.

"Careful, Dill-pickle," I admonished him, though thankfully, Rome's reflexes kicked in and he caught Dylan mid-air, lifting him up with ease.

"More magic?" Dylan asked, obviously trying to figure out exactly why Rome had come.

"Not today, buddy," I answered for my co-star. "Go tell Grandma we're here, okay?"

He ran off and we could both hear him excitedly telling my mom about his unexpected guest while Rome tried hard not to smile, not fully succeeding.

My mom waited in the doorway of the kitchen when we stepped into the living room. "So, this is the famous Wome Taylor, is it?"

She pronounced Rome's name as Dylan did, making Rome smile again as he strode over to her and offered his hand. "It's a pleasure to meet you, Mrs Rose. You can call me Rome if you prefer."

"That might be easier," she agreed, shaking his hand before casting a curious glance in my direction. "Are you joining us for dinner?"

"I don't want to intrude," Rome demurred, but of course my mom wouldn't have any of that. She insisted he stay, and told Dylan to show Rome his cars while she and I set an extra place at the table.

"Is this what kept you at rehearsal?" she whispered to me over the sound of the dishes.

I shook my head. "Not like you're thinking. Rome's just being a friend. I stayed late because..." The words caught in my throat, but I forced them out anyway, despite the tightness. "Matthew has joined the show. He's our new director."

The plate in her hand clattered down onto the counter as she looked over at me, her eyes wide in disbelief. "You're joking."

I truly wished I was. "Unfortunately not. I spoke to him after the show and found out that not only does he already know about Dylan, he wants to meet him."

My mom's jaw clenched in much the same way Rome's had. We all shared the same protective instinct when it came to Dylan. "And Rome knows about all of this?"

I nodded. "He was there while I talked to Matthew."

I hadn't told my mom about sleeping with Rome the night before, though I knew she had her suspicions. She just hadn't had a moment to question me about it yet, and I still had trouble believing it really happened myself. With everything else going on that day, I'd barely had a moment to let it sink in.

We all sat down to eat with Dylan dominating the conversation even more than usual thanks to his excitement over having Rome there. As soon as dinner finished, he pulled him away to take him to his room and show him his favourite toys. Rome asked me if that would be okay before he agreed, which I appreciated.

"He's falling hard for that little boy," my mom warned me once they were out of earshot and the two of us set to work cleaning up the kitchen.

"It looks that way," I had to agree. "He's not exactly known for sticking around, though."

The words felt unfair even as I said them, but I couldn't deny the truth of them. Long-term relationships were not Rome's thing. Everyone knew that, even Rome himself.

Besides, at the moment, I had other things on my mind, which my mom quickly acknowledged. "What are you going to do about Matthew?"

"He has a right to meet his son," I replied, as much as it pained me to say it. I'd been thinking about it all during dinner as Dylan's chatter kept everyone else entertained. "However, I'm going to lay down some firm ground rules. He can't tell Dylan he's his dad unless he plans to actually be one to him, permanently. I can introduce him as a friend, the same as I did with Rome."

I couldn't help hoping that Dylan would shy away from him as naturally as he'd been drawn to Rome, but I knew that wasn't very likely. By nature, Dylan was open and friendly, giving everyone an equal chance to be his friend, a chance that Matthew didn't really deserve at this point.

"Well, you don't need to rush into anything," my mom suggested. "He can't give you a timeline, so take your time and think it over. And in the meantime, don't let it distract you from the other good things in your life right now."

She made a pointed glance towards the kitchen door, through which we could hear the happy squeals of my son as he and Rome played together.

"I always thought that getting cast in a show would change my life, but I didn't realize it would be this much," I tried to joke. It felt like everything had been turned upside down ever since that audition. Would it have been better if I just kept my head down and didn't shoot so high? Things were so much less complicated before.

Before my mom could reply, Rome appeared in the doorway, out of breath, his blue eyes shining, and a shot of pure desire ran through me. Sometimes, with everything else going on, I forgot how truly breathtaking he could be. "Can I borrow your colander?"

Without even asking why, my mom pulled it out of the cupboard and handed it to him. Rome gave us a wink as he placed it on his head and headed back down the hall to Dylan's room.

"I think some changes are worth it," my mom said, smiling as she shook her head, and on that point, I was tempted to agree.

If only it could be easier to know just how much of a chance to take.

Chapter Twelve

~Rome~

Despite having been going at full-tilt for more than half an hour, Dylan still had so much energy, he practically bounced off the walls. "Let's play hide-and-seek now! You hide!"

I looked around his small, single bedroom, not seeing a single place where I could conceal myself. "That sounds great, but how about you hide instead?"

"No, you!" he insisted, so I gave in, though I imagined the game would be over pretty quickly. As he counted, I pulled the bed out from the wall and lay down on the floor behind it, tucking my legs up as much as I could since my body was longer than the bed itself. Even with all that effort, my feet were still sticking out the bottom.

With my head resting on the floor, I tried to ignore the tightness in my chest. It had been a long time since I played this game, and not just because of being grown up. Hide-and-seek was one of my few concrete memories with my mother. We played it a lot. I always thought I had a real talent for it; not until much later did I realize the reason it took her so long to find me was that she hadn't been looking. She must have just figured it kept me busy while she chatted with her friends or boyfriends.

My mother had never returned to my life, not as a child and not as an adult either. I had no idea whether she was even alive or dead. It went without saying that my father hadn't ever shown up either. If either of them had, would I have accepted them back happily? At Dylan's age, I probably would have. A few years later, once the bitterness and wariness took hold, it would have been a different story, but before that feeling of abandonment became fully ingrained, I would have jumped at the chance to have a family of my own rather than the foster homes I stayed in where I always felt like an outsider.

Dylan liked me, but would he like Matthew better? The thought left a completely unreasonable bitter taste in my mouth. Dylan didn't belong to me, not in any way, and I should want things to work out with him and his dad. I had done my best that whole day not to let my baser emotions win, and I didn't plan on losing the fight then either, at least externally.

"What are you doing, Dylan?" Freya's voice came from the door as Dylan finished counting to twenty, having circled back on the numbers a few times.

"Hide-and-seek!" he exclaimed gleefully. "Wome is hiding."

"Is he?" From her amused reply, I must have been about as hidden as I felt, which was not at all. Her voice went quieter, whispering something to her son, and a moment later, little fingers began to tickle my exposed feet.

"Rawwwr!" With a great roar, I sprang up as Dylan shrieked happily and ran behind Freya's legs, giggling the whole time.

"Okay, it's time for bed now," Freya told her son, shaking her head at me as she tried not to smile.

Dylan's face immediately fell. "No, please, Mommy! Ten more minutes."

I would have agreed, but Freya stood firm. "Nope, no more minutes. But if you're nice and quick about getting into your jammies and brushing your teeth, maybe Rome will read you a bedtime story before he goes home."

She threw me a hopeful look, and of course I nodded. I was in no hurry to go anywhere.

Dylan dropped his protest, running to his dresser to pull out some pajamas before he and Freya went down the hall to the bathroom together to get him ready for bed. I put his bed back in place against the wall and stepped over to his bookshelf to see what our options were. There were a few books I recognized and a lot I didn't.

I didn't have the chance to choose anyway. Dylan already had one in mind as he ran back into the room and pulled The Pout-Pout Fish off the shelf, handing it to me before taking my hand and leading me over to the bed. Once he had climbed in, I sat down next to him and read the story, putting on different voices for each character as he giggled beside me.

When we were finished, he asked me to read it again, but Freya, who had been standing in the doorway the whole time watching us, shook her head. "You know the rules, Dill-pickle. One story, that's it. Say goodnight to Rome."

"Goodnight, Wome," he repeated dutifully before throwing his little arms wide and giving me a hug. "I love you."

The words came out of him so easily, so naturally, making it clear once again that he had never doubted that love would be returned to him. I wasn't about to let him down, and I hoped Matthew wouldn't either. "I love you too, buddy. Good night."

I stepped out into the hall while Freya went to give him a kiss before turning off the light and closing the door behind her.

"Will he stay in bed now?" I wondered.

"He's usually pretty good." She gave me a grateful smile as we stepped back into the living room. "Thank you for playing with him tonight, he loved that. I would have stepped in if you needed rescuing, but you seemed to have it all under control."

"I loved it too," I assured her. "It was my pleasure. Where's your mom?" The living room was empty and I couldn't see her in the kitchen either.

"She's gone to her room," Freya explained with a wry smile. "I think she wanted to give us some privacy. She's not exactly subtle, but if you need to go, that's fine."

"There's nothing I need to do tonight. How are you feeling?"

We made ourselves comfortable on the sofa and Freya told me what she and her mom had talked about while Dylan and I played. It sounded like she had decided to let Matthew meet Dylan, but without telling Dylan who he was up front.

"The word 'dad' is pretty loaded for Dylan," Freya explained, chewing on her lip distractedly. "He'll have a lot of expectations that come with that, so I don't want to bring it up until I know for certain what Matthew's intentions are."

That seemed more than fair to me. "You're doing a great job, Freya. With the show, with Dylan, with dealing with all of this. You're amazing."

She shook her head, a blush rising in her cheeks. "Honestly, you're the amazing one, Rome. None of this is your problem. You don't have to be involved at all, but it means a lot to me that you're here."

"How about we agree we're both amazing, then?" I suggested, and her answering smile made me grin right back at her.

"I mean it," she insisted. "After last night, things could have been really weird or awkward between us, and they aren't at all."

The reminder of the time we shared in my apartment instantly sent a wave of heat through me, a rush of blood that settled directly in my groin. "It would only be awkward if it had been really bad. Since it wasn't, I don't see a reason for either of us to be embarrassed or uncomfortable about it."

"No, it definitely wasn't bad," she murmured under her breath, her gaze dropping to my mouth, and my desire grew even stronger. Mingled with the protectiveness and the possessiveness I'd felt earlier that day, my yearning for her felt more intense than it had ever been. If she were any other woman, if it were any other situation, I wouldn't hesitate, but in this case, I didn't want to cross any boundaries she didn't want to cross.

"Freya." Her name came out low, my tone a warning. "If you want me to go home now, tell me so. If you don't, I'm going to kiss you."

It could be either a threat and a promise, and to my great relief, she took it as the latter. "I don't want you to go," she whispered just before her lips connected with mine.

~Freya~

Exactly what we were doing at that moment wasn't entirely clear to me. When I went to Rome's apartment the night before, I laid things out very clearly: I went there for sex and nothing more. Yes, it had been incredible, and yes, it would have been very easy to read more into it, but I had done my very best not to. The one good thing about Matthew's unexpected arrival was that it stopped me from obsessing over the situation with Rome.

There in my apartment, however, where Rome had just charmed my mother and brought tears to my eyes with how sweetly he treated my son, things felt a hell of a lot deeper than just another hookup. When Dylan told Rome that he loved him and Rome said it back with no hesitation or uncertainty, it truly felt like my heart might melt. I had always wanted Dylan to have a male figure in his life who he could look up to and who could give him the things that I simply couldn't, and for Rome to step into that role so naturally while also supporting me in so many ways felt like something out of a dream. My mom said she thought Rome might be falling for Dylan, but the ground I stood on felt pretty shaky too. It felt more dangerous the more time we spent together.

Not that I didn't want to have sex with him again, because I did, and from the look in his eyes and the insistent press of his mouth on mine, I felt pretty damn sure he wanted it too. But what did it mean? Rome said earlier that night that he came there as a friend, but friends didn't kiss like this. Was he just as confused as I was?

We should probably have talked about it, but that would mean not kissing anymore, and I didn't want to stop. At that moment, his touch was like oxygen, vital and irresistible. I couldn't stop kissing him any more than I could stop breathing.

We both got to our feet, our lips still connected as we stumbled towards my bedroom, almost tripping over the coffee table as we went. Situated right next door to Dylan's room, I'd never had a man in my bedroom, but there was no reason I couldn't. We would just need to be as quiet as possible, a lot quieter than we had been in his apartment.

I broke our kiss momentarily to tell him so, but Rome was already on the same page as me, as usual. "We need to..."

"...keep it down," he finished, his blue eyes smouldering down into mine. "I got it."

Only when our clothes were on the floor, our movements growing more frantic and needy by the second, did we realize our other problem.

"I don't have a condom with me," Rome groaned as my hand circled his stiff cock. "Do you have one?"

I absolutely didn't. There hadn't been any need for me to buy any for a very long time.

When I shook my head, he groaned again, and though I felt equally disappointed, I found it rather sweet that he hadn't brought one. Obviously, he hadn't come there with any ulterior motive.

"I guess I could run out," he suggested, sounding about as thrilled with that prospect as I felt.

I squeezed his cock a little tighter. "I don't think this is going to fit back in your pants."

"Not very comfortably," he admitted, his voice tight as he tried to smile.

"So, we might just need to get creative," I suggested, and his eyebrows raised in curiosity. "Lie down on the bed."

Placing his trust in me, he did as I asked, lying down in the centre of the bed on his back, naked and irresistible. It would have been so easy to climb on top of him and sink down onto that enticing cock. My body ached for it, but I put my needs aside to focus on him.

Crawling over between his legs and with my eyes still on him, I bent down and kissed his cock just the same way I'd been kissing his mouth a moment earlier, my tongue pressing against it as I got my first taste of him. He'd gone down on me the night before; returning the favour was only fair.

"Shit," Rome muttered, his eyelids heavy with lust, but although the prospect of what I had in mine clearly tempted him, it didn't fully satisfy him. "Wait, Freya, not like that. Turn around. I need to get you off too."

He *needed* to. From the way he said it, I had no doubt he meant it, and it only made the aching inside me stronger. My legs trembling in anticipation, I crawled up beside him and turned myself around, straddling his head. As I bent over again, lifting his cock up to bring it to my lips, his hands gripped my hips and pulled me down onto his waiting mouth.

"Ermphmf." My moan of pleasure was muffled by Rome's cock, the sound pushed back down my throat as I took him in deeper. His tongue felt amazing, and I could only try to keep up as he licked along all my edges, sucking and kissing me in all the right places.

As my left hand ran across his balls, my right hand stroked the base of his shaft and my head bobbed up and down, quickly at first and then taking him all the way in, as far as I could. His groans of satisfaction were equally as muffled as mine had been, disappearing into my pussy as he pressed his mouth against me even more firmly.

At least we shouldn't have to worry about waking anyone up.

My need built higher and higher as my pace increased to match, and soon, my legs were trembling from the intensity of the pleasure he gave me. Sensing how close I was, Rome sucked down on my clit, exactly hard enough, and all the tension inside me burst. He groaned once more in appreciation, and tasting my satisfaction seemed to tip him over the edge too. His balls tightened beneath my fingers, preparing me for his release. I swallowed as he came, savouring every drop as he continued to lap up everything between my legs too.

When both our movements slowed, sated and fulfilled, I gently climbed off him. He spread his arm out in invitation and I accepted it gratefully, nuzzling against his warm body in the afterglow of our mutual pleasure.

"That was perfect," he murmured, bending down to kiss me, the taste of him on my lips mingling with the taste of me on his.

I couldn't argue; other than the night before, I couldn't remember the last time I felt so good.

We talked a while longer, still wrapped up in each other's arms, getting beneath the blankets of my bed when we began to get a little chilly. My bed wasn't nearly as big as his, so for both of us to fit comfortably, we had to be touching each other, but at that moment, it didn't seem like a problem. It felt perfectly natural to be right where I was, my head on Rome's shoulder, my hand on his chest, my naked legs entwined with his.

In fact, I felt so comfortable and relaxed that I couldn't even say for sure when I fell asleep. I only knew I had when a little voice woke me up.

"Mommy? How come Wome gets to sleep with you?"

~**Rome**~

Several times while Freya and I lay in her bed chatting, I thought that I should probably go home. Despite everything that had happened between us that day both in and outside of her room, we still weren't in a relationship, nor had she said anything about wanting to be. There were also two other people in the apartment, her mom and Dylan, who would require an explanation if they found me still there in the morning.

I knew I should go, but it felt so good in her bed, sharing in the closeness brought on by our mutual orgasms, holding her and talking about whatever came into our heads, that I thought a few more minutes wouldn't hurt. Then a few more, and a few more, until my eyes closed, and the next thing I knew, Dylan stood right beside the bed.

"Mommy? How come Wome gets to sleep with you?"

Immediately, we both pulled the covers tighter over our naked bodies even though the darkness of the room gave us some additional protection. "What... uh, what are you doing out of bed, buddy?" Freya asked, her voice still thick with sleep.

"I woke up," he explained, which, I had to admit, was a perfectly logical reason to be out of bed. "You said this bed is just for mommies."

My lips pressed together as I tried not to smile. Obviously, she must have told him that when he wanted to sleep with her, and he was calling her out on it. Clever kid.

"I get in too," Dylan announced before Freya could say anything, trying to lift up the edge of the blankets to climb in.

"No!" Freya and I called out in unison, startling Dylan into stillness.

"No," Freya repeated, a little more calmly. "It's not quite morning yet, and you need to sleep in your room. Do you need to go pee or have a drink?"

He nodded and she told him to go to the bathroom and she'd be right there. As soon as he'd left the room, Freya hopped out of bed and threw some pajamas on.

"I'm sorry about this," she apologized, but I wasn't at all upset. Other than being woken up at five in the morning, I actually found it kind of funny. He obviously didn't have any idea what me being there meant, but Freya's mom would be a different story. If she saw me in the apartment at all, she would know exactly what was going on, and I didn't want to put Freya in an awkward position. She had enough to worry about already.

"I should head home anyway. I can get in a workout before rehearsal."

Freya bit her lip in indecision. She obviously knew that would be best even if she didn't come out and say it. "I don't mean to kick you out."

"I know," I assured her, climbing out of bed myself to grab my clothes from the night before that were still on her floor. "Go look after Dylan. I'll be fine. We're good, Freya."

Flashing me a grateful smile, she headed out the door. As I stepped out into the hall a minute later, I could hear her explaining to Dylan that I would be going home to sleep in my own bed so he had to go to his too. I left the apartment with a smile on my face.

Using my phone, I had a taxi there within minutes and in the early morning traffic, it didn't take long to get back to my apartment. I did hit the gym, as I told Freya I would, but even with that, after showering and getting ready, it had only just hit seven thirty. With nothing else to do, I headed over to rehearsal early.

To my surprise, I wasn't the first one there. Matthew Blackman already sat at the table in the rehearsal room, reviewing the script in front of him, and he looked up curiously as I came in. "I'd heard you had a good work ethic, but this is a little extreme."

His expression turned more cautious as he realized I hadn't returned his smile.

"Unless you're here to talk about Freya?"

"I didn't know you'd be here," I told him honestly, walking over to the table and taking a seat across from him, though he hadn't invited me to. "And whatever's happening between you and Freya is between the two of you, unless she asks me to get involved."

That wasn't what I wanted to say. I would have much rather demanded an explanation from him about why he had left her in the first place and what his intentions were with Dylan, but I had to accept that none of that counted as my business.

Matthew nodded in understanding, but to my surprise, he didn't take the out I'd just given him. Instead of moving on, he leaned forward across the table. "Have you met her son? Dylan?"

Her son. If that didn't say volumes about how he viewed his responsibility, I didn't know what would.

I answered him honestly anyway. "Yeah, I've met him. In fact, I'm his

Chosen Family partner."

"What?" An understandable look of confusion crossed Matthew's face.

"Through the Chosen Family group," I explained. "For kids who need a father figure in their life."

That made him wince, as it should have. I meant it to.

"How long have you known them?" he asked next, clearly confused about my involvement.

"Not long," I had to admit. "I've known Freya for about a month now, since she auditioned for the show, and I met Dylan soon afterwards."

Matthew nodded, still looking somewhat surprised. "I didn't peg you for that kind of guy."

Though I didn't know exactly what he meant, it sounded like an insult. "*What* kind of guy?"

"I just mean with Freya, it's complicated, with the kid and everything. Your relationships are usually more casual."

So basically, he thought I only cared about having a good time? It was hard *not* to take that in a negative way, but I didn't want to talk about myself; I would much rather find out more about him.

"What about you? You're not seeing anyone? There are a lot of beautiful actresses in LA."

"There are," he agreed, somewhat wryly. "Many of whom would be happy to date a director if they thought it would give them a leg up in the business. I love movies but the culture there is different. Theatre people are more *real*, you know?"

I didn't, really, not having ever worked in movies myself, but I couldn't help pointing out the obvious. "Real like your son, you mean?"

That time, he didn't flinch. "Fair enough. I deserve that. Look, Rome, I don't want there to be any animosity between us. You obviously feel protective of both Freya and Dylan, and I can respect that. I'm honestly not trying to cause any trouble, and I definitely don't want to take Dylan away from her, if that's what she's worried about. You can tell her that if you want to."

She would definitely be relieved to hear that, but I shouldn't be the one she heard it from. "You could tell her yourself too."

"I will," he promised. "When she's ready to hear me out, I will."

Since we were being straight with each other, I asked him one of the questions that had been weighing on my mind since the previous day. "If you knew about Dylan all this time, why didn't you give them any kind of financial support, even if you didn't want to be involved?"

A grimace worked its way across his face. "It wasn't that I didn't want to be involved. If she'd come to me and said she needed money, I would have given it to her. Since she never did, I assumed she was doing okay without me."

That was bullshit and he knew it. "She shouldn't have had to ask you. That was your responsibility, as Dylan's father."

"I know," he agreed, holding up his hands to try to calm me. I hadn't even realized how loud my voice had gotten until he did it. "I just... I felt guilty, I guess. Guilty about the way I left and even more guilty once I realized she did have the baby. I didn't know how to make it right so I ignored it. It was selfish, I know, but I'm trying to make up for it now. That's why I'm here. If she needs money, I can give her money."

"She just landed the lead role in a major Broadway show," I pointed out. "She's doing fine *now*. She needed the money back when she was in college and unemployed and having your baby. Did that ever even cross your mind?"

The elevator door opened into the waiting room and other voices drifted over to us, making it clear we were going to have to suspend our conversation for the time being. I'd said getting involved wouldn't be appropriate, but then I had gone right ahead and got involved anyway, whether I meant to or not.

I did my best to smooth things over, keeping my voice down so we wouldn't be overheard. "Look, obviously, I do have some personal feelings about this. It's to do with Freya and Dylan, and it's also to do with my own past. However, as you said, we still need to work together and I can absolutely do that in a professional and respectful way. I know that Freya will too. The success of this show is important to all of us. But don't think you can use me as some kind of backchannel to tell Freya what you want her to know. She deserves to hear it from you."

Matthew nodded, his face tight as he gestured down to the pages in front of him. "In that case, I'll get back to work."

I knew a dismissal when I heard one, so I got up and headed out to the main room to greet the other cast members who had just arrived. We had less than a month left to get the show perfect. Normally, I had no trouble staying focused, but I had a feeling the following few weeks were going to test me like never before.

~Freya~

Walking into the rehearsal room that morning, my confidence was far higher than I would have expected it to be after the previous day. Matthew's sudden appearance had hit me like a bomb, the explosion sending a shockwave through my life, but Rome had been there to steady me and help me keep my balance. Although it could have knocked me down, it didn't. Matthew had broken me once but after all those years, my foundations were stronger. With Rome and my mom and especially Dylan in my corner, I could weather whatever storm Matthew brought.

It took my mom no time at all to find out that Rome had spent most of the night in our apartment. Dylan gleefully announced to his grandmother that he found Rome in my bed, still hoping this meant that he could start sleeping there too. My mom backed me up on the fact that Dylan still had to sleep in his own room, but as soon as he wandered out of earshot, she turned to me with a knowing smile. "Sounds like things might be getting a little more serious between you two."

Were they? I still didn't know if I wanted them to, and we hadn't talked about it at all. If anything, having Matthew turn back up highlighted exactly why Rome and I shouldn't get involved with each other. If I needed proof of how quickly things could take a bad turn, it stood right in front of me as I walked into the rehearsal room.

"Good morning, Freya." Matthew's greeting sounded casual, as though he'd been saying it to me every day for years. "We're going to start with your solo from act two today."

The day went quickly as we dove deep into the show. Feeling a lot more comfortable than I had the day before, I made some suggestions I had been hesitant to make back when the other director kept comparing my performance to Jennifer's. Matthew listened to them all with an open mind, Rome willingly tried out new line readings with me, and by the end of the day, my excitement had reached an all-time high. No matter how much personal drama came my way, I wouldn't let it stop me from making the most of this incredible opportunity I'd been given.

Rome asked me to join him for lunch again when we had our break, but I didn't want people to get the wrong idea. Some of them would have already noticed that we went off on our own the day before, and if we did it regularly, there would be talk, especially given Rome's reputation. I joined Jennifer and some of the other women instead.

As things drew to a close for the day, I asked Matthew for a moment in private to share the decision I'd come to. He agreed, and at least that time, he didn't make me feel like my request inconvenienced him.

I cut straight to the chase with no preamble. "You can meet Dylan this weekend if you want to. We'll be going to the zoo in the park on Sunday and you can meet us there."

Surprise flashed in his eyes, along with something that almost looked like gratitude. "Thank you, Freya. I can't wait to…"

"I'm not finished." I cut him off before he could put his own spin on things. "I'll introduce you as a friend from work. I'm not telling him that you're his dad, and you can't tell him either, not until we agree the time is right. *If* we agree the time is right. If you can't abide by that, you're not meeting him."

My firmness seemed to take him by surprise again, but to my relief, he agreed immediately. "That's fine. I don't want to upset him, I just want to get to know him."

That sounded reasonable, but our history made me wary and I laid it out even more bluntly. "If you decide he's not your problem again, you'll break his heart. Before you get involved, you better be damn sure you mean it."

"I understand," he promised. "I'll follow your lead. Should I pick up tickets or something?"

"You can pay for yourself when you get there. Dylan and I have annual passes."

Rome would have picked up on that clue. If we had annual passes, it must be something Dylan enjoyed, and Rome would have asked me why or what he liked so much about it. Matthew didn't ask anything of the kind.

Instead, he tried to make an awkward segue. "If you want, I can reimburse you for the membership. Or if you need money for anything else..."

"Let's see how Sunday goes." I didn't want to talk about money with him. Things were getting clearer to me that he must have been having some kind of crisis of conscience, after all that time, and if that worked out for Dylan, then I would learn to live with it. But if he thought we were both going to fall at his feet if he offered us cash, he would be sorely mistaken.

When Rome treated Dylan, he did it for no other reason than to make my son happy. He had no obligation to do it, and they had just as much fun together with no expense involved.

When Matthew offered, it felt like something he thought he *should* do, not simply because he wanted to. It felt like him trying to buy his way into Dylan's life and I didn't like it. Maybe that was unfair, but I felt that way anyway.

"Okay," Matthew agreed. "If you have time, maybe we could also talk that day, in private? Over coffee or something?"

"We'll see how it goes," I repeated simply. "I need to get home now. I'll see you tomorrow."

Without waiting for a reply, I left the room, feeling not quite satisfied, but not nearly as helpless as I did the day before either. I still had some power over the situation, and I intended to use it.

The rest of the week sped by, the days full of intense but rewarding work and the evenings spent at home with Dylan. He'd already been excited about his next Chosen Family outing with Rome on Saturday, and when I told him we were going to the zoo on Sunday too, life couldn't have gotten any better.

Rome and I didn't have a chance to spend any time alone together, but he did text me regularly in the evenings, keeping the conversation light and friendly. We still hadn't talked about what the night he spent at my place meant, but we didn't let it make anything awkward. We talked about the show and we talked about Dylan, but we avoided talking about Matthew by unspoken agreement. Rome knew about the meeting at the zoo on Sunday, but he hadn't said anything about it other than to let me know he would support me if I needed him.

By the time he arrived on Saturday to pick Dylan up for their afternoon out, I'd made up my mind about how he could help. "If it's not too much to ask, Rome, do you mind watching Dylan for a little while tomorrow? Matthew says he'd like to talk to me. I don't know what it's about, but it would be better if we did it away from Dylan, and my mom already has plans."

"Of course," he agreed readily, not even bothering to check his calendar. "Just tell me where and when and I'll be there."

"Wome coming to zoo too?" Dylan asked from below us, where he'd been listening to every word, apparently. The excitement on his face made it clear he wanted that to be the case.

"Not exactly. We'll figure it all out tomorrow, okay? You guys have fun today!"

I gave Dylan a kiss as he squirmed in my arms, eager to get going, and then I went to give Rome a kiss on the cheek. Before my lips connected, he turned his head so that my mouth landed directly on his. His hand went around my waist as he held me there, a moment longer than necessary. His touch brought to mind all the longer, deeper kisses we'd shared, and my body flared with desire.

"Have a good day, Freya," he murmured as he pulled away, his blue eyes taking on a slightly mischievous hue, as if he knew exactly what that kiss had done to me. "Don't miss us too much."

With that, he and my son headed out the door, leaving my head spinning.

Chapter Thirteen

Since our partnership had only just begun, Dylan and I were spending the day doing another group activity with Chosen Family. Once we'd built up more of a rapport, we'd be allowed to do things on our own, but that day, there would be lunch, a movie in the hall, and games outside afterwards. Usually, the child would still be brought directly to the building by their parent or guardian, but when we talked about it at rehearsal on Friday, I offered to pick Dylan up so that Freya didn't have to make the trip, and it made me smile when she accepted.

"It means a lot to me that you trust me with him." Clearly, Dylan meant more to her than anything else in the world, and in the grand scheme of things, we still barely knew each other.

"You're kind of famous," she pointed out in reply, her hazel eyes sparkling as she teased me. "If I called the cops and told them Broadway star Rome Taylor kidnapped my kid, the whole city would be looking for you. It seems pretty low-risk."

She might be joking, and it definitely made me laugh, but I knew there was more to it than that. She really did trust me, and the idea filled me with a warm contentment. No one had ever placed quite so much faith in me before, at least not on a personal level, and I would do my best to never let her down.

That week, she impressed me more than ever. First, there had been the dignified way she handled the whole situation with Matthew, and then, the work she did on the show blew me away. Though I hated to admit it, under Matthew's direction, she had found a whole new level to her performance. Before, she had been engaging, but that week, she was electrifying. We were watching a star in the making and I felt honoured just to be a part of it. When the show opened, her career would launch into the stratosphere, I had no doubts about it.

Dylan chatted excitedly while we walked, telling me all about what he'd been doing all week. He demanded my full attention which I gave to him happily, and once we'd arrived, had lunch and said hi to the kids he had met the week before, we were invited to sit down on the bean bag chairs set up in the hall to watch the movie with the other kids and their Chosen Family partners. He quickly got caught up in the animated film while my mind began to wander.

When I kissed Freya in her apartment just before we left, I hadn't planned to do it in advance. Since I spent the night on Monday, we'd done a good job at keeping our distance from each other sexually. It seemed like the best course of action with everything else going on, and since we only saw each other at rehearsal, sticking to it hadn't been that difficult. However, as soon as we were back in her apartment and she leaned in to kiss my cheek, I made a split-second decision. If she wanted to continue our 'casual' arrangement, I would be open to it, and I wanted to make that clear. From the way she reacted, the intake of breath, the way she leaned into me and the wide-eyed look she gave me afterwards, it seemed I got the message across. Hopefully, she would be thinking about it just as much as I did that afternoon.

Once the movie ended and Dylan and I played outside with some of the other kids for a while, it was time for me to take him home and I'd already decided on a plan of action. I would invite them all out to dinner: Freya, Dylan and her mom. If all went well, I'd try to find a way of inviting Freya back to my place afterwards while her mom took Dylan home. With the next day being Sunday, Freya could stay overnight at my place and go home in the morning since she didn't have to rush off to work.

Although I'd enjoyed spending the night with her at her apartment, mine definitely had some advantages, including being as loud as we wanted and getting a full night's sleep with no interruptions.

Freya's mom answered the door when we arrived back at the apartment and Dylan immediately launched into a full play-by-play of the movie we'd watched while his grandmother did her best to keep up.

"Go tell Mommy all about it," she said, giving him a kiss on the top of his head. "I'll be right there."

Dylan ran off to do that, while I gave Mrs Rose a curious smile. It seemed pretty clear to me that she wanted to get me alone, but why, I couldn't guess.

She quickly made it clear: "You and Freya should have a night out."

The words were blunt, to the point, and almost exactly what I'd been hoping for myself.

Just as quickly, I provided my own thoughts on the subject. "Actually, I wanted to invite all of you to join me for dinner, you and Dylan too. I'd love to treat you all."

Mrs Rose shook her head firmly. "Having Dylan around doesn't make having an adult conversation very easy. You took him all day so I'm happy to watch him tonight. The two of you can go have a nice, relaxing evening together and help take her mind off tomorrow."

She didn't specify exactly how I would do that, but from the way her lips twitched, I could guess what she meant, and I couldn't deny I wanted exactly the same thing.

I put up one more weak protest, to be polite. "If you're sure…"

"Freya!" she called out as she turned and walked into the living room, leaving me trailing behind. "Rome's taking you out for dinner. Hurry and get dressed."

"What?" Freya sat on the couch with Dylan next to her, hearing all about the movie, and her wide eyes moved between me and her mom curiously.

"If you want to," I quickly qualified. "Your mom suggested it, and I think it's a great idea."

She shot her mother a look of both annoyance and gratitude as she got to her feet. "Give me a few minutes to get ready then."

I thought she looked perfect already, but I didn't interfere. Dylan tried to follow after her, saying he wanted to come too, but his grandmother quickly distracted him by telling him she'd made his favourite supper and that if he went out with us, she would eat it all without him. He was clearly torn, but in the end, his love of lasagna won out. I couldn't decide whether to be relieved or a little insulted.

Only a few minutes later, Freya reappeared, and my heart literally skipped a beat. She'd changed into a beautiful red dress that highlighted her figure perfectly, the colour complimenting her brown hair that she'd left down. A pair of high heels brought her close to my own height, and as I stepped close to her, I got a whiff of her enticing vanilla and berries scent, reminding me of the first time we kissed, back on the day of her audition.

"Wow." I whispered the word, not wanting to get overly effusive with her mother standing right there, but I hoped she could tell by the way I said it that she had definitely impressed me.

It seemed to work. A blush spread across her cheeks as she looked down at herself. "Too much? I can put something else on."

She went to turn back to her bedroom, so I quickly grabbed hold of her arm to hold her in place. "It's absolutely perfect, but you might want to pack something else for the morning. Walking around like this on a Sunday morning could draw some looks."

Her eyes widened as my words sank in, and she glanced over at her mom who had heard every word.

"Maybe a toothbrush too," her mom added, trying not to smile. "Dylan, say goodnight and then you can come help me in the kitchen."

Dylan gave us both a big hug and I waited by the door as Freya went back into her room to pack a small overnight bag.

"I don't know what's happening," she whispered to me as we headed out the door together. "What are we even doing right now, Rome?"

Honestly, I didn't know either, but I sure as hell didn't want to stop.

~Freya~

I knew exactly what my mom was up to. As we ate lunch together, the apartment feeling strangely quiet without Dylan there, she let me know her thoughts as openly as she always did.

"Your experience with Matthew has made you cautious, which isn't entirely a bad thing, but if you let it get in the way of a good thing that's right in front of you, it becomes a problem."

I could hardly believe how easily she'd gone from sharing my wariness of my new co-star to being his head cheerleader, but I still did my best to remain objective about all of it. "It's not just about Matthew. That does play a part, of course, but it's about Rome too. He told me he doesn't know why his relationships don't last. I don't think he means to break any hearts but he does it anyway. Sooner or later, he loses interest."

Every word I spoke was true, but none of it deterred my mom. "There are very few people who end up marrying everyone they ever date. He's usually in a relationship for about a year, right?"

I nodded in confirmation. Rome's relationships lasted the length of his show contract, more or less.

"That's not a fling. He's giving things a chance. For the year that they're together, he's committed?"

That was also true, as far as I knew. The only cheating I'd ever heard of happened at the very end of his relationship with Jennifer, and even then, I'd only heard it through gossip. He and I had never talked about what happened then.

"So, let's be realistic," my mom continued. "It's been a very long time since I've seen you as happy as you've been these past few weeks, Freya. Some of it is because of the show, I know that, but I don't think it all is. You glow when you talk about Rome. I assume the sex is good too?"

I nearly choked on my salad. She'd never been quite *that* blunt before, but then, I hadn't really dated anyone since she moved in with me either. We were closer now than we'd ever been before, and it seemed that extended to talking about our sex lives too.

"It's... fine," I managed to sputter, taking a drink to clear my airway.

My mom rolled her eyes. "That dreamy smile I've seen on your face usually means more than fine. I don't need details, I'm just suggesting you really think about it. Maybe things would end eventually if you got together, but maybe a year of being happy would be worth it."

Honestly, I had been thinking along similar lines already, but I worried about the flip side too. If I went into it expecting things to end eventually, would I be giving it a full chance? Would he? Did we need to, if we both accepted that we were just having fun?

Nothing felt straightforward, and having Dylan to think about further complicated things. I hadn't made any progress on a decision by the time Rome brought Dylan home and my mom somehow managed to convince him to take me out for dinner.

Going on a date sat high on the list of things I hadn't done in a long time, so I might have gone overboard. I found a dress in the back of my closet that I'd worn to my last show opening off-Broadway. It probably felt more into the red-carpet category than casual date night, and when Rome's eyes widened as he saw me, I immediately felt foolish for choosing it. But when I offered to go change, he insisted I shouldn't, and then he made it very clear that he expected me to spend the night too.

What did he think this date meant? What did I want it to be? Things were still completely up in the air, so I admitted to him that I didn't really understand what we were doing and Rome just grinned back at me, taking my hand.

"We don't need a script, Freya. Let's try some improv and see how it goes."

We took a taxi to his apartment so I could leave my overnight bag and he could change into something that matched my dress a little better than his sweater and jeans. When he emerged from his bedroom in a suit with no tie and the top button of his shirt undone, just the right mix of in charge and casual, my stomach fluttered just as it had the first time he looked at me, that night I served him in the restaurant before we knew each other at all.

"What are you in the mood for?" he asked, coming over to put his arms around me. His lips were just a few inches from mine as his stunning blue eyes looked straight down into mine. "Anything you want, anywhere you've always wanted to go, let's make it happen."

What I really wanted would be to drag him back into the bedroom he'd just come out of and take that suit off piece by piece, but I tried to control myself. "How about Maybe This Time?" I suggested instead.

He groaned good-naturedly. "You wouldn't rather go somewhere that we won't be recognized?"

Saying 'we' would be recognized felt pretty generous. He certainly would, but no one knew me yet. Maybe This Time was a piano bar just down the street from the restaurant where I used to work, and the wait staff took turns performing songs while the diners ate. If Broadway stars turned up, they were often convinced to take the stage, to the delight of the other diners. They would certainly want Rome to sing, which was part of the reason I wanted to go. It gave me so much joy to watch him, it would make the night even better to see him perform.

"It could be good publicity for the show," I pointed out. If anyone saw Rome and I together and it ended up in the gossip columns on the Broadway news pages, it would lead to talk of our upcoming production.

"So, this whole night is a PR stunt?" he teased. "Is that all I am to you, Freya?"

He obviously didn't believe it for a second so I teased him right back.

"You're my meal ticket, quite literally, since I assume you're paying?"

His eyes sparkled as he laughed. "I certainly am. Come on, then, let's go. The sooner we eat, the sooner we can leave."

He couldn't be making it any clearer how he saw the night ending, and I couldn't pretend I didn't want it too.

Since we only had a few blocks to go, we walked over, even in my high heels. Several envious glances were thrown our way, especially by other women, and I couldn't blame them. Hell, even I was jealous of myself for getting to spend the night with the man at my side.

When we arrived, the hostess recognized Rome on sight and we were shown to a table close to the stage. She told him he'd be welcome to sing at any point, just to let them know, and he promised that he would before we left. First, though, we had dinner while Rome told me about his day with Dylan and we enjoyed the other performances on stage.

Finally, when we were finished, he glanced over at the stage. "I suppose I better honour my promise. Any requests?"

There were so many wonderful songs I could think of for him to sing, my brain momentarily froze up as I tried to decide on just one, and Rome laughed as he watched me struggle.

"You can choose next time," he told me with a wink. "I've got one."

He got up and went over to the pianist, letting him know his song choice, and one of the waitresses got on stage to introduce him. Hearing him applauded as the two-time Tony-winner Rome Taylor reminded me once again of just how amazing he was. When we spent time alone together, I sometimes forgot. Sometimes, he was just Rome.

I honestly had no idea what song he would choose, and when he launched into "Her Voice" from The Little Mermaid, I smiled in surprise. That surprise quickly turned to desire as he sang about the beautiful voice that haunted his dreams, keeping his eyes on me the whole time, sending wave after wave of heat through me. Though a hundred people were watching, it felt like we were the only people in the room. It felt like he might be singing about me.

When he'd finished and the applause had died down, he looked out over the rest of the crowd. "That song is dedicated to the very talented leading lady in my upcoming show. You guys might not have heard of her yet, but I promise you, in a few weeks, everyone's going to know her name. Do you want to hear her before the rest of the world discovers her?"

The crowd cheered and clapped as they all turned to look at me, following the direction of Rome's gaze. With him encouraging me too, I could hardly say no, so I got to my feet as gracefully as I could and joined Rome on stage.

"You trust me, right?" he whispered in my ear over the cheers of the crowd.

I couldn't deny it. "I do."

He gave a nod to the pianist, who immediately launched into the opening riff of "Bad Idea" from the musical Waitress, to the cheers of the crowd. Of course I knew every word, and I couldn't deny they seemed rather appropriate to our own situation.

The audience didn't know our history, though, they just enjoyed the energy and chemistry between us, and when the song ended, the crowd rose to their feet, even if they were halfway through their dinner. Rome and I took our bows and then headed out with pleas for encores echoing in our ears, buzzing with the adulation of the crowd.

And once we were on the street, he kissed me, right there in public, like we were actually a couple, and the words of the song we just sang repeated in my head once more: the two of us together were a terrible idea, but we were doing it anyway. I could only hope it would be worth it in the end.

~Rome~

When I told Freya that we should improvise that night, kissing her in the middle of 46th Street hadn't been exactly what I had in mind.

I should have waited until we got back to my apartment, but after the amazing performance we just shared, seeing how alive and natural she was in front of the crowd, not to mention the message of the song we'd just sung together, even waiting until the street tested my patience. I wanted to kiss her right there on that stage when we ended the song just inches away from each other, but too many of the diners had their phones out, recording our performance, and we didn't need our kiss being broadcast around the world.

Maybe we could have played it off as part of the song, but I didn't want to do it without her permission in such a public way. No matter how we spun it, rumours would start that we'd begun dating, that she was my next girlfriend and that my usual pattern had started, and I didn't want that to be the story. I wanted people to be talking about how damn good she was instead, because *that* mattered more than anything to do with me.

Given all that, I shouldn't have kissed her out on the street either, but when she turned to me, flush in the thrill of her success, her eyes sparkling in delight and still wearing that unbelievable red dress, I simply couldn't hold back.

It might be a bad idea, but it didn't stop me.

"How fast can you move in those heels?" I murmured into her ear as my lips trailed across her skin.

"Not fast enough," she whispered back with a bit of a laugh. "But I'm sure going to try."

Taking her hand, I led her the few blocks back to my apartment, both of us talking and laughing over the performance we'd just given.

"Did you see that girl at the table by the bar?" Freya giggled. "She looked ready to punch me out and take my place when you started touching me."

I hadn't noticed. I hadn't seen anything but Freya.

The doorman, Richard, greeted us with his usual friendly smile. "Good evening, Mr Taylor. Ms Rose."

Freya looked surprised that he remembered her name, but he had an incredible memory for names and faces, which was part of what made him so good at his job. I'd told him to call me Rome a dozen times, at least, but he couldn't seem to bring himself to do it. "Hi, Richard. Could you please add Freya to my approved visitor list? She's welcome here anytime."

"Of course, Mr Taylor. Hope you have a good evening."

I certainly intended to.

As soon as we were in the elevator, my mouth was on Freya's again, my body pressed firmly against her, pinning her against the mirrored wall. "I can't wait to get you out of this dress," I groaned between deep and needy kisses. "Ever since you put it on, I've been thinking how good it would look on my bedroom floor."

Her arms tightened around me, her breath short with desire. "You think we're going to make it to the bedroom?"

She made a good point. There were a lot of places between the front door and my room that would work just as well, and as soon as we were inside, we stumbled towards the living room instead. It was closer, and at that moment, every second I wasn't spending inside her felt like a second wasted.

Freya's dress came off quickly, just as I'd been imagining all night, and she pulled eagerly at my pants as I removed my suit jacket and unbuttoned my shirt. When her hands connected with my bare chest, I exhaled in satisfaction. The skin-to-skin contact was just what I'd been craving, and when she pressed her chest against mine to kiss me, it felt even better.

When I got changed earlier, I'd planned ahead and put a condom in the pocket of my pants so that wherever we ended up, we wouldn't have to stop. I pulled it out before removing the rest of my clothes, and rolled it on as quickly as possible. I couldn't remember the last time I'd been so impatient for sex, but my cock ached in anticipation and Freya seemed just as eager.

As soon as I had got myself ready, she pushed me down onto the couch and climbed onto my lap, on her knees as she straddled me. "I need you," she whispered as she slid my hard cock through her wetness, coating it with her own arousal. "I need this."

"Fuck," I groaned as she sank down onto me, giving me exactly what I needed too. "That's perfect."

Her chest was almost eye level with me as she began to ride me, hard and fast. Grabbing hold of one of her breasts, I brought it to my mouth, sucking and licking on the stiffened nipple as my other hand went to her clit, all while she continued to stroke my cock with her body, her head rolled back in pleasure.

None of our actions were soft or tender. Everything was rough and desperate, as if it had been months since we'd been together that way instead of just under a week. When she began to tremble with the beginning of her orgasm, I didn't let up. I was close too, painfully close, and I wanted her right there with me.

"Oh, God, Rome!" she cried out as she came, just in time since I couldn't hold back longer either. My cock pumped inside her as she pulsed around me too, just as perfectly in sync with each other as we had been on stage earlier.

The moans that had filled the room died off, replaced by the quieter sound of our heavy breathing, both of us panting as we recovered from the intensity of what we'd just shared.

A hint of laughter soon added to the soundscape as Freya chuckled above me, her body still wrapped around mine.

"What's so funny?" I grinned up at her, eager to share the joke since I was pretty sure it didn't have anything to do with what had just happened.

"My mom asked me earlier about how much I enjoyed sex with you," she explained, her lips twitching. "I said it was 'fine'. I'm such a liar."

I joined her laughter, both in surprise and amusement. The idea of her discussing me with her mom in that way embarrassed me a little bit, but it also pleased me to know she thought about me even when we were apart. I sure as hell thought about her.

"If that's really what you think, I might have to try a little harder." I pushed my hips up into her, rubbing against her still-sensitive clit and making her whimper. "It's a good thing we've got no other plans tonight."

Excitement and anticipation flared in her eyes, mirroring my own. Eventually, we were going to have to talk about exactly what that night meant, but until then, I would do my best to just enjoy it, no strings attached, and we had the whole night ahead of us to do just that.

Chapter Fourteen

~**Freya**~

One of the best things about being with Rome, besides the mind-blowing sex, was how comfortable it felt to talk and laugh with him. I could say whatever popped into my head, even telling him that my mom asked about his performance in bed, and he always caught my meaning and my mood, never misunderstanding or misjudging what I had to say.

Did that come from being an actor, from being so tuned into what the person opposite him did, or was it just simply his nature which made him such a good actor in the first place? I didn't know how to tell, and I wasn't sure if he knew either. It might be just as easy to figure out if the chicken or the egg came first.

I wanted to try to understand him better, so once we had cleaned up and put some clothes back on, me in the silky nightgown I'd brought with me and him in a pair of sweatpants, his chest still bare, we got ourselves some wine and sat down in the living room to talk. He took my legs across his lap as I turned to face him, his free hand running absent-mindedly up and down my calf as he drank his wine. The warmth of his touch distracted and soothed me at the same time. It felt easy and natural, like we'd been doing this for ages, and I could almost imagine us spending regular evenings this way, watching a movie while Dylan coloured on the floor or played with his cars.

Stop it, Freya. No matter what, I had to keep perspective.

"I still don't know an awful lot about you," I pointed out, which seemed a strange thing to say given our recent intimacy, but it didn't make it less true. "Can I be nosy now?"

"Nose away," he invited, taking a drink from his wine, looking as comfortable and confident as usual.

"You told me what happened with your parents," I reminded him, keeping things purposefully vague. "And then you said you found theatre and it saved you. What about the time in between? What were things like for you growing up?"

The grimace that crossed Rome's face let me know that he didn't have particularly happy memories of that time, but before I had a chance to tell him he didn't have to answer if he didn't want to, he started talking.

"I moved around between foster families a lot. Nobody wanted a sullen, withdrawn kid with abandonment issues. I didn't want people around but I didn't want them to go either. I was afraid to get close to anyone in case they left too, so I resisted any attempts they made to bond with me, but then I would be really clingy at times. It must have been frustrating for the people who took me in, and I don't blame them for passing me on. There were easier kids out there."

Imagining the open and giving man in front of me as a scared, scarred little boy wasn't easy, but I believed every word. If anything, he had probably glossed over how difficult it had been.

"Puberty was hard," he continued bluntly. "I thought about running away. I thought about just ending things. Nobody would even care if I disappeared. I didn't have friends because I pushed everyone away. That was probably the only thing that stopped me from getting mixed up in gangs or drugs or whatever, simply because I didn't trust anyone enough."

He stopped for another drink, his hand still on my leg as I waited patiently for him to continue, my heart full of sympathy for him.

"One of my teachers at school signed me up for Chosen Family. Through them, I went to my first show, and that's when things started to change. Everyone on stage looked so happy, like they all belonged there, and I wanted to be like that. Jordan picked up on my interest and he put on our own little production at the club. The show was awful, but I found that I loved being someone else for a while. When I played a part, I could forget everything about my own life. I could live someone else's life, and for the first time in my life, I felt free. I felt like I could choose who I wanted to be."

I could relate to that, at least, even if the rest of what he told me was completely outside of my own experience. When I stepped into a role, my own troubles disappeared. That was the magic of theatre, not only for the cast but for the audience too.

"I tried out for the school show, the first time I ever did anything extra-curricular, and my audition impressed the teacher running it so much that she got me free singing lessons too. And that was it. I never wanted to do anything else."

That summed things up quite nicely, but I still wanted to know more. "So, when you did that first show, is that when you stopped pushing people away?"

Rome nodded thoughtfully, taking another drink. "Yeah, I guess so. In any show, the cast becomes like a family. I knew they weren't going anywhere, at least until the show was over, so I let myself open up a bit. And I got my first girlfriend, which helped too."

He gave me a charming grin, letting me know in exactly which way it had helped, and I smiled back, unable to resist his infectious smile. Something scratching at the back of my brain though, a connection it wanted to make that hadn't become quite clear yet.

"So, you trusted that the cast, including your girlfriend, would be there for you as long as the show lasted, but once it ended, you weren't as sure?"

Rome's smile faltered a tiny bit. "I suppose so. I'm not sure I ever thought about it quite that way."

It made a lot of sense to me, and suddenly, his whole 'pattern' seemed a lot clearer too. People suggested that he lost interest after he stopped working with his significant other, but it made much more sense that he actually pushed them away before they could leave, breaking the relationship up as a means of self-defense. Somewhere inside, that little boy was still afraid of being left again.

Not wanting to simply blurt all that out, I broached the topic as gently as I could. "Do you think maybe that has something to do with why your relationships are tied to your shows in general? It's not that you can't commit, or you can't make it work, but that deep down, you're still afraid that they'll leave when there's nothing making them stay?"

Hopefully, that didn't sound too presumptuous. Insulting him or making accusations wasn't my intention, but he'd told me he didn't know why his relationships didn't last, and to me, what I'd just suggested sounded completely plausible. Our pasts formed the basis of our present decisions, in exactly the same way that my experience with Matthew affected my willingness to give a relationship with Rome a chance.

To his credit, Rome thought it over, not getting defensive or closing himself off. "That might be part of it, actually. I don't do it on purpose, but it's hard to completely erase that feeling of not being good enough on your own. If my own mother couldn't stick around, why should anyone else? I felt that way for so long, and maybe on some level, I still do."

I admired him so much for being able to look at it so rationally and clear-headed, but my heart ached at the sadness that haunted those words. Being let down so completely by the one person meant to love him above all else would be a hard thing to bear.

It brought to mind something else I'd wanted to ask him about, though I couldn't be sure I wanted to know the answer. "If she had come back a few years after she left and apologized and said she wanted to be part of your life, would that have helped?"

Reading me just as easily as he always did, Rome knew exactly what I was really asking. "You're talking about Dylan and Matthew."

The parallels hadn't been lost on me. "From my point of view, life would be a lot easier without Matthew in it, but I'm trying to think of what's best for Dylan. I don't want him thinking his dad didn't want him if it's not the whole truth."

Rome swallowed hard, thinking it over. "I guess to answer that, you need to know the full truth. You need to know exactly why Matthew left and why he came back now. But if he's sincere about wanting to be a dad to him now, then I don't think there's such a thing as too many people to love a kid, especially a kid like Dylan."

I had to agree, as difficult as it might be for me. Hopefully, when Matthew and I had a chance to talk the next day, I could get the answers to those questions. Making a decision in the meantime felt impossible.

And on that note, I had brought the mood down long enough. Taking Rome's wine glass from his hand, I downed the rest of it, along with the contents of my own glass. Rome's lips twitched as he watched me, picking up on my change of mood instantly, his eyes sparkling once more.

"I think we should go to your room now," I stage-whispered. "I don't think you showed me all your awards last time."

His laugh warmed me even more than the wine did. "There are a lot of things I haven't shown you yet, Freya. I'd love to see what we can discover together."

~Rome~

The rest of the night was just as good as I expected it to be. After our conversation, we went to my room where I showed Freya more of my awards, which was not a euphemism. She actually wanted to see my trophies and she had questions for me about the shows and my performances. Talking to another fan of the art form who also understood the ins and outs of performance was always enjoyable for me. I loved getting her perspective on things.

Our conversation and laughter eventually turned to touching and teasing, and soon, we were naked again. That time, we took things a lot slower, no longer feeling the same urgency as before but just as much passion. When I slid into her, my body covering hers, it felt like we had all the time in the world and I intended to take advantage of it.

When we'd finally finished, her more than once, Freya went into the bathroom to get ready for bed and came out joking about the size of my bathtub, claiming she could fit her entire kitchen in it. I didn't need any further encouragement to explore its size with her, and after getting each other off one more time in the tub, we finally lay down to sleep.

Freya's breathing soon evened out, her body feeling warm and soft and perfect in my arms, but despite how comfortable I felt, my mind wouldn't completely switch off. It kept returning to the things Freya said back in the living room, about how the reason my relationships ended might be tied to my childhood fear of abandonment.

It made a lot of sense, and I couldn't understand how I'd never put the pieces together before. People had always assumed that I simply had a short attention span, that when someone was no longer in front of me at all times, I'd lose interest, or that my feelings were tied to the way that my character felt, so when I took on a different character, the feelings vanished too. Though I didn't think either of those things were true, I hadn't been able to come up with a better explanation.

But after knowing me for a relatively short period of time, Freya had seen through all of that to get to the deeper issue. Maybe it had something to do with her being a mom and knowing just how important a parent could be to a little boy's self-confidence? Or maybe something in her just naturally saw me for who I really was, beyond the character that I'd created for myself to play, the one the rest of the world saw.

The person she saw might still be a little bit broken, but she didn't like him any less for it. In fact, she made me feel stronger by not treating me any differently than she had from the very start, when she only knew me by my public image. She still cared for me enough to spend the night with me, and trusted me enough to put her son in my care. She knew my reputation and she let me into her life anyway, even after she'd been abandoned by someone in a way that had to remind her of my past relationships.

She was incredible, but as much as I admired and appreciated her, the night's revelations worried me too. What if this fear of mine was so deeply ingrained that I couldn't overcome it? What if I hurt her, and Dylan, without meaning to? What if we went into this relationship for real, all in, like I truly wanted to, and it ended just the same way all the others had?

Would it be fair to ask her to give me that chance? Or was I being selfish for even considering it?

Those were the thoughts that plagued me as I tried to sleep, and which woke me early in the morning too. Freya was still asleep when I woke up, though she probably wouldn't want me to let her sleep much longer. As gently as I could, I disentangled myself from her and headed out to the kitchen to make some breakfast. Cooking had never been my strong suit, but I could manage breakfast well enough, and I returned to the bedroom just as Freya emerged from the bathroom. When she caught sight of the tray in my hands with fruit, yogurt, a bagel, and coffee, her face broke into a grin.

"This is better than a five-star hotel," she teased me. "Endless orgasms *and* breakfast in bed?"

"Not all our guests get quite that level of service," I teased her right back. "You got the deluxe package."

"Hmmmm, I certainly did." As she came over to kiss me, her hand went to the front of my pants, nearly making me drop the tray as my cock sprang back to life. The twinkle in her eyes when she pulled back told me she knew exactly what she did to me, but her satisfaction was twinned with a look of affection. "This is wonderful, Rome, thank you."

We ate together before getting dressed, and all too soon, the time came for her to leave. At least she let me call her a taxi that time.

"We're meeting Matthew at the zoo at two o'clock," she told me, checking the calendar on her phone. "I figured an hour would be a good amount of time for him to spend with Dylan, and then we can talk about whatever it is he wants to talk to me about. Could you meet us at three by the Delacorte Clock so you can take Dylan?"

The clock was just outside the zoo entrance and not far from the carousel and one of the park's playgrounds. There would be plenty to keep me and Dylan occupied. "That sounds perfect. I'll see you then."

I kissed her once more before she headed out the door, fully aware that we still hadn't talked about exactly what our night together meant, but I knew she had other things to think about right then, understandably. Dylan came first, and him meeting his father for the first time was a huge deal. She *should* be focused on that. That day, I only had a supporting role to play.

The hours seemed to drag as I checked my phone every five minutes, paranoid about being late. Freya trusted me to help her out and I wouldn't let her down. I ended up getting to the clock half an hour early, just in case, but ten minutes had passed after three o'clock before they finally arrived.

Picking up on emotional cues was one of the skills that helped me as an actor, but I found Freya's mood almost impossible to read. Her face was closed off in a way I'd never really seen it before. Matthew looked more relaxed as he gave me a friendly nod of greeting. "Rome."

Though I nodded back, my gaze strayed to the little boy whose eyes lit up when he saw me and came barrelling towards me, as usual. "Hi, Wome!"

"Hey, Dylan." I crouched down as he approached and he threw his arms around me with his usual enthusiasm. "Are you ready to go play for a while?"

"Can I, Mommy?" He looked up at Freya in eager anticipation.

"Yes, it's time to play with Rome now. I'll come and find you in a little while." Her voice missed its usual warmth even though she smiled at her son with love. That smile faded a little as she looked over at me. "I'll text you when we're finished."

She looked so tense and uncertain that I would have loved to offer her some reassurance and comfort, but in the end, I couldn't do anything other than what I'd come for: to keep Dylan busy and happy while she spoke to his father.

We headed to the carousel first while Dylan told me all about what the leopards had been doing that day. Dylan chose his horse on the carousel carefully and I took the one next to him. I'd only been on a carousel once before, for a photo shoot for one of the shows I did a few years earlier. As a child, I never went on one.

We went to the playground next and had so much fun together that when Freya's text came in, it surprised me to see that almost an hour had passed. She said they would meet us at the south end of Literary Walk, not far at all from where we were.

Dylan didn't want to leave, but when I offered him a piggyback ride, he forgot his objections. His little arms circled my neck as I pretended to be a snow leopard bounding across the hills, and his shrieks of laughter echoed in my ear as we headed to the meeting spot.

Though I hadn't said anything to her about it earlier, not wanting to put any pressure on her, I hoped to take Freya and Dylan out for dinner afterwards, where we could talk about how things went with Matthew and I could help to cheer her up if she needed it. But those plans, and any other future ones that I might have had, came crashing down around me as we rounded the corner towards Literary Walk and found Freya and Matthew in the middle of a kiss.

~Freya~

Matthew stood waiting at the zoo entrance when Dylan and I got there, which didn't surprise me. He wasn't the kind of guy who turned up late or kept people waiting. He might have other flaws, but I was mature enough to recognize his good qualities too.

I picked Dylan up as we approached, partly so he'd be eye level with Matthew, and partly because of the protective feelings that washed over me as the two of them laid eyes on each other for the first time. If Matthew hurt my little boy in any way, he would regret it, and I wanted to make that as clear as possible.

"Dylan, this is Mommy's friend, Matthew."

I had told Dylan ahead of time that we were meeting with a friend of mine, trying to sound just as excited about it as when I introduced him to Rome. There was no blue car to win Dylan's loyalty, though, just a rather serious-looking man in glasses who tried to smile, but looked rather overwhelmed with the whole situation.

For a moment, they just stared at each other, two people who looked so much alike in ways I hadn't even fully appreciated until they were side-by-side. Finally, Dylan turned to me, speaking right into my ear. "He's got glasses."

"What?" Matthew asked, not picking up on Dylan's way of speaking just yet but not wanting to miss anything.

"He likes your glasses," I explained, doing my best to smile though my stomach felt like lead. "He doesn't know many people who wear them, but he's interested in them."

"Oh." Looking a bit flustered, Matthew pulled them off his face and offered them to his son. "Do you want to try them?"

Seeing him without his glasses on made my stomach twist, though I tried not to show any outward reaction. The only time I had seen him that way had been when we were in bed together.

Dylan's eyes lit up as he reached for the glasses, but I quickly grabbed them first, before he could drop them. They wouldn't be cheap and I couldn't afford to replace them. "Here, I'll do it, Dill-pickle."

One-handed, I put the glasses on him as my heart twisted even further. With them on, he looked even more like his father.

Dylan looked around curiously. "You look funny," he announced to Matthew. Luckily, Matthew knew what he meant and didn't take offense.

"They're pretty strong," Matthew apologized as I gently removed them from Dylan's face and returned them to their rightful owner. "But I need them if I want to see the animals. Should we go?"

Those were the magic words for Dylan, and I put him down as I pulled out our passes to show at the gate. For the next hour, we wandered around the zoo, looking to the outside world like any other family there. Dylan was his usual self, full of energy and excitement, especially when we got to the leopards. Matthew engaged with him in a restrained way. He listened when Dylan had something to say and he asked him some questions, but he didn't play with him like Rome did. He looked exactly how I would expect someone to look who had never spent much time around kids before, but he seemed to be trying.

Matthew and I stood apart from each other the whole time, both of us keeping our eyes on Dylan and occasionally making the odd comment about what he was doing or about the animals in general. We didn't talk about anything personal; apparently, we were saving that for later.

When three o'clock came, we were still with the leopards, and dragging Dylan away always presented a challenge. However, when I told him that Rome would be waiting, he quickly gave in.

Once Dylan and Rome went off together, Matthew suggested we head down Literary Walk where we could find a bench to sit and talk. He offered to buy me a coffee, but I didn't want to do anything that would make it feel like a date. I just wanted to get it over with and figure out exactly what he wanted.

We sat down on the bench with some space between us. The leaves in the trees above were starting to turn yellow at the edges, a sure sign that fall had arrived. Matthew wore a black coat with a red and black scarf, and, combined with his glasses, he couldn't look much more like a hipster independent film director if he tried.

"So, I owe you an explanation," he began, getting straight to the point which I appreciated. "It's not an excuse, and I'm not looking for forgiveness. I just want to be honest with you if we're going to be a part of each other's lives going forward."

The last part still felt very up in the air to me, but the first thing he said had me intrigued. "I'm listening."

"I liked you, Freya," he continued, just as bluntly as his earlier statement. "A lot. None of that was an act, nor was it just a showmance, as I told you. I needed an out, and I lied. I'm sorry."

That was something, at least; not much, but something. "So, what's the truth?"

"Right, the truth," he repeated, swallowing uncomfortably. "The truth is that when we were at the wrap party, after you and I were together in the back room, I went back to the party and there was a woman looking for me."

"What woman?"

His nose wrinkled, forcing his glasses down his nose, and he quickly pushed them back up. "Her name isn't important. The important part is that she was very wealthy, a lot older than me, and very interested in helping my career, if I would give her a few things in return."

Maybe I was being dense, but his explanation didn't make a lot of sense to me. "I don't understand."

His smile was ruefully self-deprecating. "Of course you don't. That's not who you are. Basically, she wanted to fuck me and show me off as her protégé, and she would give me a lot of money in return."

His bluntness made me wince but I appreciated him laying it out so clearly too. I definitely wouldn't have jumped to that conclusion.

"The offer surprised me, naturally, and I told her I had a girlfriend. She replied that I couldn't possibly be that stupid. With her, I could have my first film fully funded. I could do whatever I wanted without having to go through all the hoops that new filmmakers have to jump through. I'd have money and access beyond my wildest dreams, and once I had the success and the name, and once she'd grown tired of me, I'd be free to have any girl I wanted, including you."

The way he shook his head suggested he knew how ridiculous it sounded. "And you took the deal." I simply stated it, since it didn't seem to be in question.

He nodded, not looking proud of the fact, necessarily, but not looking particularly ashamed either. "I did. She offered to transfer me $25,000 right then and there if I left with her that night."

"And that's why you broke up with me." That explained the sudden shift, the complete change in him that night. While it wasn't any kind of excuse, as he'd said, at last, after all that time, I understood it. He and I had sex at the party and a few hours later, he must have been in this other woman's bed. Perhaps I should be grateful that at least he had the decency to end things with me first.

"Things moved quickly after that," he continued. "She had a house in LA so I made plans to move out there with her as soon as school was over and I already had auditions set up for my film as soon as I landed. When you turned up and told me you were pregnant, I panicked. If she found out about it, it could have ruined everything. I had already got in too deep, Freya. I couldn't go back. If I'd never met her, if you and I were still together and you found out you were pregnant, it would have been a different story, but right then, I only saw it as a problem I didn't need."

He made no attempt to sugarcoat anything, and I did appreciate that, even if I had to wonder, listening to him, how I ever thought this man was someone to be admired.

"When I didn't hear from you again, I convinced myself that you must have gone ahead with the abortion, and I put it out of my mind. Life was busy. I made my film and it got rave reviews, as I'm sure you know. I had everything I ever wanted, and then I found out that you had a son."

At last, we were getting to the real heart of the matter. Why hadn't he contacted me then, and why had he decided to come back?

"You might not think it meant anything to me, Freya, but it did. For all my success, I'd never found the kind of happiness that we had together, and to know that I had a child, that something real had come out of that time we spent together, affected me a lot. So much so that I told my benefactor that I wanted to reach out to you and do the right thing to support you."

"Why didn't you?" He had never made any kind of attempt, I knew that for sure.

"She was furious that I'd never told her about the pregnancy and she threatened to cut me off entirely. I was in the middle of my second film, still entirely funded by her. My whole life had been wrapped up in hers and it would have ruined me. She said the fact that you had never been in touch with me, when I was such a public figure and you could have easily found me, meant that you didn't want or need my help. She questioned whether the baby was even mine, though I knew he must be. The conversation wasn't a pleasant one."

If he expected sympathy, he had come to the wrong place, and he seemed to realize that, quickly moving on.

"Again, it's not an excuse, but I let myself be persuaded. She and I finally parted ways earlier this year. I've been seeing other people since then, but it's different when I'm the one in a position of wealth and power and everyone seems to want something from me. You're the last person who really liked me for me, Freya, and I didn't know how valuable that was at the time. I wanted to reach out to you, but after how long it had been, I didn't know how to do it. And then, as I already told you, I heard about the show, and things just came together. As I said at the start, I don't expect you to forgive me. I was selfish, I lied, and I hurt you. I understand all that, but it doesn't change the fact that Dylan is my son. I want to know him and be a part of his life. He's a really great kid, I can tell that already just from this afternoon."

We both fell silent for a moment as I thought over everything he'd just said. At last, there were no more secrets, and when I finally replied, I tried to be just as open with him as he'd been with me. "My priority is Dylan and always will be. If you're serious about wanting to be there for him, then I'm willing to discuss it. He deserves a father who cares about him. But if you're going to change your mind when the next golden opportunity comes along, if you're going to turn your back on him because someone offers you something better..."

Matthew held up his hands to stop me before I got carried away. "I won't, Freya. I promise. And I know my promise isn't worth much, but I've got the money and the success now. What I don't have is something real in my life, and you and Dylan, you're real. You're the most real thing I've ever known. I can't say I'll never go back to LA or wherever work takes me, but I can promise that I'll never disappear without a word again. He'll always know where I am and I'll always make time for him."

He sounded sincere, and those brown eyes pleading with me from behind the glasses, the ones so like my little boy's, softened my resolve. "We can try," I agreed, still thinking of Dylan first and foremost. "I still don't plan to tell him you're his dad until the time is right, but you can get to know him more if you're serious about this."

"I am. I really am. Thank you, Freya." His expression melted into relief and happiness, and for a moment, with his guard down, I could almost see the man I fell in love with.

"I'll let Rome know we're done," I said, pulling out my phone to send him a text with where to meet us. "You can say goodbye to Dylan before we go."

After I'd sent the text, we got up and walked back to the south end of the walk where I'd told Rome to meet us. Matthew eyed me curiously as we were waiting. "So, there's really nothing going on between you and Rome? You're just friends?"

"We're friends," I agreed. The night before had been a lot more than friendship, but so far, we hadn't talked about anything else, and I didn't intend on sharing anything with Matthew before Rome and I figured it out.

"It doesn't look that way when he kisses you," Matthew commented, his hands in his pockets. "I've worked with a lot of actors, and the chemistry between you two is intense."

I felt it too, but Matthew was the last person I wanted to discuss it with. "He's a very good actor. I'm learning a lot from him."

"I can tell. You've come a long way from the girl in college that I had to coach through her first kissing scene."

Instantly, his words took me back to the empty stage with him at our college theatre, his hands on my face as he kissed me for the first time. I could still feel the butterflies in my stomach and the thrill of excitement that raced through me.

Some of that feeling must have shown on my face, because Matthew's gaze was heated as he stepped closer to me. "I remember it too," he whispered just before lowering his mouth to mine.

In my shock, I didn't immediately push him away. It felt like a dream, like something that couldn't possibly be happening in real life, but as soon as I realized that I was definitely not dreaming, I stepped firmly away. "What do you think you're doing?"

Before he could answer me, a movement to our left caught both our eyes, and we turned to see Rome and Dylan standing there, Dylan on Rome's back, having just witnessed the whole thing. Dylan looked confused, probably because he had never seen me kiss anyone before, and Rome...

Rome's expression was completely closed off, and that was almost worse than any other emotion he might have shown. I had no idea what might have been going through his mind.

He gently placed Dylan down on the ground before crouching down to him, ignoring me and Matthew entirely. "I'll see you again soon, okay? I've got to go home now."

Dylan gave him a hug as my heart pounded painfully. He couldn't possibly think what he'd just seen was what it looked like. "Rome, wait..."

"I'll see you both at rehearsal tomorrow." With a nod to both Matthew and I, he turned and walked away without a backward glance.

Chapter Fifteen

~Rome~

I recognized the feeling almost immediately, though it had been decades since I felt it so strongly. My mouth had gone dry, my whole body felt cold, and I simultaneously wanted to hide myself away and attach myself to Freya at the same time, never letting her out of my sight. Crawling into a dark hole where I never had to see anyone else ever again or physically clinging to the person causing my anxiety; those two opposing scenarios felt like my only two options.

Giving in to the first urge, I switched my phone off, disconnecting myself from the world even if I couldn't hide from it as I walked briskly out of the park.

The feeling mirrored the way I used to feel when my mother brought home a new boyfriend, someone she found more interesting than me. That feeling carried over to each time I moved to a new foster home after my mother left. A point would come where I'd feel like they were losing interest in me, like I wasn't good enough, and I would both withdraw and become needy at the same time.

Seeing Freya with Matthew felt like the same damn thing all over again. They had a history and they had a son together. Although she was angry with him about the way he left, anger often meant there were deeper emotions buried. She had loved him before, and as a compassionate, forgiving person, who could say she wouldn't love him again? That kiss certainly seemed to indicate it might be possible. And if she did, they would be a family: Dylan would have his dad, his real dad, and what could I offer in comparison?

When it came down to it, I was just a serial dater who couldn't make a relationship last. She had never asked me for anything serious because she knew as well as I did that I wasn't the kind of guy you did that with, not when there was so much at stake. In thinking that we might be something more, I had only set myself up for failure.

The thought of going home alone filled me with loathing, and I could only think of one place to help me sort through the crushing disappointment weighing down on me. When I walked into the lobby at Chosen Family and saw Jordan in his office, the relief that rushed through me nearly made my knees buckle. He'd always been the one person I could rely on, and that afternoon, I needed my chosen brother more than ever.

"What's going on?" As soon as I appeared in his doorway, he pushed aside whatever he had been working on, even though it was probably important and urgent, like everything he did. "Sit down, Rome. You want a drink?"

I nodded mutely, expecting him to get some coffee, but instead, he pulled out a bottle of bourbon from his desk. When I raised my eyebrows, he simply chuckled.

"Some days, watered-down coffee just doesn't cut it."

He poured us both a small amount into plastic cups he kept on hand, and once I'd drained mine, the liquid warming me on the way down, I started to feel a little calmer, though I suspected that had a lot more to do with the man in front of me than the alcohol.

"So, what happened?" he asked again, leaning back in his chair like he had all the time in the world for me.

In halting, stilted sentences, I told him everything: about the quasi-relationship that had developed between me and Freya, about Dylan and my fear of hurting him, and about Matthew's sudden reappearance in Freya's life. I told him what Freya had said the night before about why she thought my relationships always ended when my shows did. When I got to that afternoon and what I'd witnessed in the park, Jordan made a little humming sound in the back of his throat, a sound that I knew very well. It meant he'd had an idea but he wouldn't just tell me about it. He would sit with me and talk with me and wait until I figured it out myself.

"It sounds like Freya's onto something, especially since you've already recognized that what you're feeling right now stems back to what happened with your mother," he said, rephrasing and summarizing what I'd already told him far more succinctly than I'd said it. "But Freya isn't the same as your mother, just like you and Matthew aren't the same person."

I sighed in frustration. "Aren't we? What he did to her is exactly what I've done to women in the past, intentional or not. She sees us as the same. That's why she doesn't want anything serious with me."

"She's scared," Jordan countered. "She's been burned before and she's afraid of it happening again, not just with you but with anyone. You said she hasn't dated anyone since her son was born, but she's dating you, whether the two of you call it that or not. That suggests to me that she *doesn't* see you as the same as him. On some level, she sees you as someone she can trust, but admitting that out loud, or even to herself, is hard. It's easier to pretend it's not serious. She had a point about you being afraid of being left again, but she's got the same fear. With you, it might be the reason your relationships end, but with her, it's stopped her from even having one in the first place."

That was a good point, and one I hadn't considered before. Maybe deep down, we did share the same doubts. Maybe that was why she understood me so well.

"I don't know why she kissed him," Jordan continued. "But there's more than one possible reason, and you won't find out what's going on until you talk to her about it."

"That's your answer for everything," I grumbled, making him laugh.

"Because it works. I'm not a mind-reader and neither are you. You can't know that she's choosing him over you unless she tells you so, and you need to find that out. You know why, don't you?"

I'd been dreading this part, the part where he always put me on the spot and forced me to sort through my feelings, searching for the truth. I hated it, and yet, his guided introspection was why I'd come there too. I needed the clarity that he could help me find.

"I need to know because it's worse not knowing," I suggested.

Jordan looked unimpressed. "Obviously, but I'm talking deeper than that. Why does it matter to you so much?"

I tried again. "It matters because of these abandonment issues I have. I need to accept that if she does choose to be with him, it's not about me. It's about her and Dylan and them being a family. Not everything is about me."

"Wrong," Jordan replied bluntly, to my surprise. He wasn't usually so black-and-white, preferring to tease things out and gently nudge me one way or another. "This time it *is* about you, Rome. Why does it matter so much to *you?*"

I'd already mentioned my fears of abandonment, so what else could it be? Taking a moment to really think about it, to think about everything that had happened between Freya and me since the first time we met, the time I'd spent with Dylan and the time I'd spent with her alone, the time at work and the times it had just been the two of us, one thought gradually became clearer until I couldn't see anything else, making me wonder exactly how I'd missed it before.

"It matters because I'm in love with her."

Jordan nodded in approval, his eyes warm with pride. "And if I were a gambling man, I'd put good money on the fact that she's in love with you too. So, before she makes any kind of choice, if that's even what's really what's going on here, then she needs to know you're an option. She needs to know that this isn't casual for you, that you're serious about being there for her and for her son."

The idea of telling her all of that terrified me, but excited me at the same time. If she really felt the same, it could change everything.

"But what about Matthew? He wants to be a part of Dylan's life and he has that right."

"Then let him," Jordan said with a shrug. "Sometimes, you wait four years for a dad and two come along at once. I don't see how that's a bad thing."

He had a point. When it came to Dylan, there was room for both me and Matthew in his life, but when it came to Freya, I wanted her all for myself.

"I should go."

Jordan chuckled again as I got to my feet. "Good luck, Rome."

"Thank you." Those words would never be enough for all he'd done for me, but he knew I meant them, smiling after me as I hurried out of his office.

In my shows, the characters I played usually ended up making some kind of grand gesture to win over the heroine in the end. Freya wouldn't want anything big and showy, that wasn't her style, but I knew the one sure way to her heart was through her son. With that in mind, I made a stop at FAO Schwarz on the way home. The huge toy store had anything anyone could ever want, and I walked out with the largest stuffed snow leopard I could find. It barely fit in the back seat of the taxi with me.

I wanted to take it to Dylan that night, but first, I wanted to stop at my apartment to get one more thing for Freya too. The giant leopard blocked most of my view as I walked into the lobby, but I could see Richard at his desk, trying not to laugh as I walked up.

"I might need to sign your guest in," he joked. "But speaking of guests, you've got a couple of others waiting for you."

He pointed over at the sofas in the lobby, to the seating area I couldn't see with the leopard in the way, but when I turned around to take a look, to my great surprise, both Freya and Dylan were sitting there.

~Freya~

While Dylan knelt on the plush carpet at the coffee table in Rome's lobby, colouring in the book that Richard the doorman had found for him somewhere, I scrolled through my phone again, hoping to see something different than I'd been staring at for the last hour. My messages to Rome were still unread, and when we arrived to try to speak to him in person, Richard told me that he hadn't returned yet after going out that afternoon. Seeing the disappointment on my face, he told us we were welcome to wait for him if we wanted to, though of course he couldn't say how long it would be. Since there didn't seem to be any other choice, we sat down to wait while I tried to figure out exactly what to say when he arrived.

After Rome walked away from us in the park earlier, Matthew turned to me, eyebrows raised. "That was abrupt."

I couldn't argue with that, but he was also the reason for Rome's sudden departure, whether he realized it or not. Although Rome and I hadn't made any kind of commitment to each other, something had shifted between us anyway, or at least, it had for me. If I saw him kissing someone else after the night we just spent together, I would feel both hurt and foolish, and the idea that he might be feeling that way because of me pained me almost as much as if it had happened to me. I needed to clear things up quickly, on both ends.

Trying to keep my voice level, aware that Dylan was listening, I laid out my position as plainly as I could to the man in front of me. "Rome probably thought he was interrupting, when in truth, there was nothing to interrupt. Kissing me like that was completely inappropriate, Matthew. What happened between us in college meant a lot to me at the time, but I've moved on. I have no feelings for you anymore, and you coming back here doesn't change anything. You can get to know Dylan, as we discussed, but as for you and me, there is no chance, absolutely none, of anything happening."

Matthew looked genuinely taken aback by the finality of my words, his eyes wide behind his glasses. "Deep down, I'm still the same guy I was then. We had something special, Freya. I rushed this today, I understand that, but if you give me a chance..."

I simply shook my head at him, not letting him finish. "The fact that you're the same guy is exactly the problem. I never knew that man. The man I fell in love with then was an illusion, a character that I created in my head. He never existed. The man I loved wouldn't have done the things you did. I guess we got carried away in the excitement of the show, but in the end, we were meant for different things."

From the way he grimaced, I could tell he recognized that I'd just repeated his own words back to him, the words he'd used when he broke up with me. "I'm sorry, Freya."

That much, I believed. He looked very sorry, at least for himself. "I'll see you at rehearsal tomorrow," I said, echoing Rome's farewell as I took Dylan's hand and headed off in the direction we'd seen Rome go. Catching up to him at Dylan's pace would be impossible, so I pulled out my phone and dialed his number. To my frustration, it went straight to voicemail.

I left a short message, straight to the point: "Rome, that wasn't what it looked like. I know that sounds like the most cliché line, but it's true. Please, call me back."

By the time we left the park, there hadn't been any reply so I sent a text, asking him to check his voicemail and to call me.

Dylan chattered away happily beside me, telling me about the carousel ride he took with Rome and the leopard piggyback ride Rome gave him, and I did my best to pay attention while my mind continued to race, trying to decide what to do next. My mom was still out with friends until later that evening; that had been the whole reason I'd needed Rome to watch Dylan in the first place. Whatever I decided to do, Dylan would be coming with me.

Going home and waiting for Rome to call me back didn't seem like a good idea. I needed to talk to him. He was so afraid of people leaving him, so afraid of it that he pushed people away preemptively, that if I didn't get through to him and clear things up quickly, he might do the same to me without even realizing it.

That idea made my heart ache for two reasons. First, the last thing I wanted to do was cause him any additional pain. He'd been through enough already, and he had been nothing but kind and supportive to me. I didn't want to let him down. And second, I didn't want him to push me away because he meant more to me than I'd let myself realize, at least until faced with the prospect of losing him.

We were never just casual, not for me. He was everything I wanted, and I'd let my fear blind me to that fact. I'd been so afraid of falling for him that I hadn't even realized it had already happened, and I needed to tell him that before I lost the chance.

Making up my mind, Dylan and I got on the subway and headed to Midtown. First, I took Dylan to the theatre where our show would be opening in just a few weeks. The marquee had gone up along with some posters at the front of the theatre, one of which had my name on it. Rome's name was above the show's title as the big star of the show, but beneath the show's logo, it read: *introducing Freya Rose.*

I pointed it out to Dylan since he had just started to learn to read. Seeing my name was exciting, but seeing Rome's thrilled him even more. I snapped a picture of us in front of the sign and sent it to Rome with a message: *We're in the neighbourhood. Are you free for dinner?*

Still, no response came, and he hadn't read my earlier message either. Out of ideas, I brought us to his building where we'd been waiting for an hour. My stomach had started to rumble and Dylan must have been getting hungry too, even if the animal colouring book managed to distract him. We would need to go soon, but I hated the idea of missing Rome, even if it seemed pretty clear by now that he had chosen to ignore me.

"Mo- Mo- Mommy!" Dylan's stunned exclamation pulled my attention away from my phone. "Leopard!"

At first, I thought he meant a leopard in the colouring book, but his eyes were wide as he stared at the door of the building, and I turned to follow his gaze just in time to see an absolutely enormous stuffed leopard coming in the building.

It didn't come in on its own, of course, but it almost looked that way. Its size completely blocked the person carrying it, and Dylan's awe-filled expression was so adorably overwhelmed that it brought tears to my eyes. He must have thought his dreams were coming true.

From the other side of the room, Richard the doorman spoke to the leopard's owner and pointed to us, so when the leopard and the man turned to us, it didn't shock me to see Rome on the other side of the huge animal, though I still felt surprised. Had he bought the leopard for Dylan? What was happening?

"Hey," Rome greeted us, almost sheepishly. "I'm sorry if you've been waiting long. I was actually on my way to see you."

If that were true, why had he been ignoring me for the last two hours? "I've been trying to reach you," I told him, holding up the phone in my hand, and he groaned.

"Oh, shi... I mean, shoot." He caught himself at the last second, looking down at Dylan whose eyes hadn't left the leopard. He was so distracted by it that he hadn't even said hello to Rome yet. "I switched my phone off and then forgot I had. I'm sorry."

If anyone needed to be apologizing, it should be me. "I need to talk to you."

The obviousness of that statement made Rome smile. Why else would I be there? "I want to talk to you too, but this guy is getting pretty heavy. Dylan, do you want to help me take him upstairs and we can have some supper?"

Dylan nodded, his eyes still wide as he hopped to his feet and went to pick up one of the leopard's legs. He hadn't figured out that Rome had bought the leopard for him yet, though he must have. What I still didn't know was why, or how, exactly, we were going to find room for it in our apartment.

I returned the colouring book and crayons to Richard at the desk, thanking him for his help before joining Dylan and Rome by the elevator where Rome and Dylan were talking about the leopard.

"He doesn't have a name yet," Rome said as I walked up to them. "Can you help me think of one?"

"No name?" Dylan repeated curiously, stroking the soft fur of the animal's leg as he pressed it against his face.

"Everybody needs to be given a name," I reminded him. We had talked about that recently when one of his daycare friends got a new baby brother. "Mommy chose your name, and now, you can choose the leopard's name. It's an important job."

Dylan nodded seriously as he thought it over, and Rome and I smiled at each other as the elevator door opened and the three of us piled in together. Rome didn't seem upset any more, which relieved me, but I didn't understand why not. I hadn't had a chance to explain anything to him yet.

In his apartment, he set Dylan up with the leopard in his living room while he took me to the kitchen and pulled out some take-out menus. "Dylan likes lasagna, right? There's a good Italian place just down the street if that works for you."

I wasn't sure how he knew about Dylan's love of lasagna, and I also didn't understand why we were ignoring the elephant in the room. "Rome, what you saw..."

He cut me off. "I want to hear all about your day, but first, we should get dinner ordered. Dylan must be hungry."

The fact that he put Dylan's needs first endeared him to me more than anything else he could have said, but I was still completely confused.

A moment later, Rome cleared it up for me, at least a little. "Freya, the fact that you and Dylan are here tells me all I need to know for right now. Let's have something to eat, and then we can really talk, just you and me. There's a lot we need to talk about."

~Rome~

My words eased the tension in Freya's frame almost immediately. She had been looking nervous and unsure ever since the lobby, but from the moment I saw her there, my own worries were lifted considerably.

She came. She'd been trying to reach me and she came there to talk to me. Those didn't seem like the actions of someone who wanted to get back together with her ex. We still had to talk, but I felt a lot more optimistic about that conversation than if I'd had to drag that huge leopard up to Harlem and stand outside her door, unsure of who might be on the other side.

We ordered some food and returned to the living room where Dylan sat staring at his new leopard in amazement, stroking its soft fur and moving its limbs around. Maybe I went a little overboard; he looked so enthralled, I didn't know how anything would ever be able to top this for him.

"You haven't told him it's for him," Freya whispered to me as we walked in. "He thinks it's yours and you're just letting him play with it."

The fact that he wouldn't automatically assume I'd bought it for him was just another sign of Freya's excellent parent, raising a great, unspoiled kid, and I knelt down on the floor next to him. "Have you picked a name yet?"

He nodded seriously. "He's New York."

"New York?" Freya repeated curiously. "That's a great name. Why did you pick it?"

I loved how she made him feel good about the choice even though she must be just as confused by it as I was. Those kinds of small affirmations were so important.

"Mrs Shaw says people can have city names, like Wome."

I didn't quite follow that, but Freya explained it to me. "Mrs Shaw is his preschool teacher. He must have told her about you."

The idea that Dylan had been talking about me to other people sent a wave of affection through me, and I thought I understood. His teacher must have told him that Rome is also a place, so if I could have the same name as a city, so could his leopard. In a way, he was naming it after me, and it truly touched me.

"That's right," I confirmed as I picked up one of the leopard's paws and swatted at Dylan with it, making him laugh. "And do you know why New York is here in my apartment?"

Dylan shook his head seriously, all his attention on me.

"I picked him up today so I could bring him to you. He wants to be your leopard, to come and live with you. Is that okay?"

His big brown eyes got even bigger as he looked at the animal and back at me. "My leopard?"

Hope and wonder filled his voice, and from the corner of my eye, I could see Freya covering her mouth with her hand, trying not to cry. "He's your leopard," I confirmed.

"Rome got him for you, Dill-pickle," Freya added. "It's a present."

The little boy still couldn't seem to quite believe it, looking between his mom and the leopard and me a few times until, finally, he launched himself into my arms. "Thank you, Wome."

I felt close to tears myself as he squeezed me as tight as he could. If only it were so easy to bring joy to everyone. "You're welcome, Dylan."

Our food arrived soon afterwards and we ate while Dylan talked excitedly about what he was going to do with New York when he got him home. When we'd finished eating, I found an animated movie on TV for him and he cuddled up on the couch with his leopard while Freya and I moved into the dining room, close enough that we could hear him but private enough that we could talk about more adult matters.

"So, what happened with Matthew?" I asked, leaving the question open-ended so she could tell me as much as she wanted.

"What you saw... *he* kissed me. I wasn't expecting it and I didn't want it. I'm so sorry you had to see that, I know what it must have looked like, but we are not getting back together. Not now, and not ever."

I'd been hoping that might be the case, and hearing her say the words so forcefully made me even happier, but I wanted to know more than that. "Back up a little bit, Freya. What happened with him and Dylan, and what did you talk about?"

She relaxed further as she realized I wasn't fixated on the kiss. I wanted the full story and she did as I requested, starting from the beginning. She told me that Dylan had been okay with Matthew and he had been okay with Dylan, and then she told me what he'd revealed to her about why he left her in the first place and why he'd stayed away.

Despite the indignation flowing through my veins on her behalf, I tried my best to keep calm. "And after all that, he had the nerve to kiss you? Like he could just pick up where you left off and you'd be grateful for it?"

My scorn made Freya smile. "Self-confidence has never been Matthew's problem. It's part of what makes him a good director and not such a great human being. In fact, I'm not entirely sure he didn't do it on purpose knowing that you might see us. He knew you were on your way and he had just been asking me about our relationship."

Finally, we were really getting to the heart of things: our relationship. "What did you tell him?"

"I told him we're just friends." That wasn't the answer I'd been hoping for, but the second sentence she added made me feel a little better. "We haven't talked about being anything else."

She couldn't have set me up much better than that. "Well, maybe we should."

"Okay." The word came out almost as a whisper, maybe not quite as enthusiastic as I'd been hoping for, but at least it meant she would be open to discussing more.

Going first was always intimidating, but after what Jordan had said to me about Freya's own fears, I knew I would have to begin. I needed to try to alleviate the valid concerns she had so that she could see a path ahead as clearly as I could.

"Freya, since the very first time we met, I've been intrigued and impressed by you."

Her eyebrows shot up, making it clear she didn't quite believe me, but I was being completely sincere and I tried to prove it to her.

"I mean it. I definitely don't remember every waitress I ever had, but you made an impression on me that night at the restaurant, and when I saw you at the audition, it just reinforced my initial conclusion that you were someone special. I probably would have asked you out right away, except that I found out about Dylan and that's what held me back. I didn't want to hurt either of you if things didn't work out, since they never do for me."

She leaned closer to me, her hazel eyes as full of empathy and understanding as always, and though her sweet, pink lips were very tempting, I held back. We needed to talk this through; kissing could come later, hopefully.

"After meeting Dylan for myself, I only respected you more, and I really care for him too. I hope you know that."

"I do, Rome," she assured me. "Whatever is between us is completely separate from you and Dylan. I understand that."

As much as I appreciated that, my point was that I didn't want it to be completely separate. I still needed to get to that part.

"When you came here last weekend and said you wanted a sexual relationship with me, no strings attached, of course I jumped at the chance because I find you irresistible, Freya. You're beautiful, inside and out, and even having you halfway would be better than not at all. But the problem is, our relationship was never completely stringless, at least not for me. There are a lot of things tying me to you: not just the show, and not just Dylan either. There's your talent, your passion, your sincerity, and the way you understand me. Those strings have been tightening, whether I wanted them to or not, and when I saw you with Matthew today and I thought they might be breaking, that's when I finally realized just how strong they already are."

She had been listening carefully, not wanting to interrupt, but when I paused there, she asked me the question that really lay at the root of everything. "What do you think we should do, then?"

Even though she still hadn't said a word about whether she felt the same, I took the leap anyway, laying it on the line for her. "I want to be with you, Freya. I want you and Dylan in my life, not casually, not just in the show, and not only through Chosen Family. I want to give us a chance and see what we could be, all three of us together."

Although interest flared in her eyes, I could see that lingering doubt too, and I did my best to address it.

"I won't promise you forever. I know that, coming from me, it's not much of a promise at all. But I will promise that I will give it everything I can. I promise I'll talk things over with you and try to work things out and not push you away. You already know me so well, Freya, and I really think this time it might be different. I think *you* are different. I guess what I'm asking is: will you give us a chance too?"

Chapter Sixteen

~Freya~

Rome's final words were nearly drowned out by the beating of my heart as it thudded in my chest. What he'd just said was possibly the sweetest thing I'd ever heard, better than any lines from any show. In front of me, I didn't see the actor, the consummate professional who gave the person opposite him whatever they needed. Instead, I saw a man trying to speak from his heart. Rather than responding to me or working off what I gave him, he forged ahead, letting me know what *he* wanted and what *he* felt in a way that he had never really done before, certainly not with me and perhaps not with anyone.

He said this felt different for him, and it felt different to me too. It felt like I was seeing the real Rome, the one who doubted himself but kept trying anyway. I could see the kid who got up on stage for the first time despite never feeling good enough in any other part of his life. I could see the man who kept giving love a chance, even when it fell apart on him every time and he didn't know why. And I could see the man who had held himself back until that night, not because he didn't care, but because he was afraid he couldn't be what Dylan and I both needed.

But that night, he took the risk. He put himself on the line to tell me that he wanted something more, and I only needed to decide whether

I wanted it too. Luckily, that was all I'd been thinking about since he walked away from me in the park.

Until that day, I'd been trying so hard to keep Rome at arm's-length and not to let myself fall because of my fear that history would repeat itself, both on his side and mine. In the end, however, that had never been fair to Rome. He wasn't Matthew, and spending time with the actual Matthew that week made that crystal clear to me. Rome's relationships ended because of his insecurities, not his ambition. He would never put his own wants first in the way that Matthew had.

If we decided to go ahead, our relationship might end someday. Nothing in life was guaranteed, but the truth was there was no one else on earth I'd rather take that chance with, and it was high time I told him so.

"I had an idea of what you were like before we met," I started, trying to be as open and honest with him as he had been with me. "When you came into the restaurant that night, Elyse told me that Romeo Taylor was in my section. I'd heard all the stories."

He winced, those stunning blue eyes clouding over with a hint of embarrassment, and I quickly pressed ahead.

"But even that night, I saw there was more to you than that. The way you took the time to speak with the fan who wanted to meet you, the way that you saw me and engaged with me, and then especially when you recognized me at the audition, those were all clues that you weren't exactly the man the press paints you to be."

His expression turned a little more optimistic, as it should be. I was still getting to the good stuff.

"And ever since then, since we started to spend time together, you've shown me again and again who you really are. The way you put me at ease at the audition and came to congratulate me afterwards, the way you've encouraged me at rehearsal and always made me feel like your equal, the way you treat Dylan..."

My throat closed up as I tried to put into words exactly how much I appreciated what Rome had done for my son, but it didn't seem like I could, not if I wanted to be able to keep going. No words could ever fully explain it, but the look in his eyes told me he understood anyway.

"... and then on top of that, there's the way you've supported me through this week with Matthew, never making it about you even though you were involved too. And that's before I even get to how much I want you, and how good you are in bed."

A grin pulled at his lips at the compliment, but he remained silent, waiting for me to get to the point, which I still hadn't done yet.

"I don't have any illusions about what we're talking about here. I know this isn't the show; I'm not Julia and you're not Victor, and there's no happy-ever-after scripted in advance. Things might not work out, but I believe in you, Rome. I trust that you mean it when you say you'll try, and I'll try too. And even if it doesn't last forever, it doesn't mean it isn't worth taking the chance."

Rome's eyes searched mine, full of hope as he waited for my final verdict. "So, you want to do this, for real?"

The ridiculousness of that statement made me laugh. "It's always been real for me, Rome. I said we could keep it casual, but I don't even really know what that means. I think I was just afraid to admit that I'm in love with you."

Relief and delight and joy flashed in his eyes, his smile lighting up his face. "You don't know how happy I am to hear that. I love you too, Freya."

When he leaned forward to kiss me, I met him halfway. It couldn't be more different from the way Matthew had kissed me earlier, with no hesitation on either side and no holding back. The chemistry we had together had always been strong, but that kiss, boosted by the declarations we'd both just made and by the knowledge that this was far from casual and far from a showmance, felt even better than ever. It felt like the real thing.

"Mommy?" Dylan's little voice at the doorway made us both pull back, smiling at each other guiltily. Dylan had never seen me kiss anyone before, and he'd caught me twice in the same day.

"What is it, Dill-pickle?"

As he rubbed his eyes, I had a pretty good idea what he would say before the words came out. "I'm tired."

I could believe it. It had been a long day for us both.

"Let's get a taxi, then," Rome offered, pulling out his phone. "We'll need an extra big one if we're taking New York too."

I loved how Rome embraced Dylan's name for the leopard. I loved how he simply took care of things without me having to ask him to. I loved how he wasn't at all upset that our romantic moment had just been interrupted.

I loved him, pure and simple.

When the taxi arrived, a 7-seater one to make sure the leopard fit, Rome climbed in with us too.

"You don't need to come along," I protested. "It's a long way to go when you have to turn around and come back."

He leaned closer to me, whispering into my ear. "Who said I'm coming back here tonight? We're together now, Freya, and I don't intend to spend a night away from you again if I can help it."

Shivers rippled down my spine at the promise those words contained.

My mom was in the living room when we arrived back at the apartment and she burst out laughing as she caught sight of the enormous leopard that entered behind Dylan. "Someone is overcompensating. A gift from Matthew?"

I didn't know if Rome would take offense to that, but he simply joined in her laughter as he walked into the room too. "Nope, I'm afraid it's me. I might have gone overboard."

"Might have?" my mom repeated, raising her eyebrows at the animal which dwarfed her grandson. "Nice to see you, Rome."

"And you, Mrs Rose. Freya, do you mind if I talk to your mom while you get Dylan ready for bed?"

That sounded rather ominous, but I didn't mind. Somehow, I got the leopard into Dylan's room and laid him down next to Dylan's bed. Dylan wanted him *in* the bed, but there honestly wasn't room for the both of them. The big cat looked even bigger in Dylan's small room than he had in Rome's apartment.

Once Dylan had changed into his pajamas and brushed his teeth and had a drink, Rome reappeared, ready to read a bedtime story. I chose one that had several different characters and we took turns putting on dramatic voices for each one as Dylan giggled and clapped.

After flipping the light off in Dylan's room, Rome and I returned to the empty living room, my mom having disappeared into her own room. My curiosity over what they'd talked about grew even stronger, but I didn't have to wait long as we sat down together, Rome pulling me onto his lap.

"I've declared my intentions to your mother," he told me, making me laugh with the rather archaic turn of phrase.

"Declared your intentions? I think you've been playing a prince for a little too long, it's starting to go to your head."

"That's entirely possible," he agreed good-naturedly. "But I know what an important part of your life she is, and of Dylan's life too, and I didn't want her to feel left out of any plans we make."

"What plans?" His train of thought was moving so fast, I had trouble keeping up.

"About how this is going to work to make sure that we have time together but you don't miss out on time with Dylan, especially once the show starts and your hours completely change."

I appreciated his concern, but I had it covered. "My mom and I have already talked about that schedule. That's why we got Dylan's new babysitter."

"I know that, but having a babysitter here in Harlem might not be the most convenient arrangement if you move in with me."

My mouth dropped open as I looked into those twinkling blue eyes. "Move in with you?"

Rome nodded, enjoying my surprise. "You don't need to decide right now, but as I already told you, I don't want to spend a night away from you, and the simple truth is that my apartment is bigger than yours.

There are a few spare rooms Dylan can have his choice of. I asked your mom if she would want to come too, but she thinks it would be better for us to have our own space and she can have this place to herself."

"You... you asked my mom to move in with you?" I sputtered in disbelief as Rome chuckled.

"It sounds kind of wrong when you say it like that, but as I said, I know how important she's been to the two of you and how much she cares about you and Dylan. I didn't want her to feel left out, and I have the space, so I made the offer. However, she said no."

He really was unbelievable, in the very best way. "That's a really big step, Rome. Especially for Dylan."

"I know," he assured me. "He'll need a new preschool and babysitter, but we can start looking for all of that as soon as you're ready."

We. Just like that, he accepted Dylan as his responsibility too. He completely understood that there was no having me without my son, and he embraced us both.

If I hadn't already accepted that I loved him, that would have completely sealed the deal.

"I will think about it," I promised. "But for now, I think I'm ready for bed."

Rome's smile turned from warm to heated in a heartbeat. "Not as ready as I am."

~Rome~

The next morning, Freya and I walked into the rehearsal hand-in-hand. Just before we arrived, we had made a quick pit-stop at my apartment so I could get changed into some fresh clothes, and while we were there, I asked her how she wanted to handle the change in our relationship status in public.

"It will bring you a lot of attention, and not in a good way," I warned her. "There will be a lot of talk about how you're my next showmance, just like the others."

I'd seen it happen enough times to know exactly how it would play out: the catty remarks from the other cast members, the way she'd be asked about it in interviews instead of focusing on the show and her performance, which should be the real story.

Freya walked right over to me and took my face in her hands. "I'm not ashamed to be with you, Rome. You told me it's different. Have you ever said that to anyone else?"

I shook my head truthfully. This kind of soul-searching and self-examination prior to getting involved with someone was completely new to me. Usually, I just dove in and hoped for the best.

"Then I trust you, and it doesn't matter to me what anyone else has to say."

Her faith in me was uplifting, and no one was particularly surprised anyway, not after the video of us singing together in the cabaret bar over the weekend had already made a splash. Freya stayed upbeat all day, even when Jennifer pulled her away for a private conversation, followed by Matthew. I had already committed to having lunch with a reporter from one of the big Broadway news websites, so I didn't get a chance to talk to Freya about her day until we were in a taxi on the way back to her apartment after rehearsal.

"Jennifer didn't pull any punches," she told me with a rueful smile. "She basically told me she thought I was smarter than this, and she reminded me about how things ended between you two."

The memory made me wince. I had never talked to Freya about what happened between me and Jennifer, but I should. I didn't want there to be any secrets between us. "I'm not proud of that. Jenn and I were still together when we both started on new shows. Our schedules were completely different, she was busy with her own rehearsals and I guess I got afraid that she had started to pull away from me, though at the time,

I didn't think of it that way. My new co-star, Sophie, invited herself over to dinner at our apartment, and I agreed rather than eating alone again. While we were there, she suggested we work on one of the scenes from our new show."

Freya grimaced, seeing it coming before I had. "Let me guess: one that involved a kiss?"

I could only nod, feeling ashamed of myself as I did every time I thought about it. "We got carried away and Jenn walked in on it. It devastated her and it was entirely my fault. I was a jerk and I hurt her. And the stupid thing was: I didn't really even like Sophie all that much, but I ended up going out with her anyway since it seemed worse to have thrown away what Jenn and I had for no good reason."

"It's not great," Freya had to agree. "But you're human, Rome. Everyone makes mistakes. Hopefully, in the same situation, you'd just talk to me about what was bothering you."

"I would," I promised her. "I will. It's never happened again, and it never will."

She also told me about what Matthew said. He asked her if she'd lied to him the day before about us not being together, and she told him the truth: we hadn't been then, but him kissing her had been the nudge we both needed to admit our true feelings to each other.

"That must have stung," I pointed out, not able to completely keep the triumph out of my voice.

"I think it did," Freya confirmed, also trying not to smile. "I think he got the message that I'm not available, at least. There shouldn't be any more ambush kissing."

I should damn well hope not.

Over the next few weeks, our lives only got busier. Freya lasted all of three days of us travelling back and forth together between each other's apartments before she had to admit I'd been right: "This would be a lot easier if we were living together."

I had movers hired within the hour, along with a decorator to transform one of my guest rooms into a perfect bedroom for Dylan. By the time they moved in with me on Sunday, the room was ready to go, still smelling of fresh paint, and when Dylan stepped inside for the first time, his eyes went adorably wide. The walls were painted with trees, vines hung from the ceiling and a large hammock was strung in one corner, with New York, the leopard, laid out in it.

"Oh my gosh, Rome." Freya's eyes filled with happy tears as Dylan ran excitedly around the room, checking out all the features. "This is insane."

"In a good way, right?" I asked, and she wrapped her arms around my waist.

"In the best way. I keep thinking you can't do anything better, and then you do."

Hopefully, I hadn't reached my peak just yet.

I called in favours to get a highly-recommended nanny for Dylan and to get him a spot in a private preschool. When Freya protested it was too much, I told her I wanted to make up for all the things I didn't have growing up, and she couldn't argue with me then. I told her none of it was conditional on her being in a relationship with me; if we broke up, it would be amicable and we could sort it all out then.

Matthew and Dylan spent a bit more time together, with Freya there. He seemed serious about wanting to get to know Dylan better and about taking Freya's lead in how hard to push. I stayed out of it since they could handle it on their own, but Freya knew I was there for her if she needed me.

As I expected, the news of our relationship hit the media just in time for the lead-up to opening night, making the buzz surrounding it even stronger. Although I did my best to keep Freya relaxed, the pressure started to weigh on her, as it would on anyone.

The final week before the show opened was tech week, which was always brutal, and that week was no exception. Once we moved from the rehearsal into the theatre space, all of the scenery and lighting cues had to be worked out by the show's technical crew. That meant being at the theatre for 12 or 13 hours a day as we ran through each scene in minute detail, making sure everything about it would be completely perfect.

When we left the theatre on the last day of tech, we had two days off before the final dress rehearsals and first preview, and I planned to make the most of them. Without a word to Freya, I had asked her mom if she would come and stay at our apartment to watch Dylan, so instead of taking us home, the taxi headed north out of the city as Freya looked around curiously. "Where are we going?"

"You'll see when we get there. You trust me, right?"

Her warm smile was all the answer I needed.

We arrived at the bed and breakfast in Connecticut a couple of hours later, and when we got to our room, the bags I'd sent ahead were already waiting for us.

"You are too good to be true," Freya said with a hint of teasing accusation. "Are you trying to ruin every other man for me?"

"That's exactly what I'm trying to do." I pulled her into my arms, my lips lingering against hers, soft and slow. "I can't pretend this isn't selfish of me though. I brought us here because I wanted you all to myself before the rest of the world figures out just how amazing you are. Now, how tired are you? Do you want to sleep, or..."

I didn't even get the rest of the sentence out before Freya pushed me down onto the bed, climbing up on top of me as I grinned up at her.

"'Or' it is, then."

She leaned down to kiss me, hard and hungry, and my body reacted instantly, as it always did with her.

"Did you know you had me half-hard most of the afternoon?" I murmured as her hands moved down my body, looking for the button of my pants.

"I'm not convinced you don't just live in that state all the time," she teased me, pulling my zipper down and pressing her hand against my cock as I groaned.

"Around you, I do. But today, specifically, you did that quick change next to me backstage and I couldn't think about anything else afterwards."

"Oh, you mean when I did this?" She had her shirt up over her head almost faster than I could blink, making me laugh.

"Exactly. And all I could think about was doing this."

I raised myself to her chest, biting her nipple gently through the fabric of her bra. Freya sighed happily, settling down on top of my cock and rocking against it, making me even harder. "I'm rather glad you didn't do that, or I might not have been able to stop myself either."

We laughed and teased each other some more until all our clothes were off, but when I went to reach for a condom in the bag I'd brought, Freya put out a hand to stop me.

"It's okay with me if you'd rather not use it."

"Are you sure?" I would love to be inside her, skin-to-skin, but I completely understood why it would make her nervous.

She must have been thinking about it, though, because she nodded in confirmation. "I'm sure. I'm on birth control, and if something goes wrong, we'll deal with it together."

She had that right. I'd never leave her to handle something that alone, and as she lowered herself onto me, I had a thought I'd never really had before, one I couldn't help voicing out loud. "I'd love to have a baby with you, Freya. Someday. When you're ready."

"You'd be an amazing dad," she assured me. "You already are. But for right now, how about we just practice?"

That sounded pretty much perfect to me, and when she took me inside her with nothing at all between us, it felt even better. My hips thrust up each time Freya sank down, our bodies working in perfect harmony until we both forgot about babies or quick changes or tech rehearsals, or anything but the perfect pleasure of being together. Her hazel eyes shone down at me as my hands roamed her body, and when she let herself fall into the bliss of her orgasm, I thought I had never seen anything more beautiful.

When I looked at her, all I saw were stars.

~Freya~

Sometimes, the stars aligned and it felt like you could do no wrong. Things fell into place so perfectly that you knew they were meant to be. Everything felt light and easy and effortless.

Opening night was one of those times.

A knock at my dressing room door brought another bouquet of flowers, which my mom took care of so I could continue getting ready. Dylan sat next to me, watching curiously in the mirror while the show's stylist finished attaching my wig, making sure my mic pack was secure and working properly, and layered on the makeup that needed to be seen from even the farthest seat in the last row of the second balcony.

It made a big change from my natural look, and Dylan was fascinated by the change in me. "I help?" he asked hopefully as he peered at the stylist's makeup tray and all its treasures.

"Not today, Dill-pickle. We can try at home if you want?"

Thankfully, he accepted that answer, and once the stylist had left, my dresser appeared to help me into my opening costume. I had seventeen different costumes for the show, and my shortest change between costumes was 52 seconds. That was the quick change Rome had teased me about on our weekend away a couple of weeks earlier, though that trip now seemed like a lifetime ago, so much had happened since then.

Rome had to change right next to me backstage on that occasion, both of us transforming from the casual version of Julia and Victor into our formal party attire. Rome's change was easier than mine; he had to switch his shirt and suit jacket for a tuxedo, while I had to go from pants and a blouse to a ballgown and a new wig. There were three people to help me and we had it down to a finely choreographed routine, but it still made my heart beat faster each time, knowing that two thousand people were waiting for me to hit my next entrance.

Beneath my costume, beneath *every* costume, I wore the shining star necklace that Rome had given me on our first day of rehearsal. It had only grown more meaningful to me with each passing day, a symbol of his support and faith in me through the gruelling process of getting the show open, and his trust in me in general.

That night marked our official opening night. We'd had three weeks of previews, performing in front of paying audiences but still making some tweaks to the show based on how it was received. That night, the show was pretty much set in stone and the critics would all be in attendance. It would be the performance that would be immortalized in their reviews, and perhaps I should have been terrified about that, but mostly, I just felt excited to go out and perform the amazing show with my wonderful co-star and all of the amazing cast. Knowing that Dylan and my mom would be in the audience only made it better.

"No one told me we got a new co-star!"

Rome's voice from the door had the same effect on Dylan as always: his face broke into a grin and he jumped up and ran into Rome's arms.

"Daddy-Wome!"

My heart melted as I watched the two of them embrace. The week before, I had finally sat Dylan down in his room to tell him that Matthew was his dad. I didn't want Matthew there for it; I figured it would be better if Dylan had time to absorb the news first. Rome, however, *was* there. He wanted to support me, and although I tried to prepare as best I could for any questions Dylan might have, the first words out of his mouth were still not what I expected.

"Wome can't be my daddy?"

There was such confusion and disappointment on his face, as if he saw it as some kind of rejection, that it nearly broke my heart. That was the last thing I wanted him to think.

Luckily, Rome was right there to speak for himself. "I love you, Dylan, and I'm not going anywhere, okay? There are lots of kinds of daddies. Matthew is one of them, and I'm another one. You're still going to live here and we're going to have so much fun, and nothing is going to change."

"You can call Matthew Daddy if you want to," I added. "But you don't have to. It's up to you."

Dylan thought all that over for a second. "Can I call Wome Daddy too?"

From the look on Rome's face, it seemed it would be fine with him. "If you want to," he told my son. "But won't it get confusing with two daddies?"

He launched into an impression of what might happen if Dylan called for his daddy and they both answered, making Dylan laugh as he forgot all about the idea that anyone didn't want him.

By the end of the skit, Dylan had a solution: "I call you Daddy-Wome," he suggested, and neither of us could argue with that.

"Be careful, Dylan," I admonished him as he wriggled in Rome's arms in my dressing room, curious about Rome's makeup and mic pack. The last thing we needed was a ripped seam in Rome's suit fifteen minutes before curtain time.

They both ignored me, whispering to each other about something I couldn't even guess at. Soon, the call came over the backstage loud-speaker for all audience members to take their seats, and my mom gave me a tight hug. "I'm so proud of you, Freya."

Tears gathered in the corners of her eyes and I blinked quickly before mine could do the same. "Don't start! The makeup artist will kill me."

She laughed and gave me one more squeeze before taking Dylan to sit down, and Rome came over to hug me instead. "Enjoy every second of it tonight. This is your first opening night, Freya. Not the last, I'm certain, but you'll never get another first one. Just be there for it, and have fun."

That was exactly what I intended to do. The reception from the preview audiences had been amazing, so even if the critics didn't like it, for whatever reasons critics had for not liking things, people were enjoying it and that mattered most of all. Women had been coming up to me at the stage door every night to tell me that they could see themselves in Julia, and in me too: a single mom whose life's adventures didn't end with her child.

Places were called and I took my spot in the wings, holding hands with the little boy who was playing my son that night as we listened to the orchestra tuning, that wonderful moment of anticipation just before the show began.

And once the music started, the show absolutely flew by. Every word, every note, every step all hit exactly where they were supposed to. The laughter and applause of the crowd lifted me higher and higher until I felt like I was flying. During my solo in the second act, I found my mom in the crowd, tears not just in her eyes but streaming down her face, and Dylan next to her, fast asleep, which only made me smile. His bedtime had been a couple of hours ago, and I didn't take it personally.

When we took our bows at the end of the show, the crowd leapt to their feet. The show's composer, Jeffrey, wasn't there; he shied away from the spotlight, as usual, figuring his job was finished, so Matthew gave the opening night speech instead as the director. He got a huge round of applause, as he deserved. He had done an amazing job with the show, and there would almost certainly be a Tony nomination in it for him. So far, he had stuck to his promise to see Dylan regularly, and they had even spent some time together alone. Having him back in our lives was an adjustment, but one that we were learning to live with.

As he spoke, his eyes scanned the crowd until he saw Dylan, awake now thanks to all the applause, and he invited him up on stage. Only when he got to his feet did I see the rose in his hands, and immediately, I turned to Rome with a suspicious look. "Did you set this up?"

"What makes you think it was me?" Rome asked so unconvincingly that I had to laugh.

"You're an amazing actor, but a terrible liar."

My brave little boy marched right up, giving Matthew a high-five on the way before coming over to me and Rome as the audience cheered. As he handed me the rose, hundreds of phone cameras captured the moment, and I honestly couldn't imagine how life could get any better.

My mom took Dylan home after the show while Rome and I changed out of our costumes and exited the theatre through the stage door where hundreds of people waited for us. We stayed until we'd talked to them all, signing autographs and taking pictures. My hand cramped up several times and my cheeks were sore from smiling by the time we finally headed to the restaurant where our opening night party was taking place; the same restaurant where Rome and I had met, only two months earlier.

Elyse was there too, not serving that night but as my guest, and along with the rest of the cast, we laughed and talked until early in the morning. Traditionally, the opening night parties would go until the publication of the morning's papers with the reviews in them. Now that most reviews were published online, there wasn't that same ritual, but our stage manager still called out every time a review came in, reading the highlights out for everyone to hear. The one we were all on pins-and-needles for was from the New York Times, and when it came, the whole room went deathly quiet.

The music was praised along with the direction, the choreography and the costumes. The critic loved Jennifer's performance, and Rome was 'the ideal prince', 'effortlessly charming' and 'with enough clean-cut sex appeal to make teenagers, suburban moms and grandmothers swoon equally.'

I couldn't agree more. Everything in the review was so positive that I couldn't help thinking there must be a downside coming, and maybe my performance was it. The critic didn't mention me until the end.

"Freya Rose is a revelation as Julia," the stage manager read out as Rome stood behind me, his arms wrapped around me. "From her first word, the audience is rooting for her and by ten minutes in, it feels like you've known her forever. If you've ever wanted to watch a star in the making, get your tickets now."

My castmates all cheered around me as I tried to take all that in. We were a hit. That really just happened, and this really was my life.

"I'm going to need you to repeat that for me later," I whispered to

Rome. "I think I blacked out for a second."

His warm laugh reverberated in my ear. "I'll read it to you every night if you want, and every morning too. You're a star, Freya Rose, and don't you forget it."

Epilogue

One year later

~Rome~

I went over the plan with Dylan one more time before confirming we were good to go. "You got it, right, buddy?"

"I got it, Daddy." He nodded back at me solemnly, taking his responsibility very seriously.

"Remember to smile," I added, giving him a playful nudge. "We're supposed to be happy about it."

His face immediately broke into a too-wide fake grin, making us both laugh.

I could hardly believe how much Dylan had grown from the little boy I first met right there at the Bronx Zoo just over a year ago. Although still a little boy, he'd sprouted up a few inches and lost the remains of his toddler chubbiness. A wiry, active kid who had just started kindergarten two months ago, he spoke in full, confident sentences, and no longer pronounced my name Wome, which, honestly, made me a little sad. I missed hearing him call me Daddy-Wome; those days, I was just Daddy, and sometimes even just Dad. It took some getting used to, but it still sounded pretty good to me.

Matthew was Dad too. He had moved back to LA about a month after our show opened, but he kept in touch with Dylan via video chat and letters. He came to visit about once a month, and over the summer, Dylan had gone to LA with his nanny to spend two weeks there. Freya and I missed him so much, we had to laugh at each other.

"What is it going to be like when he goes to college?" she wondered, poking fun at herself when she got teary walking by his empty room one night.

"By that point, he'll be an angsty teenager," I suggested. "You'll be glad to be rid of him."

That wasn't true but it made her smile, and just the fact that she included me in discussions that looked that far into the future filled me with warmth.

Just one week earlier, Freya and I had both finished our contracts with the show. It had been an amazing year, better than even I could have predicted. The show became a huge success and one of the hottest tickets in town. We appeared together on all the national morning talk shows and some of the late-night ones too. We were voted 'Broadway's hottest couple' in an online poll. The awards shelf in my bedroom was a lot more crowded now, with Drama Desk awards and Outer Critic Circle Awards, and, best of all, two new Tony Awards - one for me, and one for her.

She had her pick of new projects with people starting to call a month before her contract ran out, and at that very moment, she was meeting with the producers of a new show they wanted her to star in. I'd offered to take Dylan to the zoo during her meeting and she could meet us there when she was finished.

As for me, I wasn't in a rush to get onto the next thing. Before, I had always tried to have something lined up before each show finished, eager to start work again as soon as possible. Thinking about it with the benefit of hindsight, I realized that it must have been at least partly because I didn't want to lose the sense of family I got from being in a cast. With Freya and Dylan, that became less of a concern. I had my own unofficial family, better than any show family, and it had no expiry date.

Soon, my phone buzzed with the text I'd been waiting for, letting me know Freya had arrived. "Alright, Mommy's here. You ready?"

"Ready." Dylan gave me a fist bump and we headed to the entrance to go and meet her.

Freya's face lit up as she saw us, her hazel eyes full of warmth, as usual. "Hope you guys didn't have too much fun without me."

"We waited for you to go to the leopards, Mommy," Dylan told her, perfectly on script. Maybe the kid would have a career in acting too. "Can we go now?"

"Of course. Are we walking this time or did Daddy hire another cart?"

She came over to give me a kiss as she teased me, and her familiar vanilla and berry scent made me smile as I pressed my lips against hers. She smelled like home. "We'll just walk if that's okay. How did the meeting go?"

"I'll tell you about it later," she promised, which made me more curious. Why couldn't she tell me then? "We better not keep the leopards waiting."

We walked over hand-in-hand, all three of us with Freya in the middle as Dylan filled her in on everything she'd missed from our zoo visit so far. When we reached the leopard enclosure, the zookeeper greeted us with a friendly wave.

Freya shot me a look of surprise. "Are we going behind the scenes again?"

"Dylan's been asking," I fibbed. "I hope you don't mind."

She sat me down about two months into our relationship to tell me I had to stop buying Dylan everything he showed any interest in. She didn't want him to think the world worked that day, and although I didn't think it would be possible to spoil a kid as good as Dylan, I trusted her judgement. Since then, I usually checked with her before splashing out, but in this case, I hadn't.

"It's been a while since the last time," she conceded, her affectionate smile a sure sign that she remembered that day just as well as I did. "Let's go see some leopards."

The three of us followed the zookeeper to the backstage area, and just as he had the last time, Dylan got a chance to feed the younger leopards, who had also grown up quite a lot in the last year. Nearly full-sized, they were still rather playful.

My heart began to race as I watched him, trying my best to appear like nothing out of the ordinary was about to happen. Freya was so focused on Dylan anyway, she didn't notice me fiddling around in my pocket.

We'd recruited the zookeeper for our plan too, so after Dylan had finished feeding the big cats, she pointed to a small white square inside the enclosure. "That must have fallen in earlier. Can you help me get it out?"

Dylan nodded seriously, using the large grabbing arm she gave him to reach safely into the leopards' enclosure and pick up the out-of-place object. A quick look at Freya's face told me she still had no suspicions.

Once Dylan had it in his hands, the zookeeper gave him his prompt. "I think it might say something on the other side. Can you read it?"

Dylan's reading skills were getting very good, so Freya watched proudly as he flipped it over and began to read, and I took the opportunity to take a step back, getting into position as my heart beat even faster.

Dylan spoke the words slowly and clearly, just as we'd practiced. "It says: 'Mommy, will you marry Daddy'?"

It took a second for her to put it together, for the words to sink in and to turn to me, only to find me down on one knee with the ring box in my hand.

"No," she whispered and my heart nearly stopped.

"No?"

Freya's eyes went wide in horror. "Wait, I didn't mean 'no'! I meant, no, this can't be happening. You're not serious."

She'd almost given me a heart attack. "I promise you I am. Isn't that right, buddy?"

Dylan came to stand next to me, still holding the little sign with the words printed on it. "Say yes, Mommy!"

It might not have been fair with the two of us ganging up on her, but eyes filled with happy tears. "Yes. Of course, yes!"

"Yay!" Dylan jumped so high in excitement that he nearly fell over. I felt just the same way as I slid the ring onto her finger and got back to my feet, giving her a kiss before picking Dylan up and bringing him into the hug. As much as the proposal was for her, it was for him too. It made us a family, officially, and I knew she understood that completely.

As Freya wiped her eyes, she gave a shaky laugh. "I guess this is as good a time as any to tell you about my meeting."

That seemed like a strange segue to me, but since I was curious about her meeting anyway, I didn't question it. "What about it? Are you taking the role?"

Maybe she meant we'd have to plan the wedding around her performance schedule?

Freya shook her head, though. "No. I turned it down."

"Oh. Okay. Why?" I supported her no matter what she decided, but she had seemed pretty excited about the show over the last few days. Something must have changed.

"Because the costumes won't fit me very well in just a few months' time."

It took me a few seconds to put it together, just as it had for her with my proposal, and Freya waited patiently as I did. When it finally hit me what she meant, my heart melted all over again, excitement rushing through my veins. "You're pregnant?"

She nodded, her eyes full of affection as she looked over at Dylan in my arms. "What do you think about having a little brother or sister, Dill-pickle?"

Dylan looked around us eagerly. "Where?"

Our combined laughter only confused him. "Not right now," Freya explained gently. "In a few months. After the wedding. We've got a lot to look forward to."

That was for damn sure.

After thanking the zookeeper, we made our way out of the zoo, eager to get home and celebrate properly. Freya called her mom to share both pieces of news and Mrs Rose immediately offered to take Dylan for the night so we could have some time alone. I had no idea why people made so many jokes about overbearing mothers-in-law; mine was absolutely amazing.

"You're happy about the baby, aren't you?" I asked Freya once we were alone. "When did you find out?"

"Yesterday. And yes, I'm happy, but I was a little worried too."

I could guess what she'd been worried about, and I hated that she would even think it, though I could completely understand why. This was the point in the relationship when I usually bailed, once the show was over.

But when she explained herself further, that wasn't exactly what she meant. "I was worried that you might think I'd done it on purpose to try to force you to stay. I know you're not the kind of guy who would ever walk away from this, but I wanted to be sure that you were sticking around because you wanted to be, not because you felt you had to be."

Did she honestly think that for even a second? "Freya, I love you. You've made my whole life make sense, that's the best way I can describe it. The thought of leaving has never even crossed my mind."

"I know that now," she assured me, looking down at the ring on her finger. "I won't doubt it again."

I hoped she would never have a reason to. "In that case, I would very much like to take my new fiancée to bed to get to work on our next rehearsal."

Her grin sent desire rushing through my whole body, as usual. "What are we rehearsing for?"

"The rest of our lives."

The world might have to wait a little longer to see Freya's next starring role, but for me, she would always be my leading lady.

~~THE END~~

More From the Author

<u>Contemporary Romance – 18+</u>

Callahan Series
A Matter of Time
A Piece of Land
A Change of Heart
A Work of Art

Christmas in the City Series
Mistletoe Mistake
Candy Cane Challenge
Tinsel Temptation
Gingerbread Gamble

Standalones
A Set of Three
Charity Case
Hired Lover
Leading Lady

Contemporary Romance – New Adult/Clean

It Figures duet
It Figures
Figuring It Out

Historical Romance – 18+

Lady in Waiting Series
Lady in Waiting
King in Training
Princess in Hiding

Paranormal Romance – 18+

Cold Lake Pack Series
The Curse and the Prophecy
The Spell and the Legacy
The Dream and the Destiny

Mismatched Mates Series
Mismatched Mates
Misguided Motives
Mistaken Meanings

Serena's Story
The Alpha's Second Chance
The Returned Mate
The Vampire's Consort

Sacrifice Series
Blood Donor
Life Giver

Paranormal Romance – New Adult/Clean

The Alpha's Prey

Keep in Touch

My Patreon account has daily updates from my works-in-progress, bonus chapters and more – join me there to comment and read along as my next books are being written:
www.patreon.com/melodytyden

You can find and follow me on Facebook at: facebook.com/melodyty den

Join the Facebook group Melody's Romance Corner for fun games, interaction with the author and exclusive news and excerpts.

You can also sign up to my newsletter at www.melodytyden.com for all the latest news.